PAPER TOWNS

ALSO BY JOHN GREEN:

Looking for Alaska

An Abundance of Katherines

Will Grayson, Will Grayson
WITH DAVID LEVITHAN

The Fault in Our Stars

Turtles All the Way Down

PAPER TOWNS

JOHN GREEN

PENGUIN BOOKS

PENGUIN BOOKS
An imprint of Penguin Random House LLC, New York

First published in the United States of America by Dutton Books,
a member of Penguin Group (USA), 2008
Published by Speak, an imprint of Penguin Group (USA), 2009, 2012
Published by Penguin Books, an imprint of Penguin Random House LLC, 2019

THE LIBRARY OF CONGRESS HAS CATALOGED THE DUTTON BOOKS EDITION AS FOLLOWS:
Green, John, date.
Paper towns / by John Green.—1st ed.
p. cm.
Summary: One month before graduation from his Central Florida high school, Quentin "Q" Jacobsen basks in the predictable boringness of his life until the beautiful and exciting Margo Roth Spiegelman, Q's neighbor and classmate, takes him on a midnight adventure and then mysteriously disappears.
ISBN 978-0-525-47818-8 (hc)
[1. Missing persons—Fiction. 2. Florida—Fiction. 3. Coming of age—Fiction. 4. Mystery and detective stories.] I. Title.
PZ7.G8233Pap 2008
[Fic]—dc22 2007052659

Penguin Books ISBN 9780142414934

Printed in the United States of America

58th Printing

To Julie Strauss-Gabel, without whom none of this could have become real

And after, when
we went outside to look at her finished lantern
from the road, I said I liked the way her light
shone through the face that flickered in the dark.
—"Jack O'Lantern," Katrina Vandenberg in *Atlas*

People say friends don't destroy one another
What do they know about friends?
—"Game Shows Touch Our Lives," The Mountain Goats

PROLOGUE

The way I figure it, everyone gets a miracle. Like, I will probably never be struck by lightning, or win a Nobel Prize, or become the dictator of a small nation in the Pacific Islands, or contract terminal ear cancer, or spontaneously combust. But if you consider all the unlikely things together, at least one of them will probably happen to each of us. I could have seen it rain frogs. I could have stepped foot on Mars. I could have been eaten by a whale. I could have married the queen of England or survived months at sea. But my miracle was different. My miracle was this: out of all the houses in all the subdivisions in all of Florida, I ended up living next door to Margo Roth Spiegelman.

Our subdivision, Jefferson Park, used to be a navy base. But then the navy didn't need it anymore, so it returned the land to the citizens of Orlando, Florida, who decided to build a massive subdivision, because that's what Florida does with land. My parents and Margo's parents ended up moving next door to one another just after the first houses were built. Margo and I were two.

Before Jefferson Park was a Pleasantville, and before it was a navy base, it belonged to an actual Jefferson, this guy Dr. Jefferson Jefferson. Dr. Jefferson Jefferson has a school named after him in Orlando and also a large charitable foundation, but the fascinating and unbelievable-but-true thing about Dr. Jefferson

Jefferson is that he was not a doctor of any kind. He was just an orange juice salesman named Jefferson Jefferson. When he became rich and powerful, he went to court, made "Jefferson" his middle name, and then changed his first name to "Dr." Capital *D*. Lowercase *r*. Period.

So Margo and I were nine. Our parents were friends, so we would sometimes play together, biking past the cul-de-sacced streets to Jefferson Park itself, the hub of our subdivision's wheel.

I always got very nervous whenever I heard that Margo was about to show up, on account of how she was the most fantastically gorgeous creature that God had ever created. On the morning in question, she wore white shorts and a pink T-shirt that featured a green dragon breathing a fire of orange glitter. It is difficult to explain how awesome I found this T-shirt at the time.

Margo, as always, biked standing up, her arms locked as she leaned above the handlebars, her purple sneakers a circuitous blur. It was a steam-hot day in March. The sky was clear, but the air tasted acidic, like it might storm later.

At the time, I fancied myself an inventor, and after we locked up our bikes and began the short walk across the park to the playground, I told Margo about an idea I had for an invention called the Ringolator. The Ringolator was a gigantic cannon that would shoot big, colored rocks into a very low orbit, giving Earth the same sort of rings that Saturn has. (I still think this would be a fine idea, but it turns out that building a cannon that can shoot boulders into a low orbit is fairly complicated.)

I'd been in this park so many times before that it was mapped in my mind, so we were only a few steps inside when I began to sense that the world was out of order, even though I couldn't immediately figure out *what* was different.

"Quentin," Margo said quietly, calmly.

She was pointing. And then I realized what was different.

There was a live oak a few feet ahead of us. Thick and gnarled and ancient-looking. That was not new. The playground on our right. Not new, either. But now, a guy wearing a gray suit, slumped against the trunk of the oak tree. Not moving. This was new. He was encircled by blood; a half-dried fountain of it poured out of his mouth. The mouth open in a way that mouths generally shouldn't be. Flies at rest on his pale forehead.

"He's dead," Margo said, as if I couldn't tell.

I took two small steps backward. I remember thinking that if I made any sudden movements, he might wake up and attack me. Maybe he was a zombie. I knew zombies weren't real, but he sure *looked* like a potential zombie.

As I took those two steps back, Margo took two equally small and quiet steps forward. "His eyes are open," she said.

"Wegottagohome," I said.

"I thought you closed your eyes when you died," she said.

"Margowegottagohomeandtell."

She took another step. She was close enough now to reach out and touch his foot. "What do you think happened to him?" she asked. "Maybe it was drugs or something."

I didn't want to leave Margo alone with the dead guy who might be an attack zombie, but I also didn't care to stand around and chat about the circumstances of his demise. I gathered my courage and stepped forward to take her hand. "Margowegotta-gorightnow!"

"Okay, yeah," she said. We ran to our bikes, my stomach churning with something that felt exactly like excitement, but wasn't. We got on our bikes and I let her go in front of me because I was crying and didn't want her to see. I could see blood on the soles of her purple sneakers. His blood. The dead guy blood.

And then we were back home in our separate houses. My parents called 911, and I heard the sirens in the distance and asked to see the fire trucks, but my mom said no. Then I took a nap.

Both my parents are therapists, which means that I am really goddamned well adjusted. So when I woke up, I had a long conversation with my mom about the cycle of life, and how death is part of life, but not a part of life I needed to be particularly concerned about at the age of nine, and I felt better. Honestly, I never worried about it much. Which is saying something, because I can do some worrying.

Here's the thing: I found a dead guy. Little, adorable nine-year-old me and my even littler and more adorable playdate found a guy with blood pouring out of his mouth, and that blood was on her little, adorable sneakers as we biked home. It's all very dramatic and everything, but so what? I didn't know the guy. People I don't know die all the damned time. If I had a nervous breakdown every time something awful happened in the world, I'd be crazier than a shithouse rat.

That night, I went into my room at nine o'clock to go to bed, because nine o'clock was my bedtime. My mom tucked me in, told me she loved me, and I said, "See you tomorrow," and she said, "See you tomorrow," and then she turned out the lights and closed the door almost-all-the-way.

As I turned on my side, I saw Margo Roth Spiegelman standing outside my window, her face almost pressed against the screen. I got up and opened the window, but the screen stayed between us, pixelating her.

"I did an investigation," she said quite seriously. Even up close the screen broke her face apart, but I could tell that she was holding a little notebook and a pencil with teeth marks around the eraser. She glanced down at her notes. "Mrs. Feldman from over on Jefferson Court said his name was Robert Joyner. She told me he lived on Jefferson Road in one of those condos on top of the grocery store, so I went over there and there were a bunch of policemen, and one of them asked if I worked at the school paper, and I said our school didn't have a paper, and he said as long as I wasn't a journalist he would answer my questions. He said Robert Joyner was thirty-six years old. A lawyer. They wouldn't let me in the apartment, but a lady named Juanita Alvarez lives next door to him, and I got into her apartment by asking if I could borrow a cup of sugar, and then she said that Robert Joyner had killed himself with a gun. And then I asked why, and then she told me that he was getting a divorce and was sad about it."

She stopped then, and I just looked at her, her face gray and moonlit and split into a thousand little pieces by the weave of the window screen. Her wide, round eyes flitted back and forth from her notebook to me. "Lots of people get divorces and don't kill themselves," I said.

"I *know*," she said, excitement in her voice. "*That's* what I told Juanita Alvarez. And then she said . . ." Margo flipped the notebook page. "She said that Mr. Joyner was troubled. And then I asked what that meant, and then she told me that we should just pray for him and that I needed to take the sugar to my mom, and I said forget the sugar and left."

I said nothing again. I just wanted her to keep talking—that small voice tense with the excitement of almost knowing things, making me feel like something important was happening to me.

"I think I maybe know why," she finally said.

"Why?"

"Maybe all the strings inside him broke," she said.

While I tried to think of something to say in answer to that, I reached forward and pressed the lock on the screen between us, dislodging it from the window. I placed the screen on the floor, but she didn't give me a chance to speak. Before I could sit back down, she just raised her face up toward me and whispered, "Shut the window." So I did. I thought she would leave, but she just stood there, watching me. I waved at her and smiled, but her eyes seemed fixed on something behind me, something monstrous that had already drained the blood from her face, and I felt too afraid to turn around to see. But there was nothing behind me, of course—except maybe the dead guy.

I stopped waving. My head was level with hers as we stared at each other from opposite sides of the glass. I don't remember how it ended—if I went to bed or she did. In my memory, it doesn't end. We just stay there, looking at each other, forever.

Margo always loved mysteries. And in everything that came afterward, I could never stop thinking that maybe she loved mysteries so much that she became one.

PART ONE

The Strings

1.

The longest day of my life began tardily. I woke up late, took too long in the shower, and ended up having to enjoy my breakfast in the passenger seat of my mom's minivan at 7:17 that Wednesday morning.

I usually got a ride to school with my best friend, Ben Starling, but Ben had gone to school on time, making him useless to me. "On time" for us was thirty minutes before school actually started, because the half hour before the first bell was the highlight of our social calendars: standing outside the side door that led into the band room and just talking. Most of my friends were in band, and most of my free time during school was spent within twenty feet of the band room. But I was not in the band, because I suffer from the kind of tone deafness that is generally associated with actual deafness. I was going to be twenty minutes late, which technically meant that I'd still be ten minutes early for school itself.

As she drove, Mom was asking me about classes and finals and prom.

"I don't believe in prom," I reminded her as she rounded a corner. I expertly angled my raisin bran to accommodate the g-forces. I'd done this before.

"Well, there's no harm in just going with a friend. I'm sure you could ask Cassie Hiney." And I *could* have asked Cassie Hiney, who was actually perfectly nice and pleasant and cute, despite having a fantastically unfortunate last name.

"It's not just that I don't like prom. I also don't like people who like prom," I explained, although this was, in point of fact, untrue. Ben was absolutely gaga over the idea of going.

Mom turned into school, and I held the mostly empty bowl with both hands as we drove over a speed bump. I glanced over at the senior parking lot. Margo Roth Spiegelman's silver Honda was parked in its usual spot. Mom pulled the minivan into a cul-de-sac outside the band room and kissed me on the cheek. I could see Ben and my other friends standing in a semicircle.

I walked up to them, and the half circle effortlessly expanded to include me. They were talking about my ex-girlfriend Suzie Chung, who played cello and was apparently creating quite a stir by dating a baseball player named Taddy Mac. Whether this was his given name, I did not know. But at any rate, Suzie had decided to go to prom with Taddy Mac. Another casualty.

"Bro," said Ben, standing across from me. He nodded his head and turned around. I followed him out of the circle and through the door. A small, olive-skinned creature who had hit puberty but never hit it very hard, Ben had been my best friend since fifth grade, when we both finally owned up to the fact that neither of us was likely to attract anyone else as a best friend. Plus, he tried hard, and I liked that—most of the time.

"How ya doin'?" I asked. We were safely inside, everyone else's conversations making ours inaudible.

"Radar is going to prom," he said morosely. Radar was our other best friend. We called him Radar because he looked like a little bespectacled guy called Radar on this old TV show *M*A*S*H*, except 1. The TV Radar wasn't black, and 2. At some point after the nicknaming, our Radar grew about six inches and started wearing contacts, so I suppose that 3. He actually didn't look like the guy on *M*A*S*H* at all, but 4. With three and a half weeks left of high school, we weren't very well going to renickname him.

"That girl Angela?" I asked. Radar never told us anything about his love life, but this did not dissuade us from frequent speculation.

Ben nodded, and then said, "You know my big plan to ask a freshbunny to prom because they're the only girls who don't know the Bloody Ben story?" I nodded.

"Well," Ben said, "this morning some darling little ninth-grade honeybunny came up to me and asked me if I was Bloody Ben, and I began to explain that it was a kidney infection, and she giggled and ran away. So that's out."

In tenth grade, Ben was hospitalized for a kidney infection, but Becca Arrington, Margo's best friend, started a rumor that the real reason he had blood in his urine was due to chronic masturbation. Despite its medical implausibility, this story had haunted Ben ever since. "That sucks," I said.

Ben started outlining plans for finding a date, but I was only half listening, because through the thickening mass of humanity crowding the hallway, I could see Margo Roth Spiegelman. She was next to her locker, standing beside her boyfriend, Jase. She wore a white skirt to her knees and a blue print top. I could see her collarbone. She was laughing at something hysterical—her shoulders bent forward, her big eyes crinkling at their corners, her mouth open wide. But it didn't seem to be anything Jase had said, because she was looking away from him, across the hallway to a bank of lockers. I followed her eyes and saw Becca Arrington draped all over some baseball player like she was an ornament and he a Christmas tree. I smiled at Margo, even though I knew she couldn't see me.

"Bro, you should just hit that. Forget about Jase. God, that is one candy-coated honeybunny." As we walked, I kept taking glances at her through the crowd, quick snapshots: a photographic series entitled *Perfection Stands Still While Mortals Walk Past.* As I got closer, I thought maybe she wasn't laughing after all. Maybe she'd received a surprise or a gift or something. She couldn't seem to close her mouth.

"Yeah," I said to Ben, still not listening, still trying to see as much of her as I could without being too obvious. It wasn't even that she was so pretty. She was just so awesome, and in the literal sense. And then we were too far past her, too many people walking between her and me, and I never even got close enough to hear her speak or understand whatever the hilarious surprise had been. Ben shook his head, because he had seen me see her a thousand times, and he was used to it.

"Honestly, she's hot, but she's not *that* hot. You know who's seriously hot?"

"Who?" I asked.

"Lacey," he said, who was Margo's other best friend. "Also your mom. Bro, I saw your mom kiss you on the cheek this morning, and forgive me, but I swear to God I was like, *man, I wish I was Q. And also, I wish my cheeks had penises.*" I elbowed him in the ribs, but I was still thinking about Margo, because she was the only legend who lived next door to me. Margo Roth Spiegelman, whose six-syllable name was often spoken in its entirety with a kind of quiet reverence. Margo Roth Spiegelman, whose stories of epic adventures would blow through school like a summer storm: an old guy living in a broken-down house in Hot Coffee, Mississippi, taught Margo how to play the guitar. Margo Roth Spiegelman, who spent three days traveling with the circus—they thought she had potential on the trapeze. Margo Roth Spiegelman, who drank a cup of herbal tea with The Mallionaires backstage after a concert in St. Louis while they drank whiskey. Margo Roth Spiegelman, who got into that concert by telling the bouncer she was the bassist's girlfriend, and didn't they recognize her, and come on guys seriously, my name is Margo Roth Spiegelman and if you go back there and ask the bassist to take one look at me, he will tell you that I either am his girlfriend or he wishes I was, and then the bouncer did so, and then the bassist said "yeah that's my girlfriend let her in the show," and then later the bassist wanted to hook up with her and she *rejected the bassist from The Mallionaires.*

The stories, when they were shared, inevitably ended with, *I mean, can you believe it?* We often could not, but they always proved true.

And then we were at our lockers. Radar was leaning against Ben's locker, typing into a handheld device.

"So you're going to prom," I said to him. He looked up, and then looked back down.

"I'm de-vandalizing the Omnictionary article about a former prime minister of France. Last night someone deleted the entire entry and then replaced it with the sentence 'Jacques Chirac is a gay,' which as it happens is incorrect both factually and grammatically." Radar is a big-time editor of this online user-created reference source called Omnictionary. His whole life is devoted to the maintenance and well-being of Omnictionary. This was but one of several reasons why his having a prom date was somewhat surprising.

"So you're going to prom," I repeated.

"Sorry," he said without looking up. It was a well-known fact that I was opposed to prom. Absolutely nothing about any of it appealed to me—not slow dancing, not fast dancing, not the dresses, and definitely not the rented tuxedo. Renting a tuxedo seemed to me an excellent way to contract some hideous disease from its previous tenant, and I did not aspire to become the world's only virgin with pubic lice.

"Bro," Ben said to Radar, "the freshhoneys know about the Bloody Ben story." Radar put the handheld away finally and nodded sympathetically. "So anyway," Ben continued, "my two remaining strategies are either to purchase a prom date on the Internet or fly to Missouri and kidnap some nice corn-fed little honeybunny." I'd tried telling Ben that "honeybunny" sounded more sexist and lame than retro-cool, but he refused to abandon the practice. He called his own mother a honeybunny. There was no fixing him.

"I'll ask Angela if she knows anybody," Radar said. "Although getting you a date to prom will be harder than turning lead into gold."

"Getting you a date to prom is so hard that the hypothetical idea itself is actually used to cut diamonds," I added.

Radar tapped a locker twice with his fist to express his approval, and then came back with another. "Ben, getting you a date to prom is so hard that the American government believes the problem cannot be solved with diplomacy, but will instead require force."

I was trying to think of another one when we all three simultaneously saw the human-shaped container of anabolic steroids known as Chuck Parson walking toward us with some intent.

Chuck Parson did not participate in organized sports, because to do so would distract from the larger goal of his life: to one day be convicted of homicide. "Hey, faggots," he called.

"Chuck," I answered, as friendly as I could muster. Chuck hadn't given us any serious trouble in a couple years—someone in cool kid land laid down the edict that we were to be left alone. So it was a little unusual for him even to talk to us.

Maybe because I spoke and maybe not, he slammed his hands against the lockers on either side of me and then leaned in close enough for me to contemplate his toothpaste brand. "What do you know about Margo and Jase?"

"Uh," I said. I thought of everything I knew about them: Jase was Margo Roth Spiegelman's first and only serious boyfriend. They began dating at the tail end of last year. They were both going to University of Florida next year. Jase got a baseball scholarship there. He was never over at her house, except to pick her up. She never acted as if she liked him all that much, but then she never acted as if she liked anyone all that much. "Nothing," I said finally.

"Don't shit me around," he growled.

"I barely even *know* her," I said, which had become true.

He considered my answer for a minute, and I tried hard to stare at his close-set eyes. He nodded very slightly, pushed off the lockers, and walked away to attend his first-period class: The Care and Feeding of Pectoral Muscles. The second bell rang. One minute to class. Radar and I had calc; Ben had finite mathematics. The classrooms were adjacent; we walked toward them together, the three of us in a row, trusting that the tide of classmates would part enough to let us by, and it did.

I said, "Getting you a date to prom is so hard that a thousand monkeys typing at a thousand typewriters for a thousand years would never once type *'I will go to prom with Ben.'*"

Ben could not resist tearing himself apart. "My prom prospects are so poor that Q's grandma turned me down. She said she was waiting for Radar to ask her."

Radar nodded his head slowly. "It's true, Q. Your grandma loves the brothers."

It was so pathetically easy to forget about Chuck, to talk about prom even though I didn't give a shit about prom. Such was life that morning: nothing really mattered that much, not the good things and not the bad ones. We were in the business of mutual amusement, and we were reasonably prosperous.

I spent the next three hours in classrooms, trying not to look at the clocks above various blackboards, and then looking at the clocks, and then being amazed that only a few minutes had passed since I last looked at the clock. I'd had nearly four years of experience looking at these clocks, but their sluggishness never ceased to surprise. If I am ever told that I have one day to live, I will head straight for the hallowed halls of Winter Park High School, where a day has been known to last a thousand years.

But as much as it felt like third-period physics would never end, it did, and then I was in the cafeteria with Ben. Radar had fifth-period lunch with most of our other friends, so Ben and I generally sat together alone, a couple seats between us and a group of drama kids we knew. Today, we were both eating mini pepperoni pizzas.

"Pizza's good," I said. He nodded distractedly. "What's wrong?" I asked.

"Nuffing," he said through a mouthful of pizza. He swallowed. "I know you think it's dumb, but I want to go to prom."

"1. I do think it's dumb; 2. If you want to go, just go; 3. If I'm not mistaken, you haven't even asked anyone."

"I asked Cassie Hiney during math. I wrote her a note." I raised my eyebrows questioningly. Ben reached into his shorts and slid a heavily folded piece of paper to me. I flattened it out:

Ben,
I'd love to go to prom with you, but I'm already going with Frank. Sorry!
—C

I refolded it and slid it back across the table. I could remember playing paper football on these tables. "That sucks," I said.

"Yeah, whatever." The walls of sound felt like they were closing in on us, and we were silent for a while, and then Ben looked at me very seriously and said, "I'm going to get so much play in college. I'm going to be in the *Guinness Book of World Records* under the category 'Most Honeybunnies Ever Pleased.'"

I laughed. I was thinking about how Radar's parents actually *were* in the *Guinness Book* when I noticed a pretty African-American girl with spiky little dreads standing above us. It took me a moment to realize that the girl was Angela, Radar's I-guess-girlfriend.

"Hi," she said to me.

"Hey," I said. I'd had classes with Angela and knew her a little, but we didn't say hello in the hallway or anything. I motioned for her to sit. She scooted a chair to the head of the table.

"I figure that you guys probably know Marcus better than anyone," she said, using Radar's real name. She leaned toward us, her elbows on the table.

"It's a shitty job, but someone's got to do it," Ben answered, smiling.

"Do you think he's, like, embarrassed of me?"

Ben laughed. "What? No," he said.

"Technically," I added, "*you* should be embarrassed of *him*."

She rolled her eyes, smiling. A girl accustomed to compliments. "But he's never, like, invited me to hang out with you, though."

"Ohhhh," I said, getting it finally. "That's because he's embarrassed of *us*."

She laughed. "You seem pretty normal."

"You've never seen Ben snort Sprite up his nose and then spit it out of his mouth," I said.

"I look like a demented carbonated fountain," he deadpanned.

"But really, you wouldn't worry? I mean, we've been dating for five weeks, and he's never even taken me to his house." Ben and I exchanged a knowing glance, and I scrunched up my face to suppress laughter. "What?" she asked.

"Nothing," I said. "Honestly, Angela. If he was forcing you to hang out with us and taking you to his house all the time—"

"Then it would definitely mean he *didn't* like you," Ben finished.

"Are his parents weird?"

I struggled with how to answer that question honestly. "Uh, no. They're cool. They're just kinda overprotective, I guess."

"Yeah, overprotective," Ben agreed a little too quickly.

She smiled and then got up, saying she had to go say hi to someone before lunch was over. Ben waited until she was gone to say anything. "That girl is awesome," Ben said.

"I know," I answered. "I wonder if we can replace Radar with her."

"She's probably not that good with computers, though. We need someone who's good at computers. Plus I bet she sucks at Resurrection," which was our favorite video game. "By the way," Ben added, "nice call saying that Radar's folks are overprotective."

"Well, it's not my place to tell her," I said.

"I wonder how long till she gets to see the Team Radar Residence and Museum." Ben smiled.

The period was almost over, so Ben and I got up and put our trays onto the conveyer belt. The very same one that Chuck Parson had thrown me onto freshman year, sending me into the terrifying netherworld of Winter Park's dishwashing corps. We walked over to Radar's locker and were standing there when he raced up just after the first bell.

"I decided during government that I would actually, literally suck donkey balls if it meant I could skip that class for the rest of the semester," he said.

"You can learn a lot about government from donkey balls," I said. "Hey, speaking of reasons you wish you had fourth-period lunch, we just dined with Angela."

Ben smirked at Radar and said, "Yeah, she wants to know why she's never been over to your house."

Radar exhaled a long breath as he spun the combination to open his locker. He breathed for so long I thought he might pass out. "Crap," he said finally.

"Are you embarrassed about something?" I asked, smiling.

"Shut up," he answered, poking his elbow into my gut.

"You live in a lovely home," I said.

"Seriously, bro," added Ben. "She's a really nice girl. I don't see why you can't introduce her to your parents and show her Casa Radar."

Radar threw his books into his locker and shut it. The din of conversation around us quieted just a bit as he turned his eyes toward the heavens and shouted, "IT IS NOT MY FAULT THAT MY PARENTS OWN THE WORLD'S LARGEST COLLECTION OF BLACK SANTAS."

I'd heard Radar say "the world's largest collection of black Santas" perhaps a thousand times in my life, and it never became any less funny to me. But he wasn't kidding. I remembered the first time I visited. I was maybe thirteen. It was spring, many months past Christmas, and yet black Santas lined the windowsills. Paper cutouts of black Santas hung from the stairway banister. Black Santa candles adorned the dining room table. A black Santa oil painting hung above the mantel, which was itself lined with black Santa figurines. They had a black Santa Pez dispenser purchased from Namibia. The light-up plastic black Santa that stood in their postage-stamp front yard from Thanksgiving to New Year's spent the rest of the year proudly keeping watch in the corner of the guest bathroom, a bathroom with homemade black Santa wallpaper created with paint and a Santa-shaped sponge. In every room, save Radar's, their home was awash in black Santadom—plaster and plastic and marble and clay and wood and resin and cloth. In total, Radar's parents owned more than twelve hundred black Santas of various sorts. As a plaque beside their front door proclaimed, Radar's house was an officially registered Santa Landmark according to the Society for Christmas.

"You just gotta tell her, man," I said. "You just gotta say, 'Angela, I really like you, but there's something you need to know: when we go to my house and hook up, we'll be watched by the twenty-four hundred eyes of twelve hundred black Santas."

Radar ran a hand through his buzz cut and shook his head. "Yeah, I don't think I'll put it exactly like that, but I'll deal with it."

I headed off to government, Ben to an elective about video game design. I watched clocks through two more classes, and then finally the relief radiated out of my chest when I was finished—the end of each day like a dry run for our graduation less than a month away.

I went home. I ate two peanut butter and jelly sandwiches as an early dinner. I watched poker on TV. My parents came home at six, hugged each other, and hugged me. We ate a macaroni casserole as a proper dinner. They asked me about school. They asked me about prom. They marveled at what a wonderful job they'd done raising me. They told me about their days dealing with people who had been raised less brilliantly. They went to watch TV. I went to my room to check my e-mail. I wrote a little bit about *The Great Gatsby* for English. I read some of *The Federalist Papers* as early prep for my government final. I IM'ed with Ben, and then Radar came online. In our conversation, he used the phrase "the world's largest collection of black Santas" four times, and I laughed each time. I told him I was happy for him, having a girlfriend. He said it would be a great summer. I agreed. It was May fifth, but it didn't have to be. My days had a pleasant identicalness about them. I had always liked that: I liked routine. I liked being bored. I didn't want to, but I did. And so May fifth could have been any day—until just before midnight, when Margo Roth Spiegelman slid open my screenless bedroom window for the first time since telling me to close it nine years before.

2.

I swiveled around when I heard the window open, and Margo's blue eyes were staring back at me. Her eyes were all I could see at first, but as my vision adjusted, I realized she was wearing black face paint and a black hoodie. "Are you having cybersex?" she asked.

"I'm IM'ing with Ben Starling."

"That doesn't answer my question, perv."

I laughed awkwardly, then walked over and knelt by the window, my face inches from hers. I couldn't imagine why she was here, in my window, like this. "To what do I owe the pleasure?" I asked. Margo and I were still friendly, I guess, but we weren't meet-in-the-dead-of-night-wearing-black-face-paint friendly. She had friends for that, I'm sure. I just wasn't among them.

"I need your car," she explained.

"I don't have a car," I said, which was something of a sore point for me.

"Well, I need your mom's car."

"You have your own car," I pointed out.

Margo puffed out her cheeks and sighed. "Right, but the thing is that my parents have taken the keys to my car and locked them inside a safe, which they put under their bed, and Myrna Mountweazel"—who was her dog—"is sleeping inside their room. And Myrna Mountweazel has a freaking aneurysm whenever she catches sight of me. I mean, I could totally sneak in there and steal the safe and crack it and get my keys out and drive away, but the thing is that it's not even worth trying because Myrna Mountweazel is just going to bark like crazy if I so much as crack open the door. So like I said, I need a car. Also, I need you to drive it, because I have to do eleven things tonight, and at least five of them involve a getaway man."

When I let my sight unfocus, she became nothing but eyes, floating in the ether. And then I locked back on her, and I could see the outline of her face, the paint still wet against her skin. Her cheekbones triangulating into her chin, her pitch-black lips barely turned to a smile. "Any felonies?" I asked.

"Hmm," said Margo. "Remind me if breaking and entering is a felony."

"No," I answered firmly.

"No it's not a felony or no you won't help?"

"No I won't help. Can't you enlist some of your underlings to drive you around?" Lacey and/or Becca were always doing her bidding.

"They're part of the problem, actually," Margo said.

"What's the problem?" I asked.

"There are eleven problems," she said somewhat impatiently.

"No felonies," I said.

"I swear to God that you will not be asked to commit a felony."

And right then, the floodlights came on all around Margo's house. In one swift motion, she somersaulted through my window, into my room, and then rolled beneath my bed. Within seconds, her dad was standing on the patio outside. "Margo!" he shouted. "I saw you!"

From beneath my bed, I heard a muffled, "Oh, Christ." Margo scooted out from under the bed, stood up, walked to the window, and said, "Come on, Dad. I'm just trying to have a chat with Quentin. You're always telling me what a fantastic influence he could be on me and everything."

"Just chatting with Quentin?"

"Yes."

"Then why are you wearing black face paint?"

Margo faltered for only the briefest moment. "Dad, to answer that question would take hours of backstory, and I know that you're probably very tired, so just go back t—"

"In the house," he thundered. "This minute!"

Margo grabbed hold of my shirt, whispered "Back in a minute" in my ear, and then climbed out the window.

As soon as she left, I grabbed my car keys from my desk. The *keys* are mine; the car, tragically, is not. On my sixteenth birthday, my parents gave me a very small gift, and I knew the moment they handed it to me that it was a car key, and I about peed myself, because they'd said over and over again that they couldn't afford to give me a car. But when they handed me the tiny wrapped box, I knew they'd been tricking me, that I was getting a car after all. I tore off the wrapping paper and popped open the little box. Indeed, it contained a key.

Upon close inspection, it contained a Chrysler key. A key for a Chrysler minivan. The one and the same Chrysler minivan owned by my mother.

"My present is a key to your car?" I asked my mom.

"Tom," she said to my dad, "I told you he would get his hopes up."

"Oh, don't blame me," my dad said. "You're just sublimating your own frustration with my income."

"Isn't that snap analysis a tad passive-aggressive?" my mother asked.

"Aren't rhetorical accusations of passive aggression inherently passive-aggressive?" my dad responded, and they went on like that for a while.

The long and short of it was this: I had access to the vehicular awesomeness that is a late-model Chrysler minivan, except for when my mom was driving it. And since she drove to work every morning, I could only use the car on weekends. Well, weekends and the middle of the goddamned night.

It took Margo more than the promised minute to return to my window, but not much more. But in the time she was gone, I'd started to waffle again. "I've got school tomorrow," I told her.

"Yeah, I know," Margo answered. "There's school tomorrow and the day after that, and thinking about that too long could make a girl bonkers. So, yeah. It's a school night. That's why we've got to get going, because we've got to be back by morning."

"I don't know."

"Q," she said. "Q. Darling. How long have we been dear friends?"

"We're not friends. We're neighbors."

"Oh, Christ, Q. Am I not nice to you? Do I not order my various and sundry minions to be kind to you at school?"

"Uh-huh," I answered dubiously, although in point of fact I'd always figured it was Margo who had stopped Chuck Parson and his ilk from screwing with us.

She blinked. She'd even painted her eyelids. "Q," she said, "we have to go."

And so I went. I slid out the window, and we ran along the side of my house, heads down, until we opened the doors of the minivan. Margo whispered not to close the doors—too much noise—so with the doors open, I put it in neutral, pushed off the cement with my foot, and then let the minivan roll down the driveway. We rolled slowly past a couple houses before I turned on the engine and the headlights. We closed the doors, and then I drove through the serpentine streets of Jefferson Park's endlessness, the houses all still new-looking and plastic, like a toy village housing tens of thousands of real people.

Margo started talking. "The thing is they don't even really *care*; they just feel like my exploits make them look bad. Just now, do you know what he said? He said, 'I don't care if you screw up your life, but don't embarrass us in front of the Jacobsens—they're our *friends*.' Ridiculous. And you have no idea how hard they've made it to get out of that goddamned house. You know how in prison-escape movies they put bundled-up clothes under the blankets to make it look like there's a person in there?" I nodded. "Yeah, well, Mom put a goddamned baby monitor in my room so she could hear my sleep-breathing all night. So I just had to pay Ruthie five bucks to sleep in my room, and then I put bundled-up clothes in *her* room." Ruthie is Margo's little sister. "It's *Mission Impossible* shit now. Used to be I could just sneak out like a regular goddamned American—just climb out the window and jump off the roof. But God, these days, it's like living in a fascist dictatorship."

"Are you going to tell me where we're going?"

"Well, first we're going to Publix. Because for reasons I'll explain later, I need you to go grocery shopping for me. And then to Wal-Mart."

"What, we're just gonna go on a grand tour of every commercial establishment in Central Florida?" I asked.

"Tonight, darling, we are going to right a lot of wrongs. And we are going to wrong some rights. The first shall be last; the last shall be first; the meek shall do some earth-inheriting. But before we can radically reshape the world, we need to shop." I pulled into the Publix then, the parking lot almost entirely empty, and parked.

"Listen," she said, "how much money do you have on you right now?"

"Zero dollars and zero cents," I answered. I turned off the ignition and looked over at her. She wriggled a hand into a pocket of her tight, dark jeans and pulled out several hundred-dollar bills. "Fortunately, the good Lord has provided," she said.

"What the hell?" I asked.

"Bat mitzvah money, bitch. I'm not allowed to access the account, but I know my parents' password because they use 'myrnamountw3az3l' for everything. So I made a withdrawal." I tried to blink away the awe, but she saw the way I was looking at her and smirked at me. "Basically," she said, "this is going to be the best night of your life."

3.

The thing about Margo Roth Spiegelman is that really all I could ever do was let her talk, and then when she stopped talking encourage her to go on, due to the facts that 1. I was incontestably in love with her, and 2. She was absolutely unprecedented in every way, and 3. She never really asked me any questions, so the only way to avoid silence was to keep her talking.

And so in the parking lot of Publix she said, "So, right. I made you a list. If you have any questions, just call my cell. Listen, that reminds me, I took the liberty of putting some supplies in the back of the van earlier."

"What, like, before I agreed to all this?"

"Well, yes. Technically yes. Anyway, just call me if you have any questions, but with the Vaseline, you want the one that's bigger than your fist. There's like a Baby Vaseline, and then there's a Mommy Vaseline, and then there's a big fat Daddy of a Vaseline, and that's the one you want. If they don't have that, then get, like, three of the Mommies." She handed me the list and a hundred-dollar bill and said, "That should cover it."

Margo's list:

3 whole Catfish, Wrapped separately
Veet (It's for Shaving your legs Only you don't Need A razor It's with all the Girly cosmetic stuff)

Vaseline
six-pack, Mountain Dew
One dozen Tulips
one Bottle Of water
Tissues
one Can of blue Spray paint

"Interesting capitalization," I said.

"Yeah. I'm a big believer in random capitalization. The rules of capitalization are so unfair to words in the middle."

Now, I'm not sure what you're supposed to say to the checkout woman at twelve-thirty in the morning when you put thirteen pounds of catfish, Veet, the fat-daddy-size tub of Vaseline, a six-pack of Mountain Dew, a can of blue spray paint, and a dozen tulips on the conveyor belt. But here's what I said: "This isn't as weird as it looks."

The woman cleared her throat but didn't look up. "Still weird," she muttered.

"I really don't want to get in any trouble," I told Margo back in the minivan as she used the bottled water to wipe the black paint off her face with the tissues. She'd only needed the makeup, apparently, to get out of the house. "In my admission letter from Duke it actually explicitly says that they won't take me if I get arrested."

"You're a very anxious person, Q."

"Let's just please not get in trouble," I said. "I mean, I want to have fun and everything, but not at the expense of, like, my future."

She looked up at me, her face mostly revealed now, and she smiled just the littlest bit. "It amazes me that you can find all that shit even remotely interesting."

"Huh?"

"College: getting in or not getting in. Trouble: getting in or not getting in. School: getting A's or getting D's. Career: having or not having. House: big or small, owning or renting. Money: having or not having. It's all so boring."

I started to say something, to say that she obviously cared a little, because she had good grades and was going to the University of Florida's honors program next year, but she just said, "Wal-Mart."

We entered Wal-Mart together and picked up that thing from infomercials called The Club, which locks a car's steering wheel into place. As we walked through the Juniors department, I asked Margo, "Why do we need The Club?"

Margo managed to speak in her usual manic soliloquy without answering my question. "Did you know that for pretty much the entire history of the human species, the average life span was less than thirty years? You could count on ten years or so of real adulthood, right? There was no planning for retirement. There was no planning for a career. There was no *planning.* No time for planning. No time for a future. But then the life spans started getting longer, and people started having more and more future, and so they spent more time thinking about it. About the future. And now life has *become* the future. Every moment of your life is lived for the future—you go to high school so you can go to college so you can get a good job so you can get a nice house so you can afford to send your kids to college so they can get a good job so they can get a nice house so they can afford to send their kids to college."

It felt like Margo was just rambling to avoid the question at hand. So I repeated it. "Why do we need The Club?"

Margo patted me in the middle of the back softly. "I mean, obviously this is all going to be revealed to you before the night is over." And then, in boating supplies, Margo located an air horn. She took it out of the box and held it up in the air, and I said, "No," and she said, "No what?" And I said, "No, don't blow the air horn," except when I got to about the *b* in *blow*, she squeezed on it and it let out an excruciatingly loud honk that felt in my head like the auditory equivalent of an aneurysm, and then she said, "I'm sorry, I couldn't hear you. What was that?" And I said, "Stop b—" and then she did it again.

A Wal-Mart employee just a little older than us walked up to us then and said, "Hey, you can't use that in here," and Margo said, with seeming sincerity, "Sorry, I didn't know that," and the guy said, "Oh, it's cool. I don't mind, actually." And then the conversation seemed over, except the guy could not stop looking at Margo, and honestly I don't blame him, because she is hard to stop looking at, and then finally he said, "What are you guys up to tonight?"

And Margo said, "Not much. You?"

And he said, "I get off at one and then I'm going out to this bar down on Orange, if you want to come. But you'd have to drop off your brother; they're really strict about ID's."

Her what?! "I'm not her brother," I said, looking at the guy's sneakers.

And then Margo proceeded to lie. "He's actually my *cousin*," she said. Then she sidled up to me, put her hand around my waist so that I could feel each of her fingers taut against my hip bone, and she added, "*And* my lover."

The guy just rolled his eyes and walked away, and Margo's hand lingered for a minute and I took the opportunity to put my arm around her. "You really are my favorite cousin," I told her. She smiled and bumped me softly with her hip, spinning out of my embrace.

"Don't I know it," she said.

4.

We were driving down a blessedly empty I-4, and I was following Margo's directions. The clock on the dashboard said it was 1:07.

"It's pretty, huh?" she said. She was turned away from me, staring out the window, so I could hardly see her. "I love driving fast under streetlights."

"Light," I said, "the visible reminder of Invisible Light."

"That's beautiful," she said.

"T. S. Eliot," I said. "You read it, too. In English last year." I hadn't actually ever read the whole poem that line was from, but a couple of the parts I did read got stuck in my head.

"Oh, it's a quote," she said, a little disappointed. I saw her hand on the center console. I could have put my own hand on the center console and then our hands would have been in the same place at the same time. But I didn't. "Say it again," she said.

"Light, the visible reminder of Invisible Light."

"Yeah. Damn, that's good. That must help with your lady friend."

"Ex-lady friend," I corrected her.

"Suzie dumped you?" Margo asked.

"How do you know *she* dumped *me*?"

"Oh, sorry."

"Although she did," I admitted, and Margo laughed. The

breakup had happened months ago, but I didn't blame Margo for failing to pay attention to the world of lower-caste romance. What happens in the band room stays in the band room.

Margo put her feet up on the dashboard and wiggled her toes to the cadence of her speaking. She always talked like that, with this discernible rhythm, like she was reciting poetry. "Right, well, I'm sorry to hear that. But I can relate. My lovely boyfriend of lo these many months is fucking my best friend."

I looked over but her hair was all in her face, so I couldn't make out if she was kidding. "Seriously?" She didn't say anything. "But you were just laughing with him this morning. I saw you."

"I don't know what you're talking about. I heard about it before first period, and then I found them both talking together and I started screaming bloody murder, and Becca ran into the arms of Clint Bauer, and Jase was just standing there like a dumbass with the chaw drool running out of his stank mouth."

I had clearly misinterpreted the scene in the hallway. "That's weird, because Chuck Parson asked me this morning what I knew about you and Jase."

"Yeah, well, Chuck does as he's told, I guess. Probably trying to find out for Jase who knew."

"Jesus, why would he hook up with Becca?"

"Well, she's not known for her personality or generosity of spirit, so it's probably because she's hot."

"She's not as hot as you," I said, before I could think better of it.

"That's always seemed so ridiculous to me, that people would want to be around someone because they're pretty. It's like picking your breakfast cereals based on color instead of taste. It's the next exit, by the way. But I'm not pretty, not close up anyway. Generally, the closer people get to me the less hot they find me."

"That's— " I started.

"Whatever," she answered.

It struck me as somewhat unfair that an asshole like Jason Worthington would get to have sex with both Margo *and* Becca, when perfectly likable individuals such as myself don't get to have sex with either of them—or anyone else, for that matter. That said, I like to think that I am the type of person who wouldn't hook up with Becca Arrington. She may be hot, but she is also 1. aggressively vapid, and 2. an absolute, unadulterated, raging bitch. Those of us who frequent the band room have long suspected that Becca maintains her lovely figure by eating nothing but the souls of kittens and the dreams of impoverished children. "Becca does sort of suck," I said, trying to draw Margo back into conversation.

"Yeah," she answered, looking out the passenger window, her hair reflecting oncoming streetlights. I thought for a second she might be crying, but she rallied quickly, pulling her hoodie up and taking The Club out of the Wal-Mart bag. "Well, this'll be fun at any rate," she said as she ripped open The Club's packaging.

"May I ask where we're going yet?"

"Becca's," she answered.

"Uh-oh," I said as I pulled up to a stop sign. I put the minivan in park and started to tell Margo that I was taking her home.

"No felonies. Promise. We need to find Jase's car. Becca's street is the next one up on the right, but he wouldn't park his car on her street, because her parents are home. Try the one after. That's the first thing."

"Okay," I said, "but then we go home."

"No, then we move on to Part Two of Eleven."

"Margo, this is a bad idea."

"Just drive," she said, and so I just did. We found Jase's Lexus two blocks down from Becca's street, parked in a cul-de-sac. Before I'd even come to a complete stop, Margo jumped out of the minivan with The Club in hand. She pulled open the Lexus's driver-side door, sat down in the seat, and proceeded to attach The Club to Jase's steering wheel. Then she softly closed the door to the Lexus.

"Dumb bastard never locks that car," she mumbled as she climbed back into the minivan. She pocketed the key to The Club. She reached over and tousled my hair. "Part One—done. Now, to Becca's house."

As I drove, Margo explained Parts Two and Three to me.

"That's quite brilliant," I said, even though inside I was bursting with a shimmering nervousness.

I turned onto Becca's street and parked two houses down from her McMansion. Margo crawled into the wayback of the minivan and returned with a pair of binoculars and a digital camera. She looked through the binoculars first, and then handed them to me. I could see a light on in the house's basement, but no movement. I was mostly surprised that the house even *had* a basement—you can't dig very deep before hitting water in most of Orlando.

I reached into my pocket, grabbed my cell phone, and dialed the number that Margo recited to me. The phone rang once, twice, and then a groggy male voice answered, "Hello?"

"Mr. Arrington?" I asked. Margo wanted me to call because no one would ever recognize my voice.

"Who is this? God, what time is it?"

"Sir, I think you should know that your daughter is currently having sex with Jason Worthington in your basement." And then I hung up. Part Two: accompli.

Margo and I threw open the doors of the minivan and charged down the street, diving onto our stomachs just behind the hedge ringing Becca's yard. Margo handed me the camera, and I watched as an upstairs bedroom light came on, and then a stairway light, and then the kitchen light. And finally, the stairway down to the basement.

"Here he comes," Margo whispered, and I didn't know what she meant until, out of the corner of my eye, I noticed a shirtless Jason Worthington wiggling out of the basement window. He took off sprinting across the lawn, naked but for his boxer shorts, and as he approached I jumped up and took a picture of him, completing Part Three. The flash surprised both of us, I think, and he blinked at me through the darkness for a white-hot moment before running off into the night.

Margo tugged on my jeans leg; I looked down at her, and she was smiling goofily. I reached my hand down, helped her up, and then we raced back to the car. I was putting the key in the ignition when she said, "Let me see the picture."

I handed her the camera, and we watched it come up on the screen together, our heads almost touching. Upon seeing the stunned, pale face of Jason Worthington, I couldn't help but laugh.

"Oh, God," Margo said, and pointed. In the rush of the moment, it seemed that Jason had been unable to get Little Jason inside his boxers, and so there it was, hanging out, digitally captured for posterity.

"It's a penis," Margo said, "in the same sense that Rhode Island is a state: it may have an illustrious history, but it sure isn't big."

I looked back at the house and noticed that the basement light was now off. I found myself feeling slightly bad for Jason—it wasn't his fault he had a micropenis and a brilliantly vindictive girlfriend. But then again, in sixth grade, Jase promised not to punch my arm if I ate a live earthworm, so I ate a live earthworm and then he punched me in the face. So I didn't feel very bad for very long.

When I looked over at Margo, she was staring at the house through her binoculars. "We have to go," Margo said. "Into the basement."

"What? Why?"

"Part Four. Get his clothes in case he tries to sneak back into her house. Part Five. Leave fish for Becca."

"No."

"Yes. Now," she said. "She's upstairs getting yelled at by her parents. But, like, how long does that lecture last? I mean, what do you say? 'You shouldn't screw Margo's boyfriend in the basement.' It's a one-sentence lecture, basically. So we have to hustle."

She got out of the car with the spray paint in one hand and one of the catfish in the other. I whispered, "This is a bad idea," but I followed behind her, crouched down as she was, until we were standing in front of the still-open basement window.

"I'll go first," she said. She went in feetfirst and was standing on Becca's computer desk, half in the house and half out of it, when I asked her, "Can't I just be lookout?"

"Get your skinny ass in here," she answered, and so I did. Quickly, I grabbed all the boy-type clothes I saw on Becca's lavender-carpeted floor. A pair of jeans with a leather belt, a pair of flip-flops, a Winter Park High School Wildcats baseball cap, and a baby blue polo shirt. I turned back to Margo, who handed me the paper-wrapped catfish and one of Becca's sparkly purple pens. She told me what to write:

A message from Margo Roth Spiegelman: Your friendship with her—it sleeps with the fishes

Margo hid the fish between folded pairs of shorts in Becca's closet. I could hear footsteps upstairs, and tapped Margo on the shoulder and looked at her, my eyes bulging. She just smiled and leisurely pulled out the spray paint. I scrambled out the window, and then turned back to watch as Margo leaned over the desk and calmly shook the spray paint. In an elegant motion—the kind you associate with calligraphy or Zorro—she spray-painted the letter *M* onto the wall above the desk.

She reached her hands up to me, and I pulled her through the window. She was just starting to stand when we heard a high-pitched voice shout, "DWIGHT!" I grabbed the clothes and took off running, Margo behind me.

I heard, but did not see, the front door of Becca's house swing open, but I didn't stop or turn around, not when a booming voice shouted "HALT!" and not even when I heard the unmistakable sound of a shotgun being pumped.

I heard Margo mumble "gun" behind me—she didn't sound upset about it exactly; she was just making an observation—and then rather than walk around Becca's hedge, I dove over it headfirst. I'm not sure how I intended to land—maybe an artful somersault or something—but at any rate, I spilled onto the asphalt of the road, landing on my left shoulder. Fortunately, Jase's bundle of clothes hit the ground first, softening the blow.

I swore, and before I could even start to stand, I felt Margo's hands pulling me up, and then we were in the car and I was driving in reverse with the lights off, which is how I nearly came to run over the mostly naked starting shortstop of the Winter Park High School Wildcats baseball team. Jase was running very fast, but he didn't seem to be running anyplace in particular. I felt another stab of regret as we backed up past him, so I rolled the window halfway down and threw his polo in his general direction. Fortunately, I don't think he saw either Margo or me, and he had no reason to recognize the minivan since—and I don't want to sound bitter or anything by dwelling on this—*I can't drive it to school.*

"Why the hell would you do that?" Margo asked as I turned on the lights and, driving forward now, began to navigate the suburban labyrinth back toward the interstate.

"I felt bad for him."

"For him? Why? Because he's been cheating on me for six weeks? Because he's probably given me god-only-knows-what disease? Because he's a disgusting idiot who will probably be rich and happy his whole life, thus proving the absolute unfairness of the cosmos?"

"He just looked sort of desperate," I said.

"Whatever. We're going to Karin's house. It's on Pennsylvania, by the ABC Liquors."

"Don't be pissed at me," I said. "I just had a guy point a freaking shotgun at me for helping you, so don't be pissed at me."

"I'M NOT PISSED AT YOU!" Margo shouted, and then punched the dashboard.

"Well, you're screaming."

"I thought maybe—whatever. I thought maybe he wasn't cheating."

"Oh."

"Karin told me at school. And I guess a lot of people have known for a long time. And no one told me until Karin. I thought maybe she was just trying to stir up drama or something."

"I'm sorry," I said.

"Yeah. Yeah. I can't believe I even care."

"My heart is really pounding," I said.

"That's how you know you're having fun," Margo said.

But it didn't feel like fun; it felt like a heart attack. I pulled over into a 7-Eleven parking lot and held my finger to my jugular vein while watching the : in the digital clock blink every second. When I turned to Margo, she was rolling her eyes at me. "My pulse is dangerously high," I explained.

"I don't even remember the last time I got excited about something like that. The adrenaline in the throat and the lungs expanding."

"In through the nose out through the mouth," I answered her.

"All your little anxieties. It's just so . . ."

"Cute?"

"Is that what they're calling childish these days?" She smiled.

Margo crawled into the backseat and came back with a purse. *How much shit did she put back there?* I thought. She opened up the purse and pulled out a full bottle of nail polish so darkly red it was almost black. "While you calm down, I'm going to paint my nails," she said, smiling up at me through her bangs. "You just take your time."

And so we sat there, she with her nail polish balanced on the dash, and me with a shaky finger on the pulse of myself. It was a good color of nail polish, and Margo had nice fingers, thinner and bonier than the rest of her, which was all curves and soft edges. She had the kind of fingers you want to interlace with your own. I remembered them against my hip bone in Wal-Mart, which felt like days ago. My heartbeat slowed. And I tried to tell myself: Margo's right. There's nothing out here to be afraid of, not in this little city on this quiet night.

5.

"Part Six," Margo said once we were driving again. She was waving her fingernails through the air, almost like she was playing piano. "Leave flowers on Karin's doorstep with apologetic note."

"What'd you do to her?"

"Well, when she told me about Jase, I sort of shot the messenger."

"How so?" I asked. We were pulled up to a stoplight, and some kids in a sports car next to us were revving their engine—as if I was going to race the Chrysler. When you floored it, it whimpered.

"Well, I don't remember exactly what I called her, but it was something along the lines of 'sniveling, repulsive, idiotic, backne-ridden, snaggletoothed, fat-assed bitch with the worst hair in Central Florida—and that's saying something.'"

"Her hair *is* ridiculous," I said.

"*I know.* That was the only thing I said about her that was true. When you say nasty things about people, you should never say the true ones, because you can't really fully and honestly take those back, you know? I mean, there are highlights. And there are streaks. And then there are skunk stripes."

As I drove up to Karin's house, Margo disappeared into the way-back and returned with the bouquet of tulips. Taped to one of the flowers' stems was a note Margo'd folded to look like an envelope. She handed me the bouquet once I stopped, and I sprinted down a sidewalk, placed the flowers on Karin's doorstep, and sprinted back.

"Part Seven," she said as soon as I was back in the minivan. "Leave a fish for the lovely Mr. Worthington."

"I suspect he won't be home yet," I said, just the slightest hint of pity in my voice.

"I hope the cops find him barefoot, frenzied, and naked in some roadside ditch a week from now," Margo answered dispassionately.

"Remind me never to cross Margo Roth Spiegelman," I mumbled, and Margo laughed.

"Seriously," she said. "We bring the fucking *rain* down on our enemies."

"Your enemies," I corrected.

"We'll see," she answered quickly, and then perked up and said, "Oh, hey, I'll handle this one. The thing about Jason's house is they have this crazy good security system. And we can't have another panic attack."

"Um," I said.

Jason lived just down the road from Karin, in this uber-rich subdivision called Casavilla. All the houses in Casavilla are Spanish-style with the red-tile roofs and everything, only they weren't built by the Spanish. They were built by Jason's dad, who is one of the richest land developers in Florida. "Big, ugly homes for big, ugly people," I told Margo as we pulled into Casavilla.

"No shit. If I ever end up being the kind of person who has one kid and seven bedrooms, do me a favor and shoot me."

We pulled up in front of Jase's house, an architectural monstrosity that looked generally like an oversize Spanish hacienda except for three thick Doric columns going up to the roof. Margo grabbed the second catfish from the backseat, uncapped a pen with her teeth, and scrawled in handwriting that didn't look much like hers:

MS's love For you: it Sleeps With the Fishes

"Listen, keep the car on," she said. She put Jase's WPHS baseball hat on backward.

"Okay," I said.

"Keep it in drive," she said.

"Okay," I said, and felt my pulse rising. *In through the nose, out through the mouth. In through the nose, out through the mouth.* Catfish and spray paint in hand, Margo threw the door open, jogged across the Worthingtons' expansive front lawn, and then hid behind an oak tree. She waved at me through the darkness, and I waved back, and then she took a dramatically deep breath, puffed her cheeks out, turned, and ran.

She'd only taken one stride when the house lit up like a municipal Christmas tree, and a siren started blaring. I briefly contemplated abandoning Margo to her fate, but just kept breathing in through the nose and out through the mouth as she ran toward the house. She heaved the fish through a window, but the sirens were so loud I could barely even hear the glass breaking. And then, just because she's Margo Roth Spiegelman, she took a moment to carefully spray-paint a lovely *M* on the part of the window that wasn't shattered. Then she was running all out toward the car, and I had a foot on the accelerator and a foot on the brake, and the Chrysler felt at that moment like a Thoroughbred racehorse. Margo ran so fast her hat blew off behind her, and then she jumped into the car, and we were gone before she even got the door closed.

I stopped at the stop sign at the end of the street, and Margo said, "What the hell? Go go go go go," and I said, "Oh, right," because I had forgotten that I was throwing caution to the wind and everything. I rolled through the three other stop signs in Casavilla, and we were a mile down Pennsylvania Avenue before we saw a cop car roar past us with its lights on.

"That was pretty hardcore," Margo said. "I mean, even for me. To put it Q-style, my pulse is a little elevated."

"Jesus," I said. "I mean, you couldn't have just left it in his car? Or at least at the doorstep?"

"We bring the fucking *rain*, Q. Not the scattered showers."

"Tell me Part Eight is less terrifying."

"Don't worry. Part Eight is child's play. We're going back to Jefferson Park. Lacey's house. You know where she lives, right?" I did, although God knows Lacey Pemberton would never deign to have me over. She lived on the opposite side of Jefferson Park, a mile away from me, in a nice condo on top of a stationery store—the same block the dead guy had lived on, actually. I'd been to the building before, because friends of my parents lived on the third floor. There were two locked doors before you even got to the condos. I figured even Margo Roth Spiegelman couldn't break into that place.

"So has Lacey been naughty or nice?" I asked.

"Lacey has been *distinctly* naughty," Margo answered. She was looking out the passenger window again, talking away from me, so I could barely hear her. "I mean, we have been friends since kindergarten."

"And?"

"And she didn't tell me about Jase. But not just that. When I look back on it, she's just a *terrible* friend. I mean, for instance, do you think I'm fat?"

"Jesus, no," I said. "You're—" And I stopped myself from saying *not skinny, but that's the whole point of you; the point of you is that you don't look like a boy.* "You should not lose any weight."

She laughed, waved her hand at me, and said, "You just love my big ass." I turned from the road for a second and glanced over, and I shouldn't have, because she could read my face and my face said: Well, first off I wouldn't say it's *big* exactly and second off, it *is* kind of spectacular. But it was more than that. You can't divorce Margo the person from Margo the body. You can't see one without seeing the other. You looked at Margo's eyes and you saw both their blueness and their Margo-ness. In the end, you could not say that Margo Roth Spiegelman was fat, or that she was skinny, any more than you can say that the Eiffel Tower is or is not lonely. Margo's beauty was a kind of sealed vessel of perfection—uncracked and uncrackable.

"But she would always make these little comments," Margo continued. "'I'd loan you these shorts but I don't think they'd fit right on you.' Or, 'You're so spunky. I love how you just make guys fall in love with your personality.' Constantly undermining me. I don't think she ever said anything that wasn't an attempt at undermination."

"Undermining."

"Thank you, Annoying McMasterGrammician."

"Grammarian," I said.

"Oh my God I'm going to kill you!" But she was laughing.

I drove around the perimeter of Jefferson Park so we could avoid driving past our houses, just in case our parents had woken up and discovered us missing. We drove in along the lake (Lake Jefferson), and then turned onto Jefferson Court and drove into Jefferson Park's little faux downtown, which felt eerily deserted and quiet. We found Lacey's black SUV parked in front of the sushi restaurant. We stopped a block away in the first parking spot we could find not beneath a streetlight.

"Would you please hand me the last fish?" Margo asked me. I was glad to get rid of the fish because it was already starting to smell. And then Margo wrote on the paper wrapper in her lettering:

your Friendship with ms Sleeps with The fishes

We wove our way around the circular glow of the streetlights, walking as casually as two people can when one of them (Margo) is holding a sizable fish wrapped in paper and the other one (me) is holding a can of blue spray paint. A dog barked, and we both froze, but then it was quiet again, and soon we were at Lacey's car.

"Well, that makes it harder," Margo said, seeing it was locked. She reached into her pocket and pulled out a length of wire that had once been a coat hanger. It took her less than a minute to jimmy the lock open. I was duly awed.

Once she had the driver's-side door open, she reached over and opened my side. "Hey, help me get the seat up," she whispered. Together we pulled the backseat up. Margo slipped the fish underneath it, and then she counted to three, and in one motion we slammed the seat down on the fish. I heard the disgusting sound of catfish guts exploding. I let myself imagine the way Lacey's SUV would smell after just one day of roasting in the sun, and I'll admit that a kind of serenity washed over me. And then Margo said, "Put an *M* on the roof for me."

I didn't even have to think about it for a full second before I nodded, scrambled up onto the back bumper, and then leaned over, quickly spraying a gigantic *M* all across the roof. Generally, I am opposed to vandalism. But I am also generally opposed to Lacey Pemberton—and in the end, that proved to be the more deeply held conviction. I jumped off the car. I ran through the darkness—my breath coming fast and short—for the block back to the minivan. As I put my hand on the steering wheel, I noticed my pointer finger was blue. I held it up for Margo to see. She smiled, and held out her own blue finger, and then they touched, and her blue finger was pushing against mine softly and my pulse failed to slow. And then after a long time, she said, "Part Nine—downtown."

It was 2:49 in the morning. I had never, in my entire life, felt less tired.

6.

Tourists never go to downtown Orlando, because there's nothing there but a few skyscrapers owned by banks and insurance companies. It's the kind of downtown that becomes absolutely deserted at night and on the weekends, except for a few nightclubs half-filled with the desperate and the desperately lame. As I followed Margo's directions through the maze of one-way streets, we saw a few people sleeping on the sidewalk or sitting on benches, but nobody was moving. Margo rolled down the window, and I felt the thick air blow across my face, warmer than night ought to be. I glanced over and saw strands of hair blowing all around her face. Even though I could see her there, I felt entirely alone among these big and empty buildings, like I'd survived the apocalypse and the world had been given to me, this whole and amazing and endless world, mine for the exploring.

"You just giving me the tour?" I asked.

"No," she said. "I'm trying to get to the SunTrust Building. It's right next to the Asparagus."

"Oh," I said, because for once on this night I had useful information. "That's on South." I drove down a few blocks and then turned. Margo pointed happily, and yes, there, before us, was the Asparagus.

The Asparagus is not, technically, an asparagus spear, nor is it derived from asparagus parts. It is just a sculpture that bears an uncanny resemblance to a thirty-foot-tall piece of asparagus—although I've also heard it likened to:

1. A green-glass beanstalk
2. An abstract representation of a tree
3. A greener, glassier, uglier Washington Monument
4. The Jolly Green Giant's gigantic jolly green phallus

At any rate, it certainly does *not* look like a Tower of Light, which is the actual name of the sculpture. I pulled in front of a parking meter and looked over at Margo. I caught her staring into the middle distance just for a moment, her eyes blank, looking not at the Asparagus, but past it. It was the first time I thought something might be wrong—not my-boyfriend-is-an-ass wrong, but really *wrong*. And I should have said something. Of course. I should have said thing after thing after thing after thing. But I only said, "May I ask why you have taken me to the Asparagus?"

She turned her head to me and shot me a smile. Margo was so beautiful that even her fake smiles were convincing. "We gotta check on our progress. And the best place to do that is from the top of the SunTrust Building."

I rolled my eyes. "Nope. No. No way. You said no breaking and entering."

"This isn't breaking and entering. It's just entering, because there's an unlocked door."

"Margo, that's ridiculous. Of c—"

"I will acknowledge that over the course of the evening there has been both breaking and entering. There was entering at Becca's house. There was breaking at Jase's house. And there will be entering here. But there has never been simultaneous breaking and entering. Theoretically, the cops could charge us with breaking, and they could charge us with entering, but they could not charge us with breaking *and* entering. So I've kept my promise."

"Surely the SunTrust Building has, like, a security guard or whatever," I said.

"They do," she said, unbuckling her seat belt. "Of course they do. His name is Gus."

We walked in through the front door. Sitting behind a broad, semicircular desk sat a young guy with a struggling goatee wearing a Regents Security uniform. "What's up, Margo?" he said.

"Hey, Gus," she answered.

"Who's the kid?"

WE ARE THE SAME AGE! I wanted to shout, but I let Margo talk for me. "This is my colleague, Q. Q, this is Gus."

"What's up, Q?" asked Gus.

Oh, we're just scattering some dead fish about town, breaking some windows, photographing naked guys, hanging out in skyscraper lobbies at three-fifteen in the morning, that kind of thing. "Not much," I answered.

"Elevators are down for the night," Gus said. "Had to shut 'em off at three. You're welcome to take the stairs, though."

"Cool. See ya, Gus."

"See ya, Margo."

"How the hell do you know the security guard at the SunTrust Building?" I asked once we were safely in the stairwell.

"He was a senior when we were freshmen," she answered. "We gotta hustle, okay? Time's a-wastin'." Margo started taking the stairs two at a time, flying up, one arm on the rail, and I tried to keep pace with her, but couldn't. Margo didn't play any sports, but she liked to run—I sometimes saw her running by herself listening to music in Jefferson Park. I, however, did not like to run. Or, for that matter, engage in any kind of physical exertion. But now I tried to keep up a steady pace, wiping the sweat off my forehead and ignoring the burning in my legs. When I got to the twenty-fifth floor, Margo was standing on the landing, waiting for me.

"Check it out," she said. She opened the stairwell door and we were inside a huge room with an oak table as long as two cars, and a long bank of floor-to-ceiling windows. "Conference room," she said. "It's got the best view in the whole building." I followed her as she walked along the windows. "Okay, so there," she said pointing, "is Jefferson Park. See our houses? Lights still off, so that's good." She moved over a few panes. "Jase's house. Lights off, no more cop cars. Excellent, although it might mean he's made it home, which is unfortunate." Becca's house was too far away to see, even from up here.

She was quiet for a moment, and then she walked right up to the glass and leaned her forehead against it. I hung back, but then she grabbed my T-shirt and pulled me forward. I didn't want our collective weight against a single pane of glass, but she kept pulling me forward, and I could feel her balled fist in my side, and finally I put my head against the glass as gently as possible and looked around.

From above, Orlando was pretty well lit. Beneath us I could see the flashing DON'T WALK signs at intersections, and the streetlights running up and down the city in a perfect grid until downtown ended and the winding streets and cul-de-sacs of Orlando's infinite suburb started.

"It's beautiful," I said.

Margo scoffed. "Really? You seriously think so?"

"I mean, well, maybe not," I said, although it was. When I saw Orlando from an airplane, it looked like a LEGO set sunk into an ocean of green. Here, at night, it looked like a real place—but for the first time, a place I could see. As I walked around the conference room, and then through the other offices on the floor, I could see it all: there was school. There was Jefferson Park. There, in the distance, Disney World. There was Wet 'n Wild. There, the 7-Eleven where Margo painted her nails and I fought for breath. It was all here—my whole world, and I could see it just by walking around a building. "It's more impressive," I said out loud. "From a distance, I mean. You can't see the wear on things, you know? You can't see the rust or the weeds or the paint cracking. You see the place as someone once imagined it."

"Everything's uglier close up," she said.

"Not you," I answered before thinking better of it.

Her forehead still against the glass, she turned to me and smiled. "Here's a tip: you're cute when you're confident. And less when you're not." Before I had a chance to say anything, her eyes went back to the view and she started talking. "Here's what's not beautiful about it: from here, you can't see the rust or the cracked paint or whatever, but you can tell what the place really is. You see how fake it all is. It's not even hard enough to be made out of plastic. It's a paper town. I mean look at it, Q: look at all those cul-de-sacs, those streets that turn in on themselves, all the houses that were built to fall apart. All those paper people living in their paper houses, burning the future to stay warm. All the paper kids drinking beer some bum bought for them at the paper convenience store. Everyone demented with the mania of owning things. All the things paper-thin and paper-frail. And all the people, too. I've lived here for eighteen years and I have never once in my life come across anyone who cares about anything that matters."

"I'll try not to take that personally," I said. We were both staring into the inky distance, the cul-de-sacs and quarter-acre lots. But her shoulder was against my arm, and the backs of our hands were touching, and although I was not looking at Margo, pressing myself against the glass felt almost like pressing myself against her.

"Sorry," she said. "Maybe things would have been different for me if I'd been hanging out with you the whole time instead of—ugh. Just, God. I just hate myself so much for even caring about my, quote, friends. I mean, just so you know, it's not that I am oh-so-upset about Jason. Or Becca. Or even Lacey, although I actually liked her. But it was the last string. It was a lame string, for sure, but it was the one I had left, and every paper girl needs at least one string, right?"

And here is what I said. I said, "You would be welcome at our lunch table tomorrow."

"That's sweet," she answered, her voice trailing off. She turned to me and nodded softly. I smiled. She smiled. I believed the smile. We walked to the stairs and then ran down them. At the bottom of each flight, I jumped off the bottom step and clicked my heels to make her laugh, and she laughed. I thought I was cheering her up. I thought she was cheerable. I thought maybe if I could be confident, something might happen between us.

I was wrong.

7.

Sitting in the minivan with the keys in the ignition but the engine not yet started, she asked, "What time do your parents get up, by the way?"

"I don't know, like, six-fifteen?" It was 3:51. "I mean, we have two-plus hours and we're through with nine parts."

"I know, but I saved the most laborious one for last. Anyway, we'll get it all done. Part Ten—Q's turn to pick a victim."

"What?"

"I already picked a punishment. Now you just pick who we're going to rain our mighty wrath down on."

"Upon whom we are going to rain our mighty wrath," I corrected her, and she shook her head in disgust. "And I don't really have anyone upon whom I want to rain down my wrath," I said, because in truth I didn't. I always felt like you had to be important to have enemies. Example: Historically, Germany has had more enemies than Luxembourg. Margo Roth Spiegelman was Germany. And Great Britain. And the United States. And czarist Russia. Me, I'm Luxembourg. Just sitting around, tending sheep, and yodeling.

"What about Chuck?" she asked.

"Hmm," I said. Chuck Parson *was* pretty horrible in all those years before he'd been reined in. Aside from the cafeteria conveyor belt debacle, he once grabbed me outside school while I waited for the bus and twisted my arm and kept saying, "Call yourself a faggot." That was his all-purpose, I-have-a-vocabulary-of-twelve-words-so-don't-expect-a-wide-variety-of-insults insult. And even though it was ridiculously childish, in the end I had to call myself a faggot, which really annoyed me, because 1. I don't think that word should ever be used by anyone, let alone me, and 2. As it happens, I am not gay, and furthermore, 3. Chuck Parson made it out like calling yourself a faggot was the ultimate humiliation, even though there's nothing at all embarrassing about being gay, which I was trying to say while he twisted my arm farther and farther toward my shoulder blade, but he just kept saying, "If you're so proud of being a faggot, why don't you admit that you're a faggot, faggot?"

Clearly, Chuck Parson was no Aristotle when it came to logic. But he was six three, and 270 pounds, which counts for something.

"You could make a case for Chuck," I acknowledged. And then I turned on the car and started to make my way back toward the interstate. I didn't know where we were going, but we sure as hell weren't staying downtown.

"Remember at the Crown School of Dance?" she asked. "I was just thinking about that tonight."

"Ugh. Yeah."

"I'm sorry about that, by the way. I have no idea why I went along with him."

"Yeah. It's all good," I said, but remembering the godforsaken Crown School of Dance pissed me off, and I said, "Yeah. Chuck Parson. You know where he lives?"

"I knew I could bring out your vengeful side. He's in College Park. Get off at Princeton." I turned onto the interstate entrance ramp and floored it. "Whoa there," Margo said. "Don't break the Chrysler."

In sixth grade, a bunch of kids including Margo and Chuck and me were forced by our parents to take ballroom dancing lessons at the Crown School of Humiliation, Degradation, and Dance. And how it worked was the boys would stand on one side and the girls would stand on the other and then when the teacher told us to, the boys would walk over to the girls and the boy would say, "May I have this dance?" and the girl would say, "You may." Girls were *not allowed* to say no. But then one day—we were doing the fox-trot—Chuck Parson convinced every single girl to say no to me. Not anyone else. Just me. So I walked across to Mary Beth Shortz and I said, "May I have this dance?" and she said no. And then I asked another girl, and then another, and then Margo, who also said no, and then another, and then I started to cry.

The only thing worse than getting rejected at dance school is crying about getting rejected at dance school, and the only thing worse than that is going to the dance teacher and saying through your tears, "The girls are saying no to me and they're not *supposedtuh*." So of course I went weeping to the teacher, and I spent the majority of middle school trying to live down that one embarrassing event. So, long story short, Chuck Parson kept me from ever dancing the fox-trot, which doesn't seem like a particularly horrible thing to do to a sixth-grader. And I wasn't really pissed about it anymore, or about everything else he'd done to me over the years. But I certainly wasn't going to lament his suffering.

"Wait, he won't know it's me, will he?"

"Nope. Why?"

"I don't want him to think I give enough of a shit about him to hurt him." I put a hand down on the center console and Margo patted it. "Don't worry," she said. "He'll never know what depilatated him."

"I think you just misused a word, but I don't know what it means."

"I know a word you don't know," Margo chanted. "I'M THE NEW QUEEN OF VOCABULARY! I'VE USURPED YOU!"

"Spell *usurped*," I told her.

"No," she answered, laughing. "I'm not giving up my crown over *usurped*. You'll have to do better."

"Fine." I smiled.

We drove through College Park, a neighborhood that passes for Orlando's historic district on account of how the houses were mostly built thirty whole years ago. Margo couldn't remember Chuck's exact address, or what his house looked like, or even for sure what street it was on ("I'm almost like ninety-five percent positive it's on Vassar."). Finally, after the Chrysler had prowled three blocks of Vassar Street, Margo pointed to her left and said, "That one."

"Are you sure?" I asked.

"I'm like ninety-seven-point-two percent sure. I mean, I'm pretty sure his bedroom is right there," she said, pointing. "One time he had a party, and when the cops came I shimmied out his window. I'm pretty sure it's the same window."

"This seems like we could get in trouble."

"But if the window is open, there's no breaking involved. Only entering. And we *just* did entering at the SunTrust, and it wasn't that big of a deal, right?"

I laughed. "It's like you're turning me into a badass."

"That's the idea. Okay, supplies: get the Veet, the spray paint, and the Vaseline."

"Okay." I grabbed them.

"Now don't freak out on me, Q. The good news is that Chuck sleeps like a hibernating bear—I know because I had English with him last year and he wouldn't wake up even when Ms. Johnston swatted him with *Jane Eyre*. So we're going to go up to his bedroom window, we're gonna open it, we're gonna take off our shoes, and then very quietly go inside, and I'm going to screw with Chuck. Then you and I are going to fan out to opposite sides of the house, and we're going to cover every door handle in Vaseline, so even if someone wakes up, they'll have a hella hard time getting out of the house in time to catch us. Then we'll screw with Chuck some more, paint his house a little, and we're out of there. And no talking."

I put my hand to my jugular, but I was smiling.

We were walking away from the car together when Margo reached down for my hand, laced her fingers in mine, and squeezed. I squeezed back and then glanced at her. She nodded her head solemnly, and I nodded back, and then she let go of my hand. We scampered up to the window. I gently pushed the wooden casing up. It squeaked ever so quietly but opened in one motion. I looked in. It was dark, but I could see a body in a bed.

The window was a little high for Margo, so I put my hands together and she stepped a socked foot onto my hand and I boosted her up. Her silent entrance into the house would have made a ninja jealous. I proceeded to jump up, get my head and shoulders into the window, and then attempt, via a complicated torso undulation, to dance the caterpillar into the house. That might have worked fine except I racked my balls against the windowsill, which hurt so bad that I groaned, which was a pretty sizable mistake.

A bedside light came on. And there, lying in bed, was some old guy—decidedly not Chuck Parson. His eyes were wide with terror; he didn't say a thing.

"Um," said Margo. I thought about shoving off and running back to the car, but for Margo's sake I stayed there, the top half of me in the house, parallel to the floor. "Um, I think we have the wrong house." She turned around then and looked at me urgently, and only then did I realize I was blocking Margo's exit. So I pushed myself back out the window, grabbed my shoes, and took off.

We drove to the other side of College Park to regroup.

"I think we share the blame on that one," Margo said.

"Um, *you picked the wrong house*," I said.

"Right, but *you* were the one who made noise." It was quiet for a minute, and we were just driving in circles, and then finally I said, "We could probably get his address off the Internet. Radar has a log-in to the school directory."

"Brilliant," Margo said.

So I called Radar, but his phone went straight to voice mail. I contemplated calling his house, but his parents were friends with my parents, so that wouldn't work. Finally, it occurred to me to call Ben. He wasn't Radar, but he did know all of Radar's passwords. I called. It went to voice mail, but only after ringing. So I called again. Voice mail. I called again. Voice mail. Margo said, "He's obviously not answering," and as I dialed again, I said, "Oh, he'll answer." And after just four more calls, he did.

"You'd better be calling me to say that there are eleven naked honeybunnies in your house, and that they're asking for the Special Feeling that only Big Daddy Ben can provide."

"I need you to use Radar's login to the student directory and look up an address. Chuck Parson."

"No."

"Please," I said.

"No."

"You'll be glad you did this, Ben. I promise."

"Yeah yeah, I just did it. I was doing it while saying no—can't help but help. Four-two-two Amherst. Hey, why do you want Chuck Parson's address at four-twelve in the morning?"

"Get some sleep, Benners."

"I'm going to assume this is a dream," Ben answered, and hung up.

Amherst was only a couple blocks down. We parked on the street in front of 418 Amherst, got our supplies together, and jogged across Chuck's lawn, the morning dew shaking off the grass and onto my calves.

At his window, which was fortunately lower than that of Random Old Guy, I climbed in quietly and then pulled Margo up and in. Chuck Parson was asleep on his back. Margo walked over to him, tiptoeing, and I stood behind her, my heart pounding. He'd kill us both if he woke up. She pulled out the Veet, sprayed a dob of what looked like shaving cream onto her palm, and then softly and carefully spread it across Chuck's right eyebrow. He didn't so much as twitch.

Then she opened the Vaseline—the lid made what seemed like a deafeningly loud *clorp*, but again Chuck showed no sign of waking. She scooped a huge gob of it into my hand, and then we headed off to opposite sides of the house. I went to the entryway first and slathered Vaseline on the front door's doorknob, and then to the open door of a bedroom, where I Vaselined the inner knob and then quietly, with only the slightest creak, shut the door to the room.

Finally I returned to Chuck's room—Margo was already there—and together we closed his door and then Vaselined the hell out of Chuck's doorknob. We slathered every surface of his bedroom window with the rest of the Vaseline, hoping it would make it hard to open the window after we closed it shut on our way out.

Margo glanced at her watch and held up two fingers. We waited. And for those two minutes we just stared at each other, and I watched the blue in her eyes. It was nice—in the dark and the quiet, with no possibility of me saying anything to screw it up, and her eyes looking back, like there was something in me worth seeing.

Margo nodded then, and I walked over to Chuck. I wrapped my hand in my T-shirt, as she'd told me to do, leaned forward, and—as softly as I could—pressed my finger against his forehead and then quickly wiped away the Veet. With it came every last hair that had been Chuck Parson's right eyebrow. I was standing above Chuck with his right eyebrow on my T-shirt when his eyes shot open. Lightning fast, Margo grabbed his comforter and threw it over him, and when I looked up, the little ninja was already out the window. I followed as quickly as I could, as Chuck screamed, "MAMA! DAD! ROBBERY ROBBERY!"

I wanted to say, *The only thing we stole was your eyebrow,* but I kept mum as I swung myself feetfirst out the window. I damn near landed on Margo, who was spray-painting an *M* onto the vinyl siding of Chuck's house, and then we both grabbed our shoes and hauled ass to the minivan. When I looked back at the house, lights were on but no one was outside yet, a testament to the brilliant simplicity of the well-Vaselined doorknob. By the time Mr. (or possibly Mrs., I couldn't really see) Parson pulled open the living room curtains and looked outside, we were driving in reverse back toward Princeton Street and the interstate.

"Yes!" I shouted. "God, that was brilliant."

"Did you see it? His face without the eyebrow? He looks permanently doubtful, you know? Like, 'oh, really? You're saying I only have one eyebrow? Likely story.' And I love making that asshole choose: better to shave off Lefty, or paint on Righty? Oh, I just love it. And how he yelled for his mama, that sniveling little shit."

"Wait, why do *you* hate him?"

"I didn't say I hated him. I said he was a sniveling little shit."

"But you were always kind of friends with him," I said, or at least I thought she had been.

"Yeah, well, I was always kind of friends with a lot of people," she said. Margo leaned across the minivan and put her head on my bony shoulder, her hair falling against my neck. "I'm tired," she said.

"Caffeine," I said. She reached into the back and grabbed us each a Mountain Dew, and I drank it in two long chugs.

"So we're going to SeaWorld," she told me. "Part Eleven."

"What, are we going to Free Willy or something?"

"No," she said. "We're just going to go to SeaWorld, that's all. It's the only theme park I haven't broken into yet."

"We can't break into SeaWorld," I said, and then I pulled over into an empty furniture store parking lot and turned off the car.

"We're in a bit of a time crunch," she told me, and then reached over to start the car again.

I pushed her hand away. "We can't break into SeaWorld," I repeated.

"There you go with the breaking again." Margo paused and opened another Mountain Dew. Light reflected off the can onto her face, and for a second, I could see her smiling at the thing she was about to say. "We're not going to *break* anything. Don't think of it as *breaking in* to SeaWorld. Think of it as visiting SeaWorld in the middle of the night for free."

8.

"Well, first off, we will get caught," I said. I hadn't started the minivan and was laying out the reasons I wouldn't start it and wondering if she could see me in the dark.

"Of course we'll get caught. So what?"

"It's illegal."

"Q, in the scheme of things, what kind of trouble can SeaWorld get you into? I mean, Jesus, after everything I've done for you tonight, you can't do one thing for me? You can't just shut up and calm down and stop being so goddamned terrified of every little adventure?" And then under her breath she said, "I mean, God. Grow some nuts."

And now I was mad. I ducked underneath my shoulder belt so I could lean across the console toward her. "After everything YOU did for ME?" I almost shouted. She wanted confident? I was getting confident. "Did you call MY friend's father who was screwing MY boyfriend so no one would know that I was calling? Did you chauffeur MY ass all around the world not because you are oh-so-important to me but because I needed a ride and you were close by? Is that the kind of shit you've done for me tonight?"

She wouldn't look at me. She just stared straight ahead at the vinyl siding of the furniture store. "You think I needed you? You don't think I could have given Myrna Mountweazel a Benadryl so she'd sleep through my stealing the safe from under my parents' bed? Or snuck into your bedroom while you were sleeping and taken your car key? I didn't need you, you idiot. I *picked* you. And then you picked me back." Now she looked at me. "And that's like a promise. At least for tonight. In sickness and in health. In good times and in bad. For richer, for poorer. Till dawn do us part."

I started the car and pulled out of the parking lot, but all her teamwork stuff aside, I still felt like I was getting badgered into something, and I wanted the last word. "Fine, but when SeaWorld, Incorporated, or whatever sends a letter to Duke University saying that miscreant Quentin Jacobsen broke into their facility at four-thirty in the morning with a wild-eyed lass at his side, Duke University will be mad. Also, my parents will be mad."

"Q, you're going to go to Duke. You're going to be a very successful lawyer-or-something and get married and have babies and live your whole little life, and then you're going to die, and in your last moments, when you're choking on your own bile in the nursing home, you'll say to yourself: 'Well, I wasted my whole goddamned life, but at least I broke into SeaWorld with Margo Roth Spiegelman my senior year of high school. At least I carpe'd that one diem.'"

"*Noctem*," I corrected.

"Okay, you are the Grammar King again. You've regained your throne. Now take me to SeaWorld."

As we drove silently down I-4, I found myself thinking about the day that the guy in the gray suit showed up dead. *Maybe that's the reason she chose me*, I thought. And that's when, finally, I remembered what she said about the dead guy and the strings—and about herself and the strings.

"Margo," I said, breaking our silence.

"Q," she said.

"You said . . . When the guy died, you said maybe all the strings inside him broke, and then you just said that about yourself, that the last string broke."

She half laughed. "You worry too much. I don't want some kids to find me swarmed with flies on a Saturday morning in Jefferson Park." She waited a beat before delivering the punch line. "I'm too vain for that fate."

I laughed, relieved, and exited the interstate. We turned onto International Drive, the tourism capital of the world. There were a thousand shops on International Drive, and they all sold the exact same thing: crap. Crap molded into seashells, key rings, glass turtles, Florida-shaped refrigerator magnets, plastic pink flamingos, whatever. In fact, there were several stores on I-Drive that sold actual, literal armadillo crap—$4.95 a bag.

But at 4:50 in the morning, the tourists were sleeping. The Drive was completely dead, like everything else, as we drove past store after parking lot after store after parking lot.

"SeaWorld is just past the parkway," Margo said. She was in the wayback of the minivan again, rifling through a backpack or something. "I got all these satellite maps and drew our plan of attack, but I can't freaking find them anywhere. But anyway, just go right past the parkway, and on your left there will be this souvenir shop."

"On my left, there are about seventeen thousand souvenir shops."

"Right, but there will only be one right after the parkway."

And sure enough, there was only one, and so I pulled into the empty parking lot and parked the car directly beneath a streetlight, because cars are always getting stolen on I-Drive. And while only a truly masochistic car thief would ever think of jacking the Chrysler, I still didn't relish the thought of explaining to my mom how and why her car went missing in the small hours of a school night.

We stood outside, leaning against the back of the minivan, the air so warm and thick I felt my clothes clinging to my skin. I felt scared again, as if people I couldn't see were looking at me. It had been too dark for too long, and my gut ached from the hours of worrying. Margo had found her maps, and by the light of the street lamp, her spray-paint-blue fingertip traced our route. "I think there's a fence right there," she said, pointing to a wooden patch we'd hit just after crossing the parkway. "I read about it online. They installed it a few years ago after some drunk guy walked into the park in the middle of the night and decided to go swimming with Shamu, who promptly killed him."

"Seriously?"

"Yeah, so if that guy can make it in drunk, surely we can make it in sober. I mean, we're ninjas."

"Well, maybe *you're* a ninja," I said.

"You're just a really loud, awkward ninja," Margo said, "but we are both ninjas." She tucked her hair behind her ears, pulled up her hood, and scrunched it shut with a drawstring; the streetlight lit up the sharp features of her pale face. Maybe we were both ninjas, but only she had the outfit.

"Okay," she said. "Memorize the map." By far the most terrifying part of the half-mile-long journey Margo had plotted for us was the moat. SeaWorld was shaped like a triangle. One side was protected by a road, which Margo figured was regularly patrolled by night watchmen. The second side was guarded by a lake that was at least a mile around, and the third side had a drainage ditch; from the map, it looked to be about as wide as a two-lane road. And where there are water-filled drainage ditches near lakes in Florida, there are often alligators.

Margo grabbed me by both shoulders and turned me toward her. "We're going to get caught, probably, and when we do, just let me talk. You just look cute and be that weird mix of innocent and confident, and we'll be fine."

I locked the car, tried to pat down my puffy hair, and whispered, "I'm a ninja." I didn't mean for Margo to hear, but she piped up. "Damned right you are! Now let's go."

We jogged across I-Drive and then started bushwhacking through a thicket of tall shrubs and oak trees. I started to worry about poison ivy, but ninjas don't worry about poison ivy, so I led the trail, my arms in front of me, pushing aside briars and brush as we walked toward the moat. Finally the trees stopped and the field opened up, and I could see the parkway on our right and the moat straight ahead of us. People could have seen us from the road if there had been any cars, but there weren't. Together we took off running through the brush, and then made a sharp turn toward the parkway. Margo said, "Now, now!" and I dashed across the six lanes of highway. Even though it was empty, something felt exhilarating and wrong about running across a road that big.

We made it across and then knelt down in the knee-high grass beside the parkway. Margo pointed to the strip of trees between SeaWorld's endlessly gigantic parking lot and the black standing water of the moat. We ran for a minute along that line of trees, and then Margo pulled on the back of my shirt, and said quietly, "Now the moat."

"Ladies first," I said.

"No, really. Be my guest," she answered.

And I didn't think about the alligators or the disgusting layer of brackish algae. I just got a running start and jumped as far as I could. I landed in waist-deep water and then high-stepped across. The water smelled rank and felt slimy on my skin, but at least I wasn't wet above my waist. Or at least I wasn't until Margo jumped in, splashing water all over me. I turned around and splashed her. She faux-retched.

"Ninjas don't splash other ninjas," Margo complained.

"The true ninja doesn't make a splash at all," I said.

"Ooh, touché."

I was watching Margo pull herself up out of the moat. And I was feeling thoroughly pleased about the lack of alligators. And my pulse was acceptable, if brisk. And beneath her unzipped hoodie, her black T-shirt had become clingy in the water. In short, a lot of things were going pretty well when I saw in my peripheral vision a slithering in the water beside Margo. Margo started to step out of the water, and I could see her Achilles tendon tensing, and before I could even say anything, the snake lashed out and bit her left ankle, right below the line of her jeans.

"Shit!" Margo said, and she looked down and then said "Shit!" again. The snake was still attached. I dove down and grabbed the snake by the tail and ripped it from Margo's leg and threw it into the moat. "Ow, God," she said. "What was it? Was it a moccasin?"

"I don't know. Lie down lie down," I said, and then I took her leg in my hands, and I pulled up her jeans. There were two drops of blood coming out where the fangs had been, and I leaned down and put my mouth on the wound and sucked as hard as I could, trying to draw out the venom. I spit, and was going to go back to her leg when she said, "Wait, I see it." I jumped up, terrified, and she said, "No no, God, it's just a garter snake." She was pointing into the moat, and I followed her finger and could see the little garter snake skirting along the surface, swimming beneath a floodlight's skirt. From the well-lit distance, the thing didn't look much scarier than a baby lizard.

"Thank God," I said, sitting down next to her and catching my breath.

After looking at the bite and seeing that the bleeding had already stopped, she asked, "How was making out with my leg?"

"Pretty good," I said, which was true. She leaned her body into mine a little and I could feel her upper arm against my ribs.

"I shaved this morning for *precisely* that reason. I was like, 'Well, you never know when someone is going to clamp down on your calf and try to suck out the snake poison.'"

There was a chain-link fence before us, but it was only about six feet tall. As Margo put it, "Honestly, first garter snakes and now this fence? This security is sort of insulting to a ninja." She scampered up, swung her body around, and climbed down like it was a ladder. I managed not to fall.

We ran through a small thicket of trees, hugging tight against these huge opaque tanks that might have stored animals, and then we came out to an asphalt path and I could see the big amphitheater where Shamu splashed me when I was a kid. The little speakers lining the walkway were playing soft Muzak. Maybe to keep the animals calm. "Margo," I said, "we're in SeaWorld."

And she said, "Seriously," and then she jogged away and I followed her. We ended up by the seal tank, but it seemed like there were no seals inside it.

"Margo," I said again. "We're in SeaWorld."

"Enjoy it," she said without moving her mouth much. "'Cause here comes security." I dashed through a stand of waist-high bushes, but when Margo didn't run, I stopped. A guy strolled up wearing a SEAWORLD SECURITY vest and very casually asked, "How y'all?" He held a can of something in his hand—pepper spray, I guessed.

To stay calm, I wondered to myself, *Does he have regular handcuffs, or does he have special SeaWorld handcuffs? Like, are they shaped like two curved dolphins coming together?*

"We were just on our way out, actually," said Margo.

"Well, that's certain," the man said. "The question is whether you walkin' out or gettin' driven out by the Orange County sheriff."

"If it's all the same to you," Margo said, "we'd rather walk." I shut my eyes. This, I wanted to tell Margo, was no time for snappy comebacks. But the man laughed.

"You know a man got kilt here a couple years ago jumping in the big tank, and they told us we cain't never let anybody go if they break in, no matter if they're pretty." Margo pulled her shirt out so it wouldn't look so clingy. And only then did I realize he was talking to her breasts.

"Well, then I guess you have to arrest us."

"But that's the thing. I'm 'bout to get off and go home and have a beer and get some sleep, and if I call the police they'll take their sweet time in coming. I'm just thinkin' out loud here," he said, and then Margo raised her eyes in recognition. She wiggled a hand into a wet pocket and pulled out one moat-water-soaked hundred-dollar bill.

The guard said, "Well, y'all best be getting on now. If I were you, I wouldn't walk out past the whale tank. It's got all-night security cameras all 'round it, and we wouldn't want anyone to know y'all was here."

"Yessir," Margo said demurely, and with that the man walked off into the darkness. "Man," Margo mumbled as the guy walked away, "I really didn't want to pay that perv. But, oh well. Money's for spendin'." I could barely even hear her; the only thing happening was the relief shivering out of my skin. This raw pleasure was worth all the worry that preceded it.

"Thank God he's not turning us in," I said.

Margo didn't respond. She was staring past me, her eyes squinting almost closed. "I felt this exact same way when I got into Universal Studios," she said after a moment. "It's kind of cool and everything, but there's nothing much to see. The rides aren't working. Everything cool is locked up. Most of the animals are put into different tanks at night." She turned her head and appraised the SeaWorld we could see. "I guess the pleasure isn't being inside."

"What's the pleasure?" I asked.

"Planning, I guess. I don't know. Doing stuff never feels as good as you hope it will feel."

"This feels pretty good to me," I confessed. "Even if there isn't anything to see." I sat down on a park bench, and she joined me. We were both looking out at the seal tank, but it contained no seals, just an unoccupied island with rocky outcroppings made of plastic. I could smell her next to me, the sweat and the algae from the moat, her shampoo like lilacs, and the smell of her skin like crushed almonds.

I felt tired for the first time, and I thought of us lying down on some grassy patch of SeaWorld together, me on my back and she on her side with her arm draped against me, her head on my shoulder, facing me. Not doing anything—just lying there together beneath the sky, the night here so well lit that it drowns out the stars. And maybe I could feel her breathe against my neck, and maybe we could just stay there until morning and then the people would walk past as they came into the park, and they would see us and think that we were tourists, too, and we could just disappear into them.

But no. There was one-eyebrowed Chuck to see, and Ben to tell the story to, and classes and the band room and Duke and the future.

"Q," Margo said.

I looked up at her, and for a moment I didn't know why she'd said my name, but then I snapped out of my half-sleep. And I heard it. The Muzak from the speakers had been turned up, only it wasn't Muzak anymore—it was real music. This old, jazzy song my dad likes called "Stars Fell on Alabama." Even through the tinny speakers you could hear that whoever was singing it could sing a thousand goddamned notes at once.

And I felt the unbroken line of me and of her stretching back from our cribs to the dead guy to acquaintanceship to now. And I wanted to tell her that the pleasure for me wasn't planning or doing or leaving; the pleasure was in seeing our strings cross and separate and then come back together—but that seemed too cheesy to say, and anyway, she was standing up.

Margo's blue blue eyes blinked and she looked impossibly

beautiful right then, her jeans wet against her legs, her face shining in the gray light.

I stood up and reached out my hand and said, "May I have this dance?" Margo curtsied, gave me her hand, and said, "You may," and then my hand was on the curve between her waist and her hip, and her hand was on my shoulder. And then step-step-sidestep, step-step-sidestep. We fox-trotted all the way around the seal tank, and still the song kept going on about the stars falling. "Sixth-grade slow dance," Margo announced, and we switched positions, her hands on my shoulders and mine on her hips, elbows locked, two feet between us. And then we fox-trotted some more, until the song ended. I stepped forward and dipped Margo, just as they'd taught us to do at Crown School of Dance. She raised one leg and gave me all her weight as I dipped her. She either trusted me or wanted to fall.

9.

We bought dish towels at a 7-Eleven on I-Drive and tried our best to wash the slime and stink from the moat off our clothes and skin, and I filled the gas tank to where it had been before we drove the circumference of Orlando. The Chrysler's seats were going to be a little bit wet when Mom drove to work, but I held out hope that she wouldn't notice, since she was pretty oblivious. My parents generally believed that I was the most well-adjusted and not-likely-to-break-into-SeaWorld person on the planet, since my psychological well-being was proof of their professional talents.

I took my time going home, avoiding interstates in favor of back roads. Margo and I were listening to the radio, trying to figure out what station had been playing "Stars Fell on Alabama," but then she turned it down and said, "All in all, I think it was a success."

"Absolutely," I said, although by now I was already wondering what tomorrow would be like. Would she show up by the band room before school to hang out? Eat lunch with me and Ben? "I do wonder if it will be different tomorrow," I said.

"Yeah," she said. "Me, too." She left it hanging in the air, and then said, "Hey, speaking of tomorrow, as thanks for your hard work and dedication on this remarkable evening, I would like to give you a small gift." She dug around beneath her feet and then produced the digital camera. "Take it," she said. "And use the Power of the Tiny Winky wisely."

I laughed and put the camera in my pocket. "I'll download the pic when we get home and then give it back to you at school?" I asked. I still wanted her to say, *Yes, at school, where things will be different, where I will be your friend in public, and also decidedly single,* but she just said, "Yeah, or whenever."

It was 5:42 when I turned into Jefferson Park. We drove down Jefferson Drive to Jefferson Court and then turned onto our road, Jefferson Way. I killed the headlights one last time and idled up my driveway. I didn't know what to say, and Margo wasn't saying anything. We filled a 7-Eleven bag with trash, trying to make the Chrysler look and feel as if the past six hours had not happened. In another bag, she gave me the remnants of the Vaseline, the spray paint, and the last full Mountain Dew. My brain raced with fatigue.

With a bag in each hand, I paused for a moment outside the van, staring at her. "Well, it was a helluva night," I said finally.

"Come here," she said, and I took a step forward. She hugged me, and the bags made it hard to hug her back, but if I dropped them I might wake someone. I could feel her on her tiptoes and then her mouth was right up against my ear and she said, very clearly, "I. Will. Miss. Hanging. Out. With. You."

"You don't have to," I answered aloud. I tried to hide my disappointment. "If you don't like them anymore," I said, "just hang out with me. My friends are actually, like, nice."

Her lips were so close to me that I could feel her smile. "I'm afraid it's not possible," she whispered. She let go then, but kept looking at me, taking step after step backward. She raised her eyebrows finally, and smiled, and I believed the smile. I watched her climb up a tree and then lift herself onto the roof outside of her second-floor bedroom window. She jimmied her window open and crawled inside.

I walked through my unlocked front door, tiptoed through the kitchen to my bedroom, peeled off my jeans, threw them into a corner of the closet back near the window screen, downloaded the picture of Jase, and got into bed, my mind booming with the things I would say to her at school.

PART TWO
The Grass

1.

I'd been asleep for just about thirty minutes when my alarm clock went off at 6:32. But I did not personally notice that my alarm clock was going off for seventeen minutes, not until I felt hands on my shoulders and heard the distant voice of my mother saying, "Good morning, sleepyhead."

"Uhh," I responded. I felt significantly more tired than I had back at 5:55, and I would have skipped school, except I had perfect attendance, and while I realized that perfect attendance is not particularly impressive or even necessarily admirable, I wanted to keep the streak alive. Plus, I wanted to see how Margo would act around me.

When I walked into the kitchen, Dad was telling Mom something while they ate at the breakfast counter. Dad paused when he saw me and said, "How'd you sleep?"

"I slept fantastically," I said, which was true. Briefly, but well.

He smiled. "I was just telling your mom that I have this recurring anxiety dream," he said. "So I'm in college. And I'm taking a Hebrew class, except the professor doesn't speak Hebrew, and the tests aren't in Hebrew—they're in gibberish. But everyone is acting like this made-up language with a made-up alphabet *is* Hebrew. And so I have this test, and I have to write in a language I don't know using an alphabet I can't decipher."

"Interesting," I said, although in point of fact it wasn't. Nothing is as boring as other people's dreams.

"It's a metaphor for adolescence," my mother piped up. "Writing in a language—adulthood—you can't comprehend, using an alphabet—mature social interaction—you can't recognize." My mother worked with crazy teenagers in juvenile detention centers and prisons. I think that's why she never really worried about me—as long as I wasn't ritually decapitating gerbils or urinating on my own face, she figured I was a success.

A normal mother might have said, "Hey, I notice you look like you're coming down off a meth binge and smell vaguely of algae. Were you perchance dancing with a snakebit Margo Roth Spiegelman a couple hours ago?" But no. They preferred dreams.

I showered, put on a T-shirt and a pair of jeans. I was late, but then again, I was always late.

"You're late," Mom said when I made it back to the kitchen. I tried to shake the fog in my brain enough to remember how to tie my sneakers.

"I am aware," I answered groggily.

Mom drove me to school. I sat in the seat that had been Margo's. Mom was mostly quiet on the drive, which was good, because I was entirely asleep, the side of my head against the minivan window.

As Mom pulled up to school, I saw Margo's usual spot empty in the senior parking lot. Couldn't blame her for being late, really. Her friends didn't gather as early as mine.

As I walked up toward the band kids, Ben shouted, "Jacobsen, was I dreaming or did you—" I gave him the slightest shake of my head, and he changed gears midsentence—"and me go on a wild adventure in French Polynesia last night, traveling in a sailboat made of bananas?"

"That was one delicious sailboat," I answered. Radar raised his eyes at me and ambled into the shade of a tree. I followed him. "Asked Angela about a date for Ben. No dice." I glanced over at Ben, who was talking animatedly, a coffee stirrer dancing in his mouth as he spoke.

"That sucks," I said. "It's all good, though. He and I will hang out and have like a marathon session of Resurrection or something."

Ben came over then, and said, "Are you trying to be subtle? Because I know you're talking about the honeybunnyless prom tragedy that is my life." He turned around and headed inside. Radar and I followed him, talking as we went past the band room, where freshmen and sophomores were sitting and chatting amid a slew of instrument cases.

"Why do you even want to go?" I asked.

"Bro, it's our *senior prom*. It's my last best chance to be some honeybunny's fondest high school memory." I rolled my eyes.

The first bell rang, meaning five minutes to class, and like Pavlov's dogs, people started rushing around, filling up the hallways. Ben and Radar and I stood by Radar's locker. "So why'd you call me at three in the morning for Chuck Parson's address?"

I was mulling over how to best answer that question when I saw Chuck Parson walking toward us. I elbowed Ben's side and cut my eyes toward Chuck. Chuck, incidentally, had decided that the best strategy was to shave off Lefty. "Holy shitstickers," Ben said.

Soon enough, Chuck was in my face as I scrunched back against the locker, his forehead deliciously hairless. "What are you assholes looking at?"

"Nothing," said Radar. "We're certainly not looking at your eyebrows." Chuck flicked Radar off, slammed an open palm against the locker next to me, and walked away.

"You did that?" Ben asked, incredulous.

"You can never tell anyone," I said to both of them. And then quietly added, "I was with Margo Roth Spiegelman."

Ben's voice rose with excitement. "You were with Margo Roth Spiegelman last night? At THREE A.M.?" I nodded. "Alone?" I nodded. "Oh my God, if you hooked up with her, you have to tell me every single thing that happened. You have to write me a term paper on the look and feel of Margo Roth Spiegelman's breasts. Thirty pages, minimum!"

"I want you to do a photo-realistic pencil drawing," Radar said.

"A sculpture would also be acceptable," Ben added.

Radar half raised his hand. I dutifully called on him. "Yes, I was wondering if it would be possible for you to write a sestina about Margo Roth Spiegelman's breasts? Your six words are: *pink*, *round*, *firmness*, *succulent*, *supple*, and *pillowy*."

"Personally," Ben said, "I think at least one of the words should be *buhbuhbuhbuh*."

"I don't think I'm familiar with that word," I said.

"It's the sound my mouth makes when I'm giving a honey-bunny the patented Ben Starling Speedboat." At which point Ben mimicked what he would do in the unlikely event that his face ever encountered cleavage.

"Right now," I said, "although they have no idea why, thousands of girls all across America are feeling a chill of fear and disgust run down their spines. Anyway, I didn't hook up with her, perv."

"Typical," Ben said. "I'm the only guy I know with the balls to give a honeybunny what she wants, and the only one with no opportunities."

"What an amazing coincidence," I said. It was life as it had always been—only more fatigued. I had hoped that last night would change my life, but it hadn't—at least not yet.

The second bell rang. We hustled off to class.

I became extremely tired during calc first period. I mean, I had been tired since waking, but combining fatigue with calculus seemed unfair. To stay awake, I was scribbling a note to Margo—nothing I'd ever send to her, just a summary of my favorite moments from the night before—but even that could not keep me awake. At some point, my pen just stopped moving, and I found my field of vision shrinking and shrinking, and then I was trying to remember if tunnel vision was a symptom of fatigue. I decided it must be, because there was only one thing in front of me, and it was Mr. Jiminez at the blackboard, and this was the only thing that my brain could process, and so when Mr. Jiminez said, "Quentin?" I was extraordinarily confused, because the one thing happening in my universe was Mr. Jiminez writing on the blackboard, and I couldn't fathom how he could be both an auditory and a visual presence in my life.

"Yes?" I asked.

"Did you hear the question?"

"Yes?" I asked again.

"And you raised your hand to answer it?" I looked up, and sure enough my hand was raised, but I did not know how it had come to be raised, and I only sort of knew how to go about de-raising it. But then after considerable struggle, my brain was able to tell my arm to lower itself, and my arm was able to do so, and then finally I said, "I just needed to ask to go to the bathroom?"

And he said, "Go ahead," and then someone else raised a hand and answered some question about some kind of differential equation.

I walked to the bathroom, splashed water on my face, and then leaned over the sink, close to the mirror, and appraised myself. I tried to rub the bloodshotedness out of my eyes, but I couldn't. And then I had a brilliant idea. I went into a stall, put the seat down, sat down, leaned against the side, and fell asleep. The sleep lasted for about sixteen milliseconds before the second period bell rang. I got up and walked to Latin, and then to physics, and then finally it was fourth period, and I found Ben in the cafeteria and said, "I really need a nap or something."

"Let's have lunch with RHAPAW," he answered.

RHAPAW was a fifteen-year-old Buick that had been driven with impunity by all three of Ben's older siblings and was, by the time it reached Ben, composed primarily out of duct tape and spackle. Her full name was Rode Hard And Put Away Wet, but we called her RHAPAW for short. RHAPAW ran not on gasoline, but on the inexhaustible fuel of human hope. You would sit on the blisteringly hot vinyl seat and hope she would start, and then Ben would turn the key and the engine would turn over a couple times, like a fish on land making its last, meager, dying flops. And then you would hope harder, and the engine would turn over a couple more times. You hoped some more, and it would finally catch.

Ben started RHAPAW and turned the AC on high. Three of the four windows didn't even open, but the air conditioner worked magnificently, though for the first few minutes it was just hot air blasting out of the vents and mixing with the hot stale air in the car. I reclined the passenger seat all the way back, so that I was almost lying down, and I told him everything: Margo at my window, the Wal-Mart, the revenge, the SunTrust Building, entering the wrong house, SeaWorld, the I-will-miss-hanging-out-with-you.

He didn't interrupt me once—Ben was a good friend in the not-interrupting way—but when I finished, he immediately asked me the most pressing question in his mind.

"Wait, so about Jase Worthington, how small are we talking?"

"Shrinkage may have played a role, since he was under significant anxiety, but have you ever seen a pencil?" I asked him, and Ben nodded. "Well, have you ever seen a pencil eraser?" He nodded again. "Well, have you ever seen the little shavings of rubber left on the paper after you erase something?" More nodding. "I'd say three shavings long and one shaving wide," I said. Ben had taken a lot of crap from guys like Jason Worthington and Chuck Parson, so I figured he was entitled to enjoy it a little. But he didn't even laugh. He was just shaking his head slowly, awestruck.

"God, she is such a badass."

"I know."

"She's the kind of person who either dies tragically at twenty-seven, like Jimi Hendrix and Janis Joplin, or else grows up to win, like, the first-ever Nobel Prize for Awesome."

"Yeah," I said. I rarely tired of talking about Margo Roth Spiegelman, but I was rarely this tired. I leaned back against the cracked vinyl headrest and fell immediately asleep. When I woke up, a Wendy's hamburger was sitting in my lap with a note. *Had to go to class, bro. See you after band.*

Later, after my last class, I translated Ovid while sitting up against the cinder-block wall outside the band room, trying to ignore the groaning cacophony coming from inside. I always hung around school for the extra hour during band practice, because to leave before Ben and Radar meant enduring the unbearable humiliation of being the lone senior on the bus.

After they got out, Ben dropped Radar off at his house right by the Jefferson Park "village center," near where Lacey lived. Then he took me home. I noticed Margo's car was not parked in her driveway, either. So she hadn't skipped school to sleep. She'd skipped school for another adventure—a *me-less* adventure. She'd probably spent her day spreading hair-removal cream on the pillows of other enemies or something. I felt a little left out as I walked into the house, but of course she knew I would never have joined her anyway—I cared too much about a day of school. And who even knew if it would be just a day for Margo. Maybe she was off on another three-day jaunt to Mississippi, or temporarily joining the circus. But it wasn't either of those, of course. It was something I couldn't imagine, that I would never imagine, because I couldn't be Margo.

I wondered what stories she would come home with this time. And I wondered if she would tell them to me, sitting across from me at lunch. Maybe, I thought, this is what she meant by I will miss hanging out with you. She knew she was heading somewhere for another of her brief respites from Orlando's paperness. But when she came back, who knew? She couldn't spend the last weeks of school with the friends she'd always had, so maybe she would spend them with me after all.

She didn't have to be gone long for the rumors to start. Ben called me that night after dinner. "I hear she's not answering her phone. Someone on Facebook said she'd told them she might move into a secret storage room in Tomorrowland at Disney."

"That's idiotic," I said.

"I know. I mean, Tomorrowland is by far the crappiest of the Lands. Someone else said she met a guy online."

"Ridiculous," I said.

"Okay, fine, but what?"

"She's somewhere by herself having the kind of fun we can only imagine," I said.

Ben giggled. "Are you saying that she's playing with herself?"

I groaned. "Come on, Ben. I mean she's just doing Margo stuff. Making stories. Rocking worlds."

That night, I lay on my side, staring out the window into the invisible world outside. I kept trying to fall asleep, but then my eyes would dart open, just to check. I couldn't help but hope that Margo Roth Spiegelman would return to my window and drag my tired ass through one more night I'd never forget.

2.

Margo left often enough that there weren't any Find Margo rallies at school or anything, but we all felt her absence. High school is neither a democracy nor a dictatorship—nor, contrary to popular belief, an anarchic state. High school is a divine-right monarchy. And when the queen goes on vacation, things change. Specifically, they get worse. It was during Margo's trip to Mississippi sophomore year, for example, that Becca had unleashed the Bloody Ben story to the world. And this was no different. The little girl with her finger in the dam had run off. Flooding was inevitable.

That morning, I was on time for once and got a ride with Ben. We found everyone unusually quiet outside the band room. "Dude," our friend Frank said with great seriousness.

"What?"

"Chuck Parson, Taddy Mac, and Clint Bauer took Clint's Tahoe and ran over twelve bikes belonging to freshmen and sophomores."

"That sucks," I said, shaking my head.

Our friend Ashley added, "Also, yesterday somebody posted our phone numbers in the boys' bathroom with—well, with dirty stuff."

I shook my head again, and then joined the silence. We couldn't turn them in; we'd tried that plenty in middle school, and it inevitably resulted in more punishment. Usually, we'd just have to wait until someone like Margo reminded everyone what immature jackasses they all were.

But Margo had given me a way of starting a counteroffensive. And I was just about to say something when, in my peripheral vision, I saw a large individual running toward us at a full sprint. He wore a black ski mask and carried a large, complex green water cannon. As he ran past he tagged me on the shoulder and I lost my footing, landing against the cracked concrete on my left side. As he reached the door, he turned back and shouted toward me, "You screw with us and you're gonna get *smackdown*." The voice was not familiar to me.

Ben and another of our friends picked me up. My shoulder hurt, but I didn't want to rub it. "You okay?" asked Radar.

"Yeah, I'm fine." I rubbed the shoulder now.

Radar shook his head. "Someone needs to tell him that while it is possible to get *smacked* down, and it is also possible to get *a* smackdown, it is not possible to get 'smackdown.'" I laughed. Someone nodded toward the parking lot, and I looked up to see two little freshmen guys walking toward us, their T-shirts hanging wet and limp from their narrow frames.

"It was pee!" one of them shouted at us. The other one didn't say anything; he just held his hands far away from his T-shirt, which only sort of worked. I could see rivulets of liquid snaking from his sleeve down his arm.

"Was it animal pee or human pee?" someone asked.

"How would I know! What, am I an expert in the study of pee?"

I walked over to the kid. I put my hand on the top of his head, the only place that seemed totally dry. "We'll fix this," I said.

The second bell rang, and Radar and I raced to calc. As I slid into my desk I dinged my arm, and the pain radiated into my shoulder. Radar tapped his notebook, where he'd circled a note: *Shoulder okay?*

I wrote on the corner of my notebook: *Compared to those freshmen, I spent the morning in a field of rainbows frolicking with puppies.*

Radar laughed enough for Mr. Jiminez to shoot him a look. I wrote, *I have a plan, but we have to figure out who it was.*

Radar wrote back, *Jasper Hanson,* and circled it several times. That was a surprise.

How do you know?

Radar wrote, *You didn't notice? Dumbass was wearing his own football jersey.*

Jasper Hanson was a junior. I'd always thought him harmless, and actually sort of nice—in that bumbling, dude-how's-it-going kind of way. Not the kind of guy you'd expect to see shooting geysers of pee at freshmen. Honestly, in the governmental bureaucracy of Winter Park High School, Jasper Hanson was like Deputy Assistant Undersecretary of Athletics and Malfeasance. When a guy like that gets promoted to Executive Vice President of Urine Gunning, immediate action must be taken.

So when I got home that afternoon, I created an e-mail account and wrote my old friend Jason Worthington.

From: mavenger@gmail.com
To: jworthington90@yahoo.com
Subject: You, Me, Becca Arrington's House, Your Penis, Etc.

Dear Mr. Worthington,

1. $200 in cash should be provided to each of the 12 people whose bikes your colleagues destroyed via Chevy Tahoe. This shouldn't be a problem, given your magnificent wealth.
2. This graffiti situation in the boys' bathroom has to stop.
3. Water guns? With pee? Really? Grow up.
4. You should treat your fellow students with respect, particularly those less socially fortunate than you.
5. You should probably instruct members of your clan to behave in similarly considerate ways.

I realize that it will be very difficult to accomplish some of these tasks. But then again, it will also be very difficult not to share the attached photograph with the world.

Yours truly,
Your Friendly Neighborhood Nemesis

The reply came twelve minutes later.

Look, Quentin, and yeah, I know it's you. You know it wasn't me who squirt-peed those freshmen. I'm sorry, but it's not like I control the actions of other people.

My answer:

Mr. Worthington,

I understand that you do not control Chuck and Jasper.

But you see, I am in a similar situation. I do not control the little devil sitting on my left shoulder. The devil is saying, "PRINT THE PICTURE PRINT THE PICTURE TAPE IT UP ALL OVER SCHOOL DO IT DO IT DO IT." And then on my right shoulder, there is a little tiny white angel. And the angel is saying, "Man, I sure as shit hope all those freshmen get their money bright and early on Monday morning."

So do I, little angel. So do I.

Best wishes,
Your Friendly Neighborhood Nemesis

He did not reply, and he didn't need to. Everything had been said.

Ben came over after dinner and we played Resurrection, pausing every half hour or so to call Radar, who was on a date with Angela. We left him eleven messages, each more annoying and salacious than the last. It was after nine o'clock when the doorbell rang. "Quentin!" my mom shouted. Ben and I figured it was Radar, so we paused the game and walked out into the living room. Chuck Parson and Jason Worthington were standing in my doorway. I walked over to them, and Jason said, "Hey, Quentin," and I nodded my head. Jason glanced over at Chuck, who looked at me and mumbled, "Sorry, Quentin."

"For what?" I asked.

"For telling Jasper to piss-gun those freshmen," he mumbled. He paused, and then said, "And the bikes."

Ben opened his arms, as if to hug. "C'mere, bro," he said.

"What?"

"C'mere," he said again. Chuck stepped forward. "Closer," Ben said. Chuck was standing fully in the entryway now, maybe a foot from Ben. Out of nowhere, Ben slammed a punch into Chuck's gut. Chuck barely flinched, but he immediately reared back to clobber Ben. Jase grabbed his arm, though. "Chill, bro," Jase said. "It's not like it hurt." Jase reached out his hand, to shake. "I like your guts, bro," he said. "I mean, you're an asshole. But still." I shook his hand.

They left then, getting into Jase's Lexus and backing down the driveway. As soon as I closed the front door, Ben let out a mighty groan. "*Ahhhhhhhggg.* Oh, sweet Lord Jesus, my hand." He attempted to make a fist and winced. "I think Chuck Parson had a textbook strapped to his stomach."

"Those are called abs," I told him.

"Oh, yeah. I've heard of those." I clapped him on the back and we headed back to the bedroom to play Resurrection. We'd just unpaused it when Ben said, "By the way, did you notice that Jase says 'bro'? I've totally brought *bro* back. Just with the sheer force of my own awesomeness."

"Yeah, you're spending Friday night gaming and nursing the hand you broke while trying to sucker punch somebody. No wonder Jase Worthington has chosen to hitch his star to your wagon."

"At least I'm *good* at Resurrection," he said, whereupon he shot me in the back even though we were playing in team mode.

We played for a while longer, until Ben just curled onto the floor, holding the controller up to his chest, and went to sleep. I was tired, too—it had been a long day. I figured Margo would be back by Monday anyway, but even so, I felt a little pride at having been the person who stemmed the tide of lame.

3.

Every morning, I now looked up through my bedroom window to check whether there was any sign of life in Margo's room. She always kept her rattan shades closed, but since she'd left, her mom or somebody had pulled them up, so I could see a little snippet of blue wall and white ceiling. On that Saturday morning, with her only forty-eight hours gone, I figured she wouldn't be home yet, but even so, I felt a flicker of disappointment when I saw the shade still pulled up.

I brushed my teeth and then, after briefly kicking at Ben in an attempt to wake him, walked out in shorts and a T-shirt. Five people were seated at the dining room table. My mom and dad. Margo's mom and dad. And a tall, stout African-American man with oversize glasses wearing a gray suit, holding a manila folder.

"Uh, hi," I said.

"Quentin," my mom asked, "did you see Margo on Wednesday night?"

I walked into the dining room and leaned against the wall, standing opposite the stranger. I'd thought of my answer to this question already. "Yeah," I said. "She showed up at my window at like midnight and we talked for a minute and then Mr. Spiegelman caught her and she went back to her house."

"And was that—? Did you see her after that?" Mr. Spiegelman asked. He seemed quite calm.

"No, why?" I asked.

Margo's mom answered, her voice shrill. "Well," she said, "it seems that Margo has run away. Again." She sighed. "This would be—what is it, Josh, the fourth time?"

"Oh, I've lost count," her dad answered, annoyed.

The African-American man spoke up then. "Fifth time you've filed a report." The man nodded at me and said, "Detective Otis Warren."

"Quentin Jacobsen," I said.

Mom stood up and put her hands on Mrs. Spiegelman's shoulders. "Debbie," she said, "I'm so sorry. It's a very frustrating situation." I knew this trick. It was a psychology trick called empathic listening. You say what the person is feeling so they feel understood. Mom does it to me all the time.

"I'm not frustrated," Mrs. Spiegelman answered. "I'm done."

"That's right," Mr. Spiegelman said. "We've got a locksmith coming this afternoon. We're changing the locks. She's eighteen. I mean, the detective has just said there's nothing we can do—"

"Well," Detective Warren interrupted, "I didn't quite say that. I said that she's not a missing *minor*, and so she has the right to leave home."

Mr. Spiegelman continued talking to my mom. "We're happy to pay for her to go to college, but we can't support this . . . this silliness. Connie, she's eighteen! And still so self-centered! She needs to see some consequences."

My mom removed her hands from Mrs. Spiegelman. "I would argue she needs to see *loving* consequences," my mom said.

"Well, she's not your daughter, Connie. She hasn't walked all over you like a doormat for a decade. We've got another child to think about."

"And ourselves," Mr. Spiegelman added. He looked up at me then. "Quentin, I'm sorry if she tried to drag you into her little game. You can imagine how . . . just how embarrassing this is for us. You're such a good boy, and she . . . well."

I pushed myself off the wall and stood up straight. I knew Margo's parents a little, but I'd never seen them act so bitchy. No wonder she was annoyed with them Wednesday night. I glanced over at the detective. He was flipping through pages in the folder. "She's been known to leave a bit of a bread crumb trail; is that right?"

"Clues," Mr. Spiegelman said, standing up now. The detective had placed the folder on the table, and Margo's dad leaned forward to look at it with him. "Clues everywhere. The day she ran away to Mississippi, she ate alphabet soup and left exactly four letters in her soup bowl: An *M*, an *I*, an *S*, and a *P*. She was disappointed when we didn't piece it together, although as I told her when she finally returned: 'How can we find you when all we know is *Mississippi*? It's a big state, Margo!'"

The detective cleared his throat. "And she left Minnie Mouse on her bed when she spent a night inside Disney World."

"Yes," her mom said. "The clues. The stupid clues. But you can never *follow* them anywhere, trust me."

The detective looked up from his notebook. "We'll get the word out, of course, but she can't be compelled to come home; you shouldn't necessarily expect her back under your roof in the near future."

"I don't *want* her under our roof." Mrs. Spiegelman raised a tissue to her eyes, although I heard no crying in her voice. "I know that's terrible, but it's true."

"Deb," my mom said in her therapist voice.

Mrs. Spiegelman just shook her head—the smallest shake. "What can we do? We told the detective. We filed a report. She's an adult, Connie."

"She's *your* adult," my mom said, still calm.

"Oh, come on, Connie. Look, is it sick that it's a blessing to have her out of the house? Of course it's sick. But she was a sickness in this family! How do you look for someone who announces she won't be found, who always leaves clues that lead nowhere, who runs away constantly? You can't!"

My mom and dad shared a glance, and then the detective spoke to me. "Son, I'm wondering if we can chat privately?" I nodded. We ended up in my parents' bedroom, he in an easy chair and me sitting on the corner of their bed.

"Kid," he said once he'd settled into the chair, "let me give you some advice: never work for the government. Because when you work for the government, you work for the people. And when you work for the people, you have to interact with the people, even the Spiegelmans." I laughed a little.

"Let me be frank with you, kid. Those people know how to parent like I know how to diet. I've worked with them before, and I don't like them. I don't care if you tell her parents where she is, but I'd appreciate it if you told me."

"I don't know," I said. "I really don't."

"Kid, I've been thinking about this girl. This stuff she does—she breaks into Disney World, for instance, right? She goes to Mississippi and leaves alphabet soup clues. She organizes a huge campaign to toilet paper houses."

"How do you know about *that*?" Two years before, Margo had led the TP-ing of two hundred houses in a single night. Needless to say, I wasn't invited on that adventure.

"I worked this case before. So, kid, here's where I need your help: who plans this stuff? These crazy schemes? She's the mouthpiece for it all, the one crazy enough to do everything. But who plans it? Who's sitting around with notebooks full of diagrams figuring out how much toilet paper you need to toilet paper a ton of houses?"

"It's all her, I assume."

"But she might have a partner, somebody helpin' her do all these big and brilliant things, and maybe the person who's in on her secret isn't the obvious person, isn't her best friend or her boyfriend. Maybe it's somebody you wouldn't think of right off," he said. He took a breath and was about to say something more when I cut him off.

"I don't know where she is," I said. "I swear to God."

"Just checking, kid. Anyway, you know something, don't you? So let's start there." I told him everything. I trusted the guy. He took a few notes while I talked, but nothing very detailed. And something about telling him, and his scribbling in the notebook, and her parents being so lame—something about all of it made the possibility of her being lastingly missing well up in me for the first time. I felt the worry start to snatch at my breath when I finished talking. The detective didn't say anything for a while. He just leaned forward in the chair and stared past me until he'd seen whatever he was waiting to see, and then he started talking.

"Listen, kid. This is what happens: somebody—girl usually—got a free spirit, doesn't get on too good with her parents. These kids, they're like tied-down helium balloons. They strain against the string and strain against it, and then something happens, and that string gets cut, and they just float away. And maybe you never see the balloon again. It lands in Canada or somethin', gets work at a restaurant, and before the balloon even notices, it's been pouring coffee in that same diner to the same sad bastards for thirty years. Or maybe three or four years from now, or three or four days from now, the prevailing winds take the balloon back home, because it needs money, or it sobered up, or it misses its kid brother. But listen, kid, that string gets cut all the time."

"Yeah, bu—"

"I'm not finished, kid. The thing about these balloons is that there are so goddamned many of them. The sky is choked full of them, rubbing up against one another as they float to here or from there, and every one of those damned balloons ends up on my desk one way or another, and after a while a man can get discouraged. Everywhere the balloons, and each of them with a mother or a father, or God forbid both, and after a while, you can't even see 'em individually. You look up at all the balloons in the sky and you can see all of the balloons, but you cannot see any one balloon." He paused then, and inhaled sharply, as if he was realizing something. "But then every now and again you talk to some big-eyed kid with too much hair for his head and you want to lie to him because he seems like a good kid. And you feel bad for this kid, because the only thing worse than the skyful of balloons *you* see is what he sees: a clear blue day interrupted by just the one balloon. But once that string gets cut, kid, you can't uncut it. Do you get what I'm saying?"

I nodded, although I wasn't sure I *did* understand. He stood up. "I do think she'll be back soon, kid. If that helps."

I liked the image of Margo as a balloon, but I figured that in his urge for the poetic, the detective had seen more worry in me than the pang I'd actually felt. I knew she'd be back. She'd deflate and float back to Jefferson Park. She always had.

I followed the detective back to the dining room, and then he said he wanted to go back over to the Spiegelmans' house and pick through her room a little. Mrs. Spiegelman gave me a hug and said, "You've always been such a good boy; I'm sorry she ever got you caught up in this ridiculousness." Mr. Spiegelman shook my hand, and they left. As soon as the door closed, my dad said, "Wow."

"Wow," agreed Mom.

My dad put his arm around me. "Those are some very troubling dynamics, eh, bud?"

"They're kind of assholes," I said. My parents always liked it when I cursed in front of them. I could see the pleasure of it in their faces. It signified that I trusted them, that I was myself in front of them. But even so, they seemed sad.

"Margo's parents suffer a severe narcissistic injury whenever she acts out," Dad said to me.

"It prevents them from parenting effectively," my mom added.

"They're assholes," I repeated.

"Honestly," my dad said, "they're probably right. She probably is in need of attention. And God knows, I would need attention, too, if I had those two for parents."

"When she comes back," my mom said, "she's going to be devastated. To be abandoned like that! Shut out when you most need to be loved."

"Maybe she could live here when she comes back," I said, and in saying it I realized what a fantastically great idea it was. My mom's eyes lit up, too, but then she saw something in my dad's expression and answered me in her usual measured way.

"Well, she'd certainly be welcome, although that would come

with its own challenges—being next door to the Spiegelmans. But when she returns to school, please do tell her that she's welcome here, and that if she doesn't want to stay with us, there are many resources available to her that we're happy to discuss."

Ben came out then, his bedhead seeming to challenge our basic understanding of the force gravity exerts upon matter. "Mr. and Mrs. Jacobsen—always a pleasure."

"Good morning, Ben. I wasn't aware you were staying the night."

"Neither was I, actually," he said. "What's wrong?"

I told Ben about the detective and the Spiegelmans and Margo being technically a missing adult. And when I had finished, he nodded and said, "We should probably discuss this over a piping hot plate of Resurrection." I smiled and followed him back to my room. Radar came over shortly thereafter, and as soon as he arrived, I was kicked off the team, because we were facing a difficult mission and despite being the only one of us who actually owned the game, I wasn't very good at Resurrection. As I watched them tramp through a ghoul-infested space station, Ben said, "Goblin, Radar, goblin."

"I see him."

"Come here you little bastard," Ben said, the controller twisting in his hand. "Daddy's gonna put you on a sailboat across the River Styx."

"Did you just use Greek mythology to talk trash?" I asked.

Radar laughed. Ben started pummeling buttons, shouting, "Eat it, goblin! Eat it like Zeus ate Metis!"

"I would think that she'd be back by Monday," I said. "You don't want to miss too much school, even if you're Margo Roth Spiegelman. Maybe she can stay here till graduation."

Radar answered me in the disjointed way of someone playing Resurrection. "I don't even get why she left, was it just *imp six o'clock no dude use the ray gun* like because of lost love? I would have figured her to be *where is the crypt is it to the left* immune to that kind of stuff."

"No," I said. "It wasn't that, I don't think. Not just that, anyway. She kind of hates Orlando; she called it a paper town. Like, you know, everything so fake and flimsy. I think she just wanted a vacation from that."

I happened to glance out my window, and I saw immediately that someone—the detective I guessed—had lowered the shade in Margo's room. But I wasn't seeing the shade. Instead, I was seeing a black-and-white poster, taped to the back of the shade. In the photograph, a man stands, his shoulders slightly slumped, staring ahead. A cigarette dangles out of his mouth. A guitar is slung over his shoulder, and the guitar is painted with the words THIS MACHINE KILLS FASCISTS.

"There's something in Margo's window." The game music stopped, and Radar and Ben knelt down on either side of me.

"That's new?" asked Radar.

"I've seen the back of that shade a million times," I answered, "but I've never seen that poster before."

"Weird," Ben said.

"Margo's parents just said this morning that she sometimes leaves clues," I said. "But never anything, like, concrete enough to find her before she comes home."

Radar already had his handheld out; he was searching Omnictionary for the phrase. "The picture's of Woody Guthrie," he said. "A folksinger, 1912 to 1967. Sang about the working class.

'This Land Is Your Land.' Bit of a Communist. Um, inspired Bob Dylan." Radar played a snippet of one of his songs—a high-pitched scratchy voice sang about unions.

"I'll e-mail the guy who wrote most of this page and see if there are any obvious connections between Woody Guthrie and Margo," Radar said.

"I can't imagine she likes his songs," I said.

"Seriously," Ben said. "This guy sounds like an alcoholic Kermit the Frog with throat cancer."

Radar opened the window and stuck his head out, swiveling it around. "It sure seems she left this for you, though, Q. I mean, does she know anyone else who could see this window?" I shook my head no.

After a moment, Ben added, "The way he's staring at us—it's like, 'pay attention to me.' And his head like that, you know? It's not like he's standing on a stage; it's like he's standing in a doorway or something."

"I think he wants us to come inside," I said.

4.

We didn't have a view of the front door or the garage from my bedroom: for that, we needed to sit in the family room. So while Ben continued playing Resurrection, Radar and I went out to the family room and pretended to watch TV while keeping watch on the Spiegelmans' front door through a picture window, waiting for Margo's mom and dad to leave. Detective Warren's black Crown Victoria was still in the driveway.

He left after about fifteen minutes, but neither the garage door nor the front door opened again for an hour. Radar and I were watching some half-funny stoner comedy on HBO, and I had started to get into the story when Radar said, "Garage door." I jumped off the couch and got close to the window so that I could see clearly who was in the car. Both Mr. and Mrs. Spiegelman. Ruthie was still at home. "Ben!" I shouted. He was out in a flash, and as the Spiegelmans turned off Jefferson Way and onto Jefferson Road, we raced outside into the muggy morning.

We walked through the Spiegelmans' lawn to their front door. I rang the doorbell and heard Myrna Mountweazel's paws scurrying on the hardwood floors, and then she was barking like crazy, staring at us through the sidelight glass. Ruthie opened the door. She was a sweet girl, maybe eleven.

"Hey, Ruthie."

"Hi, Quentin," she said.

"Hey, are your parents here?"

"They just left," she said, "to go to Target." She had Margo's big eyes, but hers were hazel. She looked up at me, her lips pursed with worry. "Did you meet the policeman?"

"Yeah," I said. "He seemed nice."

"Mom says that it's like if Margo went to college early."

"Yeah," I said, thinking that the easiest way to solve a mystery is to decide that there is no mystery to solve. But it seemed clear to me now that she had left the clues to a mystery behind.

"Listen, Ruthie, we need to look in Margo's room," I said. "But the thing is—it's like when Margo would ask you to do top-secret stuff. We're in the same situation here."

"Margo doesn't like people in her room," Ruthie said. "'Cept me. And sometimes Mommy."

"But we're her friends."

"She doesn't like her friends in her room," Ruthie said.

I leaned down toward her. "Ruthie, please."

"And you don't want me to tell Mommy and Dad," she said.

"Correct."

"Five dollars," she said. I was about to bargain with her, but then Radar produced a five-dollar bill and handed it to her. "If I see the car in the driveway, I'll let you know," she said conspiratorially.

I knelt down to give the aging-but-always-enthusiastic Myrna Mountweazel a good petting, and then we raced upstairs to Margo's room. As I put my hand on the doorknob, it occurred to me that I had not seen Margo's entire room since I was about ten years old.

I walked in. Much neater than you'd expect Margo to be, but

maybe her mom had just picked everything up. To my right, a closet packed-to-bursting with clothes. On the back of the door, a shoe rack with a couple dozen pairs of shoes, from Mary Janes to prom heels. It didn't seem like much could be missing from that closet.

"I'm on the computer," Radar said. Ben was fiddling with the shade. "The poster is taped on," he said. "Just Scotch tape. Nothing strong."

The great surprise was on the wall next to the computer desk: bookcases as tall as me and twice as long, filled with vinyl records. *Hundreds* of them. "John Coltrane's *A Love Supreme* is in the record player," Ben said.

"God, that is a brilliant album," Radar said without looking away from the computer. "Girl's got taste." I looked at Ben, confused, and then Ben said, "He was a sax player." I nodded.

Still typing, Radar said, "I can't believe Q has never heard of Coltrane. Trane's playing is literally the most convincing proof of God's existence I've ever come across."

I began to look through the records. They were organized alphabetically by artist, so I scanned through, looking for the G's. Dizzy Gillespie, Jimmie Dale Gilmore, Green Day, Guided by Voices, George Harrison. "She has, like, every musician in the world *except* Woody Guthrie," I said. And then I went back and started from the A's.

"All her schoolbooks are still here," I heard Ben say. "Plus some other books by her bedside table. No journal."

But I was distracted by Margo's music collection. She liked *everything*. I could never have imagined her listening to all these old records. I'd seen her listening to music while running, but I'd never suspected this kind of obsession. I'd never heard of most of the bands, and I was surprised to learn that vinyl records were even being produced for the newer ones.

I kept going through the *A*'s and then the *B*'s—making my way through the Beatles and the Blind Boys of Alabama and Blondie—and I started to rifle through them more quickly, so quickly that I didn't even see the back cover of Billy Bragg's *Mermaid Avenue* until I was looking at the Buzzcocks. I stopped, went back, and pulled out the Billy Bragg record. The front was a photograph of urban row houses. But on the back, Woody Guthrie was staring at me, a cigarette hanging out of his lips, holding a guitar that said THIS MACHINE KILLS FASCISTS.

"Hey," I said. Ben looked over.

"Holy shitstickers," he said. "Nice find." Radar spun around the chair and said, "Impressive. Wonder what's inside."

Unfortunately, only a record was inside. The record looked exactly like a record. I put it on Margo's record player and eventually figured out how to turn it on and put down the needle. It was some guy singing Woody Guthrie songs. He sang better than Woody Guthrie.

"What is it, just a crazy coincidence?"

Ben was holding the album cover. "Look," he said. He was pointing at the song list. In thin black pen, the song title "Walt Whitman's Niece" had been circled.

"Interesting," I said. Margo's mom had said that Margo's clues never led anywhere, but I knew now that Margo had created a chain of clues—and she had seemingly made them for me. I immediately thought of her in the SunTrust Building, telling me I was better when I showed confidence. I turned the record over and played it. "Walt Whitman's Niece" was the first song on side two. Not bad, actually.

I saw Ruthie in the doorway then. She looked at me. "Got any clues for us, Ruthie?" She shook her head. "I already looked," she said glumly. Radar looked at me and gestured his head toward Ruthie.

"Can you please keep watch for your mom for us?" I asked. She nodded and left. I closed the door.

"What's up?" I asked Radar. He motioned us over to the computer. "In the week before she left, Margo was on Omnictionary a bunch. I can tell from minutes logged by her username, which she stored in her passwords. But she erased her browsing history, so I can't tell what she was looking at."

"Hey, Radar, look up who Walt Whitman was," Ben said.

"He was a poet," I answered. "Nineteenth century."

"Great," Ben said, rolling his eyes. "Poetry."

"What's wrong with that?" I asked.

"Poetry is just so emo," he said. "Oh, the pain. The pain. It always rains. In my soul."

"Yeah, I believe that's Shakespeare," I said dismissively. "Did Whitman have any nieces?" I asked Radar. He was already on Whitman's Omnictionary page. A burly guy with this huge beard. I'd never read him, but he *looked* like a good poet.

"Uh, no one famous. Says he had a couple brothers, but no mention of whether they had kids. I can probably find out if you want." I shook my head. That didn't seem right. I went back to looking around the room. The bottom shelf of her record collection included some books—middle school yearbooks, a beat-up copy of *The Outsiders*—and some back issues of teen magazines. Nothing relating to Walt Whitman's niece, certainly.

I looked through the books by her bedside table. Nothing of interest. "It would make sense if she had a book of his poetry," I said. "But she doesn't seem to."

"She does!" Ben said excitedly. I went over to where he had knelt by the bookshelves, and saw it now. I'd looked right past the slim volume on the bottom shelf, wedged between two yearbooks. Walt Whitman. *Leaves of Grass.* I pulled out the book. There was a photograph of Whitman on the cover, his light eyes staring back at me.

"Not bad," I told Ben.

He nodded. "Yeah, now can we get out of here? Call me old-fashioned, but I'd rather not be here when Margo's parents get back."

"Is there anything we're missing?"

Radar stood up. "It really seems like she's drawing a pretty straight line; there's gotta be something in that book. It's weird, though—I mean, no offense, but if she always left clues for her parents, why would she leave them for you this time?"

I shrugged my shoulders. I didn't know the answer, but of course I had my hopes: maybe Margo needed to see my confidence. Maybe this time she *wanted* to be found, and to be found by *me.* Maybe—just as she had chosen me on the longest night, she had chosen me again. And maybe untold riches awaited he who found her.

Ben and Radar left soon after we got back to my house, after they'd each looked through the book and not found any obvious clues. I grabbed some cold lasagna from the fridge for lunch and went to my room with Walt. It was the Penguin Classics version of the first edition of *Leaves of Grass.* I read a little from the introduction and then paged through the book. There were several quotes highlighted in blue, all from the epically long poem known as "Song of Myself." And there were two lines from the poem that were highlighted in green:

Unscrew the locks from the doors!
Unscrew the doors themselves from their jambs!

I spent most of my afternoon trying to make sense of that quote, thinking maybe it was Margo's way of telling me to become more of a badass or something. But I also read and reread everything highlighted in blue:

You shall no longer take things at second or third hand . . . .
nor look through the eyes of the dead . . . . nor feed on
the spectres in books.

I tramp a perpetual journey

All goes onward and outward . . . . and nothing collapses,
And to die is different from what any one supposed, and
luckier.

If no other in the world be aware I sit content,
And if each and all be aware I sit content.

The final three stanzas of "Song of Myself" were also highlighted.

I bequeath myself to the dirt to grow from the grass I love,
If you want me again look for me under your bootsoles.

You will hardly know who I am or what I mean,
But I shall be good health to you nevertheless,
And filter and fibre your blood.

Failing to fetch me at first keep encouraged,
Missing me one place search another,
I stop some where waiting for you

It became a weekend of reading, of trying to see her in the fragments of the poem she'd left for me. I could never get anywhere with the lines, but I kept thinking about them anyway, because I didn't want to disappoint her. She wanted me to play out the string, to find the place where she had stopped and was waiting for me, to follow the bread crumb trail until it dead-ended into her.

5.

Monday morning, an extraordinary event occurred. I was late, which was normal; and then my mom dropped me off at school, which was normal; and then I stood outside talking with everyone for a while, which was normal; and then Ben and I headed inside, which was normal. But as soon as we swung open the steel door, Ben's face became a mix of excitement and panic, like he'd just been picked out of a crowd by a magician for the get-sawn-in-half trick. I followed his gaze down the hall.

Denim miniskirt. Tight white T-shirt. Scooped neck. Extraordinarily olive skin. Legs that make you care about legs. Perfectly coiffed curly brown hair. A laminated button reading ME FOR PROM QUEEN. Lacey Pemberton. Walking toward us. By the *band room*.

"*Lacey Pemberton*," Ben whispered, even though she was about three steps from us and could clearly hear him, and in fact flashed a faux-bashful smile upon hearing her name.

"Quentin," she said to me, and more than anything else, I found it impossible that she knew my name. She motioned with her head, and I followed her past the band room, over to a bank of lockers. Ben kept pace with me.

"Hi, Lacey," I said once she stopped walking. I could smell her perfume, and I remembered the smell of it in her SUV, remembered the crunch of the catfish as Margo and I slammed her seat down.

"I hear you were with Margo."

I just looked at her.

"That night, with the fish? In my car? And in Becca's closet? And through Jase's window?"

I kept looking. I wasn't sure what to say. A man can live a long and adventurous life without ever being spoken to by Lacey Pemberton, and when that rare opportunity does arise, one does not wish to misspeak. So Ben spoke for me. "Yeah, they hung out," Ben said, as if Margo and I were tight.

"Was she mad at me?" Lacey asked after a moment. She was looking down; I could see her brown eye shadow.

"What?"

She spoke quietly then, the tiniest crack in her voice, and all at once Lacey Pemberton was not Lacey Pemberton. She was just—like, a person. "Was she, you know, pissed at me about something?"

I thought about how to answer that for a while. "Uh, she was a little disappointed that you didn't tell her about Jase and Becca, but you know Margo. She'll get over it."

Lacey started walking down the hall. Ben and I let her go, but then she slowed down. She wanted us to walk with her. Ben nudged me, and then we started walking together. "I didn't even *know* about Jase and Becca. That's the thing. God, I hope I can explain that to her soon. For a while, I was really worried that maybe she had like really left, but then I went into her locker 'cause I know her combination and she still has all her pictures up and everything, and all her books are stacked there."

"That's good," I said.

"Yeah, but it's been like four days. That's almost a record for her. And you know, this has really sucked, because Craig knew, and I was so pissed at him for not telling me that I broke up with him, and now I'm out a prom date, and my best friend is off wherever, in New York or whatever, thinking I did something I would NEVER do." I shot a look to Ben. Ben shot a look back to me.

"I have to run to class," I said. "But why do you say she's in New York?"

"I guess she told Jase like two days before she left that New York was the only place in America where a person could actually live a halfway livable life. Maybe she was just saying it. I don't know."

"Okay, I gotta run," I said.

I knew Ben would never convince Lacey to go to prom with him, but I figured he at least deserved the opportunity. I jogged through the halls toward my locker, rubbing Radar's head as I ran past him. He was talking to Angela and a freshman girl in band. "Don't thank me. Thank Q," I heard him say to the freshman, and she called out, "Thank you for my two hundred dollars!" Without looking back I shouted, "Don't thank me, thank Margo Roth Spiegelman!" because of course she'd given me the tools I needed.

I made it to my locker and grabbed my calc notebook, but then I just stayed, even after the second bell rang, standing still in the middle of the hallway while people rushed past me in both directions, like I was the median in their freeway. Another kid thanked me for his two hundred dollars. I smiled at him. The school felt more *mine* than in all my four years there. We'd gotten a measure of justice for the bikeless band geeks. Lacey Pemberton had spoken to me. Chuck Parson had apologized.

I knew these halls so well—and finally it was starting to feel like they knew me, too. I stood there as the third bell rang and the crowds dwindled. Only then did I walk to calc, sitting down just after Mr. Jiminez had started another interminable lecture.

I'd brought Margo's copy of *Leaves of Grass* to school, and I started reading the highlighted parts of "Song of Myself" again, under the desk while Mr. Jiminez scratched away at the blackboard. There were no direct references to New York that I could see. I handed it to Radar after a few minutes, and he looked at it for a while before writing on the corner of his notebook closest to me, *The green highlighting must mean something. Maybe she wants you to open the door of your mind?* I shrugged, and wrote back, *Or maybe she just read the poem on two different days with two different highlighters.*

A few minutes later, as I glanced toward the clock for only the thirty-seventh time, I saw Ben Starling standing outside the classroom door, a hall pass in his hand, dancing a spastic jig.

When the bell rang for lunch, I raced to my locker, but somehow Ben had beaten me there, and somehow he was talking to Lacey Pemberton. He was crowding her, slumping slightly so he could talk toward her face. Talking to Ben could make me feel a little claustrophobic sometimes, and I wasn't even a hot girl.

"Hey, guys," I said when I got up to them.

"Hey," Lacey answered, taking an obvious step back from Ben. "Ben was just bringing me up-to-date on Margo. No one ever went into her room, you know. She said her parents didn't allow her to have friends over."

"Really?" Lacey nodded. "Did you know that Margo owns, like, a thousand records?"

Lacey threw up her hands. "No, that's what Ben was saying!

Margo never talked about music. I mean, she would say she liked something on the radio or whatever. But—no. She's so *weird*."

I shrugged. Maybe she was weird, or maybe the rest of us were weird. Lacey kept talking. "But we were just saying that Walt Whitman was from New York."

"And according to Omnictionary, Woody Guthrie lived there for a long time, too," Ben said.

I nodded. "I can totally see her in New York. I think we have to figure out the next clue, though. It can't end with the book. There must be some code in the highlighted lines or something."

"Yeah, can I look at it during lunch?"

"Yeah," I said. "Or I can make you a copy in the library if you want."

"Nah, I can just read it. I mean, I don't know crap about poetry. Oh, but anyway, I have a cousin in college there, at NYU, and I sent her a flyer she could print. So I'm going to tell her to put them up in record stores. I mean, I know there are a lot of record stores, but still."

"Good idea," I said. They started to walk to the cafeteria, and I followed them.

"Hey," Ben asked Lacey, "what color is your dress?"

"Um, it's kind of sapphire, why?"

"Just want to make sure my tux matches," Ben said. I'd never seen Ben's smile so giddy-ridiculous, and that's saying something, because he was a fairly giddy-ridiculous person.

Lacey nodded. "Well, but we don't want to be *too* matchy-matchy. Maybe if you go traditional: black tux and a black vest?"

"No cummerbund, you don't think?"

"Well, they're okay, but you don't want to get one with really fat pleats, you know?"

They kept talking—apparently, the ideal level of pleat-fatness is a conversational topic to which hours can be devoted—but I stopped listening as I waited in the Pizza Hut line. Ben had found his prom date, and Lacey had found a boy who would happily talk prom for hours. Now everyone had a date—except me, and I wasn't going. The only girl I'd want to take was off tramping some kind of perpetual journey or something.

When we sat down, Lacey started reading "Song of Myself," and she agreed that none of it sounded like anything and certainly none of it sounded like Margo. We still had no idea what, if anything, Margo was trying to say. She gave the book back to me, and they started talking about prom again.

All afternoon, I kept feeling like it wasn't doing any good to look at the highlighted quotes, but then I would get bored and reach into my backpack and put the book on my lap and go back to it. I had English at the end of the day, seventh period, and we were just starting to read *Moby Dick*, so Dr. Holden was talking quite a lot about fishing in the nineteenth century. I kept *Moby Dick* on the desk and Whitman in my lap, but even being in English class couldn't help. For once, I went a few minutes without looking at the clock, so I was surprised by the bell ringing, and took longer than everyone else to get my backpack packed. As I slung it over one shoulder and started to leave, Dr. Holden smiled at me and said, "Walt Whitman, huh?"

I nodded sheepishly.

"Good stuff," she said. "So good that I'm almost okay with you reading it in class. But not quite." I mumbled *sorry* and then walked out to the senior parking lot.

While Ben and Radar banded, I sat in RHAPAW with the doors open, a slow husky breeze blowing through. I read from *The Federalist Papers* to prepare for a quiz I had the next day in government, but my mind kept returning to its continuous loop: Guthrie and Whitman and New York and Margo. Had she gone to New York to immerse herself in folk music? Was there some secret folk music–loving Margo I'd never known? Was she maybe staying in an apartment where one of them had once lived? And why did she want to tell *me* about it?

I saw Ben and Radar approaching in the sideview mirror, Radar swinging his sax case as he walked quickly toward RHAPAW. They hustled in through the already-open door, and Ben turned the key and RHAPAW sputtered, and then we hoped, and then she sputtered again, and then we hoped some more, and finally she gurgled to life. Ben raced out of the parking lot and turned off campus before saying to me, "CAN YOU BELIEVE THIS SHIT!" He could hardly contain his glee.

He started hitting the car's horn, but of course the horn didn't work, so every time he hit it, he just yelled, "BEEP! BEEP! BEEP! HONK IF YOU'RE GOING TO PROM WITH TRUE-BLUE HONEYBUNNY LACEY PEMBERTON! HONK, BABY, HONK!"

Ben could hardly shut up the whole way home. "You know what did it? Aside from desperation? I guess she and Becca Arrington are fighting because Becca's, you know, a cheater, and I think she started to feel bad about the whole Bloody Ben thing. She didn't *say* that, but she sort of *acted* it. So in the end, Bloody Ben is going to get me some puh-lay-hey." I was happy for him and everything, but I wanted to focus on the game of getting to Margo.

"Do you guys have any ideas at all?"

It was quiet for a moment, and then Radar looked at me through the rearview mirror and said, "That doors thing is the only one marked different from the others, and it's also the most random; I really think that's the one with the clue. What is it again?"

"'Unscrew the locks from the doors! / Unscrew the doors themselves from their jambs!'" I replied.

"Admittedly, Jefferson Park is not really the best place to unscrew the doors of closed-mindedness from their jambs," Radar allowed. "Maybe that's what she's saying. Like the paper town thing she said about Orlando? Maybe she's saying that's why she left."

Ben slowed for a stoplight and then turned around to look at Radar. "Bro," he said, "I think you guys are giving Margo Honeybunny way too much credit."

"How's that?" I asked.

"Unscrew the locks from the doors," he said. "Unscrew the doors themselves from their jambs."

"Yeah," I said. The light turned green and Ben hit the gas. RHAPAW shuddered like she might disintegrate but then began to move.

"It's not *poetry*. It's not *metaphor*. It's instructions. We are supposed to go to Margo's room and unscrew the lock from the door and unscrew the door itself from its jamb."

Radar looked at me in the rearview mirror, and I looked back at him. "Sometimes," Radar said to me, "he's so retarded that he becomes kind of brilliant."

6.

After parking in my driveway, we walked across the strip of grass that separated Margo's house from mine, just as we had Saturday. Ruthie answered the door and said her parents wouldn't be home until six; Myrna Mountweazel ran excited circles around us; we went upstairs. Ruthie brought us a toolbox from the garage, and then we all stared at the door leading to Margo's bedroom for a while. We were not handy people.

"What the hell are you supposed to do?" asked Ben.

"Don't curse in front of Ruthie," I said.

"Ruthie, do you mind if I say hell?"

"We don't believe in hell," she said, by way of answering.

Radar interrupted. "People," he said. "People. The door." Radar dug out a Phillips-head screwdriver from the mess of a toolbox and knelt down, unscrewing the locking doorknob. I grabbed a bigger screwdriver and tried to unscrew the hinges, but there didn't seem to be any screws involved. I looked at the door some more. Eventually, Ruthie got bored and went downstairs to watch TV.

Radar got the doorknob loose, and we each, in turn, peered inside at the unpainted, unfinished wood around the knob. No message. No note. Nothing. Annoyed, I moved onto the hinges, wondering how to open them. I swung the door open and shut, trying to understand its mechanics. "That poem is so damned long," I said. "You'd think old Walt could have taken a line or two to tell us *how* to unscrew the door itself from its jamb."

Only when he responded did I realize Radar was sitting at Margo's computer. "According to Omnictionary," he said, "we're looking at a butt hinge. And you just use the screwdriver as a lever to pop out the pin. Incidentally, some vandal has added that butt hinges function well because they are powered by farts. Oh, Omnictionary. Wilt thou ever be accurate?"

Once Omnictionary had told us what to do, doing it proved surprisingly easy. I got the pin off each of the three hinges and then Ben pulled the door away. I examined the hinges, and the unfinished wood of the doorway. Nothing.

"Nothing on the door," Ben said. Ben and I placed the door back in place, and Radar pounded in the pins with the screwdriver's handle.

Radar and I went over to Ben's house, which was architecturally identical to mine, to play a game called Arctic Fury. We were playing this game-within-a-game where you shoot each other with paintballs on a glacier. You received extra points for shooting your opponents in the balls. It was very sophisticated. "Bro, she's definitely in New York City," Ben said. I saw the muzzle of his rifle around a corner, but before I could move, he shot me between the legs. "Shit," I mumbled.

Radar said, "In the past, it seems like her clues have pointed to a place. She tells Jase; she leaves us clues involving two people who both lived in New York City most of their lives. It does make sense."

Ben said, "Dude, that's what she wants." Just as I was creeping up on Ben, he paused the game. "She wants you to *go* to New

York. What if she arranged to make that the only way to find her? To actually *go*?"

"What? It's a city of like twelve million people."

"She could have a mole here," Radar said. "Who will tell her if you go."

"Lacey!" Ben said. "It's totally Lacey. Yes! You gotta get on a plane and go to New York City right now. And when Lacey finds out, Margo will pick you up at the airport. Yes. Bro, I am going to take you to your house, and you're gonna pack, and then I'm driving your ass to the airport, and you're gonna put a plane ticket on your emergencies-only credit card, and then when Margo finds out what a badass you are, the kind of badass Jase Worthington only *dreams* about being, all *three* of us will be taking hotties to prom."

I didn't doubt there was a flight to New York City leaving shortly. From Orlando, there's a flight to *everywhere* leaving shortly. But I doubted everything else. "If you call Lacey . . . ," I said.

"She's not going to confess!" Ben said. "Think of all the misdirection they used—they probably only acted like they were fighting so you wouldn't suspect she was the mole."

Radar said, "I don't know, that doesn't really add up." He kept talking, but I was only half listening. Staring at the paused screen, I thought it over. If Margo and Lacey were fake-fighting, did Lacey fake-break-up with her boyfriend? Had she faked her concern? Lacey had been fielding dozens of e-mails—none with real information—from the flyers her cousin had put in record stores in New York. She was no mole, and Ben's plan was idiotic. Still, the mere idea of a plan appealed to me. But there were only two and a half weeks left of school, and I'd miss at least two days if I went to New York—not to mention my parents would kill me for putting a plane ticket on my credit card. The more I thought about it, the dumber it was. Still, if I could see her tomorrow. . . . But no. "I can't miss school," I finally said. I unpaused the game. "I have a French quiz tomorrow."

"You know," Ben said, "your romanticism is a real inspiration."

I played for a few more minutes and then walked across Jefferson Park back home.

My mom told me once about this crazy kid she worked with. He was a completely normal kid until he was nine, when his dad died. And even though obviously a lot of nine-year-olds have had a lot of dead fathers and most of the time the kids don't go crazy, I guess this kid was an exception.

So what he did was he took a pencil and one of those steel compass things, and he started drawing circles onto a piece of paper. All the circles exactly two inches in diameter. And he would draw the circles until the entire piece of paper was completely black, and then he would get another piece of paper and draw more circles, and he did this every day, all day, and didn't pay attention in school and drew circles all over all of his tests and shit, and my mom said that this kid's problem was that he had created a routine to cope with his loss, only the routine became destructive. So anyway, then my mom made him cry about his dad or whatever and the kid stopped drawing circles and presumably lived happily ever after. But I think about the circles kid sometimes, because I can sort of understand him. I always liked routine. I suppose I never found boredom very boring. I doubted I could explain it to someone like Margo, but drawing circles through life struck me as a kind of reasonable insanity.

So I should have felt fine about not going to New York—it was a dumb idea, anyway. But as I went about my routine that night and the next day at school, it ate away at me, as if the routine itself was taking me farther from reuniting with her.

7.

Tuesday evening, when she had been gone six days, I talked to my parents. It wasn't a big *decision* or anything; I just did. I was sitting at the kitchen counter while Dad chopped vegetables and Mom browned some beef in a skillet. Dad was razzing me about how much time I'd spent reading such a short book, and I said, "Actually, it's not for English; it seems like maybe Margo left it for me to find." They got quiet, and then I told them about Woody Guthrie and the Whitman.

"She clearly likes to play these games of incomplete information," my dad said.

"I don't blame her for wanting attention," my mom said, and then to me added, "but that doesn't make her well-being your responsibility."

Dad scraped the carrots and onions into the skillet. "Yeah, true. Not that either of us could diagnose her without seeing her, but I suspect she'll be home soon."

"We shouldn't speculate," my mom said to him quietly, as if I couldn't hear or something. Dad was about to respond but I interrupted.

"What should *I* do?"

"Graduate," my mom said. "And trust that Margo can take of herself, for which she has shown a great talent."

"Agreed," my dad said, but after dinner, when I went back to my room and played Resurrection on mute, I could hear them talking quietly back and forth. I could not hear the words, but I could hear the worry.

Later that night, Ben called my cell.

"Hey," I said.

"Bro," he said.

"Yes," I answered.

"I'm about to go shoe shopping with Lacey."

"*Shoe* shopping?"

"Yeah. Everything's thirty percent off from ten to midnight. She wants me to help her pick out her prom shoes. I mean, she had some, but I was over at her house yesterday and we agreed that they weren't . . . you know, you want the *perfect* shoes for prom. So she's going to return them and then we're going to Burdines and we're going to like pi—"

"Ben," I said.

"Yeah?"

"Dude, I don't want to talk about Lacey's prom shoes. And I'll tell you why: I have this thing that makes me really uninterested in prom shoes. It's called a penis."

"I'm really nervous and I can't stop thinking that I actually kinda really like her not just in the she's-a-hot-prom-date way but in the she's-actually-really-cool-and-I-like-hanging-out-with-her kinda way. And, like, maybe we're going to go to prom and we'll be, like, kissing in the middle of the dance floor and everyone will be like, holy shit and, you know, everything they ever thought about me will just go out the window—"

"Ben," I said. "Stop the dork babble and you'll be fine." He kept talking for a while, but I finally got off the phone with him.

I lay down and started to feel a little depressed about prom. I refused to feel any kind of sadness over the fact that I wasn't *going* to prom, but I had—stupidly, embarrassingly—thought of finding Margo, and getting her to come home with me just in time for prom, like late on Saturday night, and we'd walk into the Hilton ballroom wearing jeans and ratty T-shirts, and we'd be just in time for the last dance, and we'd dance while everyone pointed at us and marveled at the return of Margo, and then we'd fox-trot the hell out of there and go get ice cream at Friendly's. So yes, like Ben, I harbored ridiculous prom fantasies. But at least I didn't *say mine out loud.*

Ben was such a self-absorbed idiot sometimes, and I had to remind myself why I still liked him. If nothing else, he sometimes got surprisingly bright ideas. The door thing was a good idea. It didn't work, but it was a good idea. But obviously Margo had intended it to mean something else to me.

To me.

The clue was *mine.* The doors were mine!

On my way to the garage, I had to walk through the living room, where Mom and Dad were watching TV. "Want to watch?" my mom asked. "They're about to crack the case." It was one of those solve-the-murder crime shows.

"No, thanks," I said, and breezed past them through the kitchen and into the garage. I found the widest flathead screwdriver and then stuck it in the waistband of my khaki shorts, cinching my belt tight. I grabbed a cookie out of the kitchen and then walked back through the living room, my gait only slightly awkward, and while they watched the televised mystery unfold, I removed the three pins from my bedroom door. When the last one came off, the door creaked and started to fall, so I swung it all the way open against the wall with one hand, and as I swung it, I saw a tiny piece of paper—about the size of my thumbnail—flutter down from the door's top hinge. Typical Margo. Why hide something in her own room when she could hide it in mine? I wondered when she'd done it, how she'd gotten in. I couldn't help but smile.

It was a sliver of the *Orlando Sentinel*, half straight edges and half ripped. I could tell it was the *Sentinel* because one ripped edge read "*do Sentinel* May 6, 2." The day she'd left. The message was clearly from her. I recognized her handwriting:

8328 bartlesville Avenue

I couldn't put the door back on without beating the pins back into place with the screwdriver, which would have definitely alerted my parents, so I just propped the door on its hinges and kept it all the way open. I pocketed the pins and then went to my computer and looked up a map of 8328 Bartlesville Avenue. I'd never heard of the street.

It was 34.6 miles away, way the hell out Colonial Drive almost to the town of Christmas, Florida. When I zoomed in on the satellite image of the building, it looked like a black rectangle fronted by dull silver and then grass behind. A mobile home, maybe? It was hard to get a sense of scale, because it was surrounded by so much green.

I called Ben and told him. "So I was right!" he said. "I can't wait to tell Lacey, because she totally thought it was a good idea, too!"

I ignored the Lacey comment. "I think I'm gonna go," I said.

"Well, yeah, of course you've gotta go. I'm coming. Let's go on

Sunday morning. I'll be tired from all-night prom partying, but whatever."

"No, I mean I'm going tonight," I said.

"Bro, it's *dark*. You can't go to a strange building with a mysterious address in the *dark*. Haven't you ever seen a horror movie?"

"She could be there," I said.

"Yeah, and a demon who can only be nourished by the pancreases of young boys could also be there," he said. "Christ, at least wait till tomorrow, although I've got to order her corsage after band, and then I want to be home in case Lacey IM's, because we've been IM'ing a lot—"

I cut him off. "No, tonight. I want to see her." I could feel the circle closing. In an hour, if I hurried, I could be looking at her.

"Bro, I am not letting you go to some sketchy address in the middle of the night. I will Tase your ass if necessary."

"Tomorrow morning," I said, mostly to myself. "I'll just go tomorrow morning." I was tired of having perfect attendance anyway. Ben was quiet. I heard him blowing air between his front teeth.

"I do feel a little something coming on," he said. "Fever. Cough. Aches. Pains." I smiled. After I hung up, I called Radar.

"I'm on the other line with Ben," he said. "Let me call you back."

He called back a minute later. Before I could even say hello, Radar said, "Q, I've got this terrible migraine. There's no way I can go to school tomorrow." I laughed.

After I got off the phone, I stripped down to T-shirt and boxers, emptied my garbage can into a drawer, and put the can next to the bed. I set my alarm for the ungodly hour of six in the morning, and spent the next few hours trying in vain to fall asleep.

8.

Mom came into my room the next morning and said, "You didn't even close the door last night, sleepyhead," and I opened my eyes and said, "I think I have a stomach bug." And then I motioned toward the trash can, which contained puke.

"Quentin! Oh, goodness. When did this happen?"

"About six," I said, which was true.

"Why didn't you come get us?"

"Too tired," I said, which was also true.

"You just woke up feeling ill?" she asked.

"Yeah," I said, which was untrue. I woke up because my alarm went off at six, and then I snuck into the kitchen and ate a granola bar and some orange juice. Ten minutes later, I stuck two fingers down my throat. I didn't want to do it the night before because I didn't want it stinking the room up all night. The puking sucked, but it was over quickly.

Mom took the bucket, and I could hear her cleaning it out in the kitchen. She returned with a fresh bucket, her lips pouting with worry. "Well, I feel like I should take the day—" she started, but I cut her off.

"I'm honestly fine," I said. "Just queasy. Something I ate."

"Are you sure?"

"I'll call if it gets worse," I said. She kissed my forehead. I could feel her sticky lipstick on my skin. I wasn't really sick, but still, somehow she'd made me feel better.

"Do you want me to close the door?" she asked, one hand on it. The door clung to its hinges, but only barely.

"No no no," I said, perhaps too nervously.

"Okay," she said. "I'll call school on my way to work. You let me know if you need anything. Anything. Or if you want me to come home. And you can always call Dad. And I'll check up on you this afternoon, okay?"

I nodded, and then pulled the covers back up to my chin. Even though the bucket had been cleaned, I could smell the puke underneath the detergent, and the smell of it reminded me of the act of puking, which for some reason made me want to puke again, but I just took slow, even mouth breaths until I heard the Chrysler backing down the driveway. It was 7:32. For once, I thought, I would be on time. Not to school, admittedly. But still.

I showered and brushed my teeth and put on dark jeans and a plain black T-shirt. I put Margo's scrap of newspaper in my pocket. I hammered the pins back into their hinges, and then packed. I didn't really know what to throw into my backpack, but I included the doorjamb-opening screwdriver, a printout of the satellite map, directions, a bottle of water, and in case she was there, the Whitman. I wanted to ask her about it.

Ben and Radar showed up at eight on the dot. I got in the backseat. They were shouting along to a song by the Mountain Goats.

Ben turned around and offered me his fist. I punched it softly, even though I hated that greeting. "Q!" he shouted over the music. "How good does this feel?"

And I knew exactly what Ben meant: he meant listening to the Mountain Goats with your friends in a car that runs on a Wednesday morning in May on the way to Margo and whatever Margotastic prize came with finding her. "It beats calculus," I answered. The music was too loud for us to talk. Once we got out of Jefferson Park, we rolled down the one window that worked so the world would know we had good taste in music.

We drove all the way out Colonial Drive, past the movie theaters and the bookstores that I had been driving to and past my whole life. But this drive was different and better because it occurred during calculus, because it occurred with Ben and Radar, because it occurred on our way to where I believed I would find her. And finally, after twenty miles, Orlando gave way to the last remaining orange tree groves and undeveloped ranches—the endlessly flat land grown over thick with brush, the Spanish moss hanging off the branches of oak trees, still in the windless heat. This was the Florida where I used to spend mosquito-bitten, armadillo-chasing nights as a Boy Scout. The road was dominated now by pickup trucks, and every mile or so you could see a subdivision off the highway—little streets winding for no reason around houses that rose up out of nothing like a volcano of vinyl siding.

Farther out we passed a rotting wooden sign that said GROVEPOINT ACRES. A cracked blacktop road lasted only a couple hundred feet before dead-ending into an expanse of gray dirt, signaling that Grovepoint Acres was what my mom called a pseudovision—a subdivision abandoned before it could be completed. Pseudovisions had been pointed out to me a couple times before on drives with my parents, but I'd never seen one so desolate.

We were about five miles past Grovepoint Acres when Radar turned down the music and said, "Should be in about a mile."

I took a long breath. The excitement of being somewhere other than school had started to wane. This didn't seem like a place where Margo would hide, or even visit. It was a far cry from New York City. This was the Florida you fly over, wondering why people ever thought to inhabit this peninsula. I stared at the empty asphalt, the heat distorting my vision. Ahead, I saw a strip mall wavering in the bright distance.

"Is that it?" I asked, leaning forward and pointing.

"Must be," Radar said.

Ben pushed the power button on the stereo, and we all got very quiet as Ben pulled into a parking lot long since reclaimed by the gray sandy dirt. There had once been a sign for these four storefronts. A rusted pole stood about eight feet high by the side of the road. But the sign was long gone, snapped off by a hurricane or an accumulation of decay. The stores themselves had fared little better: it was a single-story building with a flat roof, and bare cinder block was visible in places. Strips of cracked paint wrinkled away from the walls, like insects clinging to a nest. Water stains formed brown abstract paintings between the store windows. The windows were boarded up with warped sheets of particleboard. I was struck by an awful thought, the kind that cannot be taken back once it escapes into the open air of consciousness: it seemed to me that this was not a place you go to live. It was a place you go to die.

As soon as the car stopped, my nose and mouth were flooded with the rancid smell of death. I had to swallow back a rush of puke that rose up into the raw soreness in the back of my throat. Only now, after all this lost time, did I realize how terribly I had misunderstood both her game and the prize for winning it.

I get out of the car and Ben is standing next to me, and Radar next to him. And I know all at once that this isn't funny, that this hasn't been prove-to-me-you're-good-enough-to-hang-out-with-me. I can hear Margo that night as we drove around Orlando. I can hear her saying to me, "I don't want some kids to find me swarmed with flies on a Saturday morning in Jefferson Park." Not wanting to be found by some kids in Jefferson Park isn't the same thing as not wanting to die.

There is no evidence that anyone has been here in a long time except for the smell, that sickly sour stench designed to keep the living from the dead. I tell myself she can't smell like that, but of course she can. We all can. I hold my forearm up to my nose so I can smell sweat and skin and anything but death.

"MARGO?" Radar calls. A mockingbird perched on the rusted gutter of the building spits out two syllables in response. "MARGO!" he shouts again. Nothing. He digs a parabola into the sand with his foot and sighs. "Shit."

Standing before this building, I learn something about fear. I learn that it is not the idle fantasies of someone who maybe wants something important to happen to him, even if the important thing is horrible. It is not the disgust of seeing a dead stranger, and not the breathlessness of hearing a shotgun pumped outside of Becca Arrington's house. This cannot be addressed by breathing exercises. This fear bears no analogy to any fear I knew before. This is the basest of all possible emotions, the feeling that was with us before we existed, before this building existed, before the earth existed. This is the fear that made fish crawl out onto dry land and evolve lungs, the fear that teaches us to run, the fear that makes us bury our dead.

The smell leaves me seized by desperate panic—panic not like my lungs are out of air, but like the atmosphere itself is out of air. I think maybe the reason I have spent most of my life being afraid is that I have been trying to prepare myself, to train my body for the real fear when it comes. But I am not prepared.

"Bro, we should leave," Ben says. "We should call the cops or something." We have not looked at each other yet. We are all still looking at this building, this long-abandoned building that cannot possibly hold anything but corpses.

"No," Radar says. "No no no no no. We call if there's something to call about. She left the address for Q. Not for the cops. We have to find a way in there."

"*In* there?" Ben says dubiously.

I clap Ben on the back, and for the first time all day, the three of us are looking not forward but at one another. That makes it bearable. Something about seeing them makes me feel as if she is not dead until we find her. "Yeah, in there," I say.

I don't know who she is anymore, or who she was, but I need to find her.

9.

We walk around the back of the building and find four locked steel doors and nothing but ranch land, patches of palmettos dotting an expanse of gold-green grass. The stench is worse here, and I feel afraid to keep walking. Ben and Radar are just behind me, to my right and left. We form a triangle together, walking slowly, our eyes scanning the area.

"It's a raccoon!" Ben shouts. "Oh, thank God. It's a raccoon. Jesus." Radar and I walk away from the building to join him near a shallow drainage ditch. A huge, bloated raccoon with matted hair lies dead, no visible trauma, its fur falling off, one of its ribs exposed. Radar turns away and heaves, but nothing comes out. I lean down next to him and put my arm between his shoulder blades, and when he gets his breath back, he says, "I am so fucking glad to see that dead fucking raccoon."

But even so, I cannot picture her here alive. It occurs to me that the Whitman could be a suicide note. I think about things she highlighted: "To die is different from what any one supposed, and luckier." "I bequeath myself to the dirt to grow from the grass I love, / If you want me again look for me under your bootsoles." For a moment, I feel a flash of hope when I think about the last line of the poem: "I stop some where waiting for you." But then I think that the *I* does not need to be a person. The *I* can also be a body.

Radar has walked away from the raccoon and is tugging on the handle of one of the four locked steel doors. I feel like praying for the dead—saying Kaddish for this raccoon—but I don't even know how. I'm so sorry for him, and so sorry for how happy I am to see him like this.

"It's giving a little," Radar shouts to us. "Come help."

Ben and I both put our arms around Radar's waist and pull back. He puts his foot up against the wall to give himself extra leverage as he pulls, and then all at once they collapse onto me, Radar's sweat-soaked T-shirt pressed up against my face. For a moment, I'm excited, thinking we're in. But then I see Radar holding the door handle. I scramble up and look at the door. Still locked.

"Piece of shit forty-year-old goddamned doorknob," Radar says. I've never heard him talk like this before.

"It's okay," I say. "There's a way. There has to be."

We walk all the way around to the front of the building. No doors, no holes, no visible tunnels. But I need in. Ben and Radar try to peel the slabs of particleboard from the windows, but they're all nailed shut. Radar kicks at the board, but it doesn't give. Ben turns back to me. "There's no glass behind one of these boards," he says, and then he starts jogging away from the building, his sneakers splashing sand as he goes.

I give him a confused look. "I'm going to bust through the particleboard," he explains.

"You can't do that." He is the smallest of our light trio. If anyone tries to smash through the boarded-up windows, it should be me.

He balls his hands into fists and then extends his fingers out. As I walk toward him, he starts talking to me. "When my mom was trying to keep me from getting beat up in third grade, she put me in tae kwon do. I only went to like three classes, and I only learned one thing, but the thing comes in handy sometimes: we watched this tae kwon do master punch through a thick wooden block, and we were all like, dude, how did he do that, and he told us that if you move as though your hand will go through the block, and if you believe that your hand will go through the block, then it will."

I'm about to refute this idiotic logic when he takes off, running past me in a blur. His acceleration continues as he approaches the board, and then utterly without fear, he leaps up at the last possible second, twists his body sideways—his shoulder out to bear the brunt of the force—and slams into the wood. I half-expect him to burst through and leave a Ben-shaped cutout, like a cartoon. Instead, he bounces off the board and falls onto his ass in a patch of bright grass amid the sea of sandy dirt. Ben rolls onto his side, rubbing his shoulder. "It broke," he announces.

I assume he means his shoulder as I race toward him, but then he stands up, and I'm looking at a Ben-high crack in the particleboard. I start kicking at it, and the crack spreads horizontally, and then Radar and I get our fingers inside the crack and start tugging. I squint to keep the sweat from burning my eyes, and pull with all my force back and forth until the crack starts to make a jagged opening. Radar and I urge it on with silent work, until eventually he has to take a break and Ben replaces him. Finally we are able to punch a big chunk of the board into the minimall. I climb in feetfirst, landing blindly onto what feels like a stack of papers.

The hole we've carved into this building gives a little light, but I can't even make out the dimensions of the room, or whether there is a ceiling. The air in here is so stale and hot that inhaling and exhaling feel identical.

I turn around and my chin hits Ben's forehead. I find myself whispering, even though there's no reason to. "Do you have a—"

"No," he whispers back before I can finish. "Radar, did you bring a flashlight?"

I hear Radar coming through the hole. "I have one on my key chain. It's not much, though."

The light comes on, and I still can't see very well, but I can tell we've stepped into a big room filled with a labyrinth of metal shelves. The papers on the floor are pages from an old day-by-day calendar, the days scattered through the room, all of them yellowing and mouse-bit. I wonder if this might once have been a little bookstore, although it's been decades since these shelves held anything but dust.

We fall into line behind Radar. I hear something creak above us, and we all stop moving. I try to swallow the panic. I can hear each of Radar's and Ben's breaths, their shuffling footsteps. I want out of here, but that could be Margo creaking for all I know. It could also be crack addicts.

"Just the building settling," Radar whispers, but he seems less sure than usual. I stand there unable to move. After a moment, I hear Ben's voice. "The last time I was this scared, I peed myself."

"The last time I was this scared," Radar says, "I actually had to face a Dark Lord in order to make the world safe for wizards."

I made a feeble attempt. "The last time I was this scared I had to sleep in Mommy's room."

Ben chuckles. "Q, if I were you, I would get that scared Every. Single. Night."

I'm not up for laughing, but their laughter makes the room

feel safer, and so we begin to explore. We walk through each row of shelves, finding nothing but a few copies of *Reader's Digest* from the 1970s lying on the floor. After a while, I find my eyes adjusting to the darkness, and in the gray light we start walking in different directions at different speeds.

"No one leaves the room until everyone leaves the room," I whisper, and they whisper *okay's* back. I get to a side wall of the room and find the first evidence that someone has been here since everyone left. A jagged semicircular, waist-high tunnel has been cut out of the wall. The words TROLL HOLE have been spray-painted in orange above the hole, with a helpful arrow pointing down to the hole. "Guys," Radar says, so loud that the spell breaks for just a moment. I follow his voice and find him standing by the opposite wall, his flashlight illuminating another Troll Hole. The graffiti doesn't look particularly like Margo's, but it's hard to tell for sure. I've only seen her spray-paint a single letter.

Radar shines the light through the hole as I duck down and lead the way through. This room is entirely empty except for a rolled carpet in one corner. As the flashlight scans the floor, I can see glue stains on the concrete from where the carpet had once been. Across the room, I can just make out another hole cut into the wall, this time without the graffiti.

I crawl through that Troll Hole into a room lined with clothing racks, the stainless-steel poles still bolted into walls wine-stained with water damage. This room is better lit, and it takes me a moment to realize it's because there are several holes in the roof—tar paper hangs down, and I can see places where the roof sags against exposed steel girders.

"Souvenir store," Ben whispers in front of me, and I know immediately he is right.

In the middle of the room five display cases form a pentagon. The glass that once kept the tourists from their tourist crap has mostly been shattered and lies in shards around the cases. The gray paint peels off the wall in odd and beautiful patterns, each cracked polygon of paint a snowflake of decay.

Strangely, though, there's still some merchandise: there's a Mickey Mouse phone I recognize from some way back part of childhood. Moth-bit but still-folded SUNNY ORLANDO T-shirts are on display, splattered with broken glass. Beneath the glass cases, Radar finds a box filled with maps and old tourist brochures advertising Gator World and Crystal Gardens and fun houses that no longer exist. Ben waves me over and silently points out the green glass alligator tchotchke lying alone in the case, almost buried in the dust. This is the value of our souvenirs, I think: you can't give this shit away.

We make our way back through the empty room and the shelved room and crawl through the last Troll Hole. This room looks like an office only without computers, and it appears to have been abandoned in a great hurry, like its employees were beamed up to space or something. Twenty desks sit in four rows. There are still pens on some of the desks, and they all feature oversize paper calendars lying flat against the desks. On each calendar, it is perpetually February of 1986. Ben pushes a cloth desk chair and it spins, creaking rhythmically. Thousands of Post-it notes advertising The Martin-Gale Mortgage Corp. are piled beside one desk in a rickety pyramid. Open boxes contain stacks of paper from old dot matrix printers, detailing the expenses and income of the Martin-Gale Mortgage Corp. On one of the desks, someone has stacked brochures for subdivisions into a single-story house of cards. I spread the brochures out, thinking that they may hold a clue, but no.

Radar fingers through the papers, whispering, "Nothing after 1986." I start to go through the desk drawers. I find Q-tips and stickpins. Pens and pencils packed a dozen each in flimsy cardboard packaging with retro fonts and design. Napkins. A pair of golf gloves.

"Do you guys see anything," I ask, "that gives any hint that anyone has been here in the last, say, twenty years?"

"Nothing but the Troll Holes," Ben answers. It's a tomb, everything wrapped in dust.

"So why did she lead us here?" asks Radar. We are speaking now.

"Dunno," I say. She is clearly not here.

"There are some spots," Radar says, "with less dust. There's a dustless rectangle in the empty room, like something was moved. But I don't know."

"And there's that painted part," Ben says. Ben points and Radar's flashlight shows me that a piece of the far wall in this office has been brushed over with white primer, like someone got the idea to remodel the place but abandoned the project after half an hour. I walk over to the wall, and up close, I can see that there's some red graffiti behind the white paint. But I can only see occasional hints of the red paint bleeding through—not nearly enough to make anything out. There's a can of primer up against the wall, open. I kneel down and push my finger into the paint. There's a hard surface, but it breaks easily, and my finger comes up drenched in white. As the paint drips off my finger, I don't say anything, because we've all come to the same conclusion, that someone has been here recently after all, and then the building creaks again and Radar drops the flashlight and curses.

"This is freaky," he says.

"Guys," Ben says. The flashlight is still on the ground, and I take a step back, to pick it up, but then I see Ben pointing. He is pointing at the wall. A trick of the indirect light has made the graffiti letters float up through the coat of primer, a ghost-gray print I recognize immediately as Margo's.

YOU WILL GO TO THE PAPER TOWNS
AND YOU WILL NEVER COME BACK

I pick up the flashlight and shine it on the paint directly, and the message disappears. But when I shine it against a different part of the wall, I can read it again. "Shit," Radar says under his breath.

And now Ben says, "Bro, can we go now? Because the last time I was this scared . . . screw it. I'm freaked out. There's nothing funny about this shit."

There's nothing funny about this shit is the closest Ben can come to the terror I feel, maybe. And it is close enough for me. I fast-walk toward the Troll Hole. I can feel the walls closing in on us.

10.

Ben and Radar dropped me off at my house—even though they'd skipped school, they couldn't afford to skip band practice. I sat alone with "Song of Myself" for a long time, and for about the tenth time I tried to read the entire poem starting at the beginning, but the problem was that it's like eighty pages long and weird and repetitive, and although I could understand each word of it, I couldn't understand anything about it as a whole. Even though I knew the highlighted parts were probably the only important parts, I wanted to know whether it was a suicide-note kind of poem. But I couldn't make sense of it.

I was ten confusing pages into the poem when I got so freaked out that I decided to call the detective. I dug his business card out of a pair of shorts in the laundry hamper. He answered on the second ring.

"Warren."

"Hi, um, it's Quentin Jacobsen. I'm a friend of Margo Roth Spiegelman?"

"Sure, kid, I remember you. What's up?"

I told him about the clues and the minimall and about paper towns, about how she had called Orlando a paper town from the top of the SunTrust Building, but she hadn't used it in the plural, about her telling me that she wouldn't want to be found, about finding her underneath our bootsoles. He didn't even tell me not to break into abandoned buildings, or ask why I was at an abandoned building at 10 A.M. on a school day. He just waited until I stopped talking and said, "Jesus, kid, you're almost a detective. All you need now is a gun, a gut, and three ex-wives. So what's your theory?"

"I'm worried that she might have, um, I guess killed herself."

"It never crossed my mind this girl did anything but run off, kid. I can see your case, but you gotta remember she's done this before. The clues, I mean. Adds drama to the whole enterprise. Honestly, kid, if she wanted you to find her—dead or alive—you already would have."

"But don't you—"

"Kid, the unfortunate thing is that she's a legal adult with free will, you know? Let me give you some advice: let her come home. I mean, at some point, you gotta stop looking up at the sky, or one of these days you'll look back down and see that you floated away, too."

I hung up with a bad taste in my mouth—I realized it wasn't Warren's poetry that would take me to Margo. I kept thinking about those lines at the end Margo had underlined: "I bequeath myself to the dirt to grow from the grass I love, / If you want me again look for me under your bootsoles." That grass, Whitman writes in the first few pages, is "the beautiful uncut hair of graves." But where were the graves? Where were the paper towns?

I logged onto Omnictionary to see if it knew anything more about the phrase "paper towns" than I did. They had an extremely thoughtful and helpful entry created by a user named skunkbutt: "A Paper Town is a town that's got a paper mill in it." This was the shortcoming of Omnictionary: the stuff written by Radar was thorough and extremely helpful; the unedited work of skunk-butt left something to be desired. But when I searched the whole Web, I found something interesting buried forty entries down on a forum about real estate in Kansas.

> Looks like Madison Estates isn't going to get built; my husband and I bought property there, but someone called this week to say they're refunding us our deposit because they didn't presell enough houses to finance the project. Another paper town for KS! —Marge in Cawker, KS

A pseudovision! You will go to the pseudovisions and you will never come back. I took a deep breath and stared at the screen for a while.

The conclusion seemed inescapable. Even with everything broken and decided inside her, she couldn't quite allow herself to disappear for good. And she had decided to leave her body—to leave it for me—in a shadow version of *our* subdivision, where her first strings had broken. She had said she didn't want her body found by random kids—and it made sense that out of everyone she knew, she would pick me to find her. She wouldn't be hurting me in a new way. I'd done it before. I had experience in the field.

I saw that Radar was online and was clicking over to talk to him when an IM from him popped up on my screen.

OMNICTIONARIAN96: Hey.
QTHERESURRECTION: Paper towns = pseudovisions.
I think she wants me to find her body. Because she thinks

I can handle it. Because we found that dead guy when we were kids.

I sent him the link.

OMNICTIONARIAN96: Slow down. Let me look at the link.
QTHERESURRECTION: K.
OMNICTIONARIAN96: Okay, don't be so morbid. You don't know anything for sure. I think she's probably fine.
QTHERESURRECTION: No you don't.
OMNICTIONARIAN96: Okay, I don't. But if anybody's alive in the face of this evidence . . .
QTHERESURRECTION: Yeah, I guess. I'm gonna go lie down. My parents get home soon.

But I couldn't calm down, so I called Ben from bed and told him my theory.

"Pretty morbid shit, bro. But she's fine. It's all part of some game she's playing."

"You're being kind of cavalier about it."

He sighed. "Whatever, it's a little lame of her to, like, hijack the last three weeks of high school, you know? She's got you all worried, and she's got Lacey all worried, and prom is in like three days, you know? Can't we just have a fun prom?"

"Are you serious? She could be *dead*, Ben."

"She's not dead. She's a drama queen. Wants attention. I mean, I know her parents are assholes, but they know her better than we do, don't they? And they think so, too."

"You can be such a tool," I said.

"Whatever, bro. We both had a long day. Too much drama. I'll TTYS." I wanted to ridicule him for using chatspeak IRL, but I found myself lacking the energy.

After I hung up with Ben, I went back online, looking for a list of pseudovisions in Florida. I couldn't find a list anywhere, but after searching "abandoned subdivisions" and "Grovepoint Acres" and the like for a while, I managed to compile a list of five places within three hours of Jefferson Park. I printed out a map of Central Florida, tacked the map to the wall above my computer, and then added a tack for each of the five locations. Looking at the map, I could detect no pattern among them. They were randomly distributed among the far-flung suburbs, and it would take me at least a week to get to all of them. Why hadn't she left me a specific place? All these scary-as-hell clues. All this intimation of tragedy. But no *place*. Nothing to hold on to. Like trying to climb a mountain of gravel.

Ben gave me permission to borrow RHAPAW the next day, since he was going to be driving around, prom shopping with Lacey in her SUV. So for once I didn't have to sit outside the band room—the seventh-period bell rang and I raced out to his car. I lacked Ben's talent for getting RHAPAW to start, so I was one of the first people to arrive at the senior parking lot and one of the last to leave, but finally the engine caught, and I was off to Grovepoint Acres.

I drove out of town on Colonial, driving slowly, watching for any other pseudovisions I might have missed online. A long line of cars trailed behind me, and I felt anxious about holding them up; I marveled at how I could still have room to worry about such petty, ridiculous crap as whether the guy in the SUV behind me thought I was an excessively cautious driver. I wanted Margo's disappearance to change me; but it hadn't, not really.

As the line of cars snaked behind me like some kind of unwilling funeral procession, I found myself talking out loud to her. *I will play out the string. I will not betray your trust. I will find you.*

Talking like this to her kept me calm, strangely. It kept me from imagining the possibilities. I came again to the sagging wooden sign for Grovepoint Acres. I could almost hear the sighs of relief from the bottleneck behind me as I turned left onto the dead-end asphalt road. It looked like a driveway without a house. I left RHAPAW running and got out. From close up, I could see that Grovepoint Acres was more finished than it initially appeared. Two dirt roads ending in cul-de-sacs had been cut into the dusty ground, although the roads had eroded so much I could barely see their outlines. As I walked up and down both streets, I could feel the heat in my nose with each breath. The scalding sun made it hard to move, but I knew the beautiful, if morbid, truth: heat made death reek, and Grovepoint Acres smelled like nothing except cooked air and car exhaust—our cumulative exhalations held close to the surface by the humidity.

I looked for evidence she had been there: footprints or something written in the dirt or some memento. But I seemed to be the first person to walk on these unnamed dirt streets in years. The ground was flat, and not much brush had grown back yet, so I could see for a ways in every direction. No tents. No campfires. No Margo.

I got back in RHAPAW and drove to I-4 and then went northeast of town, up to a place called Holly Meadows. I drove past Holly

Meadows three times before I finally found it—everything in the area was oak trees and ranch land, and Holly Meadows—lacking a sign at its entrance—didn't stand out much. But once I drove a few feet down a dirt road through the initial roadside stand of oak and pine trees, it was every bit as desolate as Grovepoint Acres. The main dirt road just slowly evaporated into a field of dirt. There were no other roads that I could make out, but as I walked around, I did find a few spray-painted wooden stakes lying on the ground; I guessed that they had once been lot line markers. I couldn't smell or see anything suspicious, but even so I felt a fear standing on my chest, and at first I couldn't understand why, but then I saw it: when they'd clear-cut the area to build, they'd left a solitary live oak tree near the back of the field. And the gnarled tree with its thick-barked branches looked so much like the one where we'd found Robert Joyner in Jefferson Park that I felt sure she was there, on the other side of the tree.

And for the first time, I had to picture it: Margo Roth Spiegelman, slumped against the tree, her eyes silent, the black blood pouring out of her mouth, everything bloated and distorted because I had taken so long to find her. She had trusted me to find her sooner. She had trusted me with her last night. And I had failed her. And even though the air tasted like nothing but it-might-rain-later, I was sure I'd found her.

But no. It was only a tree, alone in the empty silver dirt. I sat down against the tree and let my breath come back. I hated doing this alone. I hated it. If she thought Robert Joyner had prepared me for this, she was wrong. I didn't know Robert Joyner. I didn't love Robert Joyner.

I hit at the dirt with the heels of my fists, and then pounded it again and again, the sand scattering around my hands until I was hitting the bare roots of the tree, and I kept it up, the pain shooting up through my palms and wrists. I had not cried for Margo until then, but now finally I did, pounding against the ground and shouting because there was no one to hear: I missed her I missed her I missed her I miss her.

I stayed there even after my arms got tired and my eyes dried up, sitting there and thinking about her until the light got gray.

11.

The next morning at school, I found Ben standing beside the band door talking to Lacey, Radar, and Angela in the shade of a tree with low-hanging branches. It was hard for me to listen as they talked about prom, and about how Lacey was feuding with Becca or whatever. I was waiting for a chance to tell them what I'd seen, but then when I had the chance, when I finally said, "I took a pretty long look at the two pseudovisions but didn't find much," I realized that there was nothing new to say, really.

No one even seemed that concerned, except Lacey. She shook her head as I talked about the pseudovisions, and then said, "I was reading online last night that people who are suicidal end relationships with people they're angry with. And they give away their stuff. Margo gave me like five pairs of jeans last week because she said I could wear them better, which isn't even true because she's so much more, like, curvy." I liked Lacey, but I saw Margo's point about the undermining.

Something about telling us that story made her start to cry, and Ben put an arm around her, and she tucked her head into his shoulder, which was hard to do, because in her heels she was actually taller than him.

"Lacey, we just have to find a location. I mean, talk to your friends. Did she ever mention paper towns? Did she ever talk about a specific place? Was there some subdivision somewhere that meant something to her?" She shrugged into Ben's shoulder.

"Bro, don't push her," Ben said. I sighed, but shut up.

"I'm on the online stuff," Radar said, "but her username hasn't logged on to Omnictionary since she left."

And then all at once they were back on the topic of prom. Lacey emerged from Ben's shoulder still looking sad and distracted, but she tried to smile as Radar and Ben swapped tales of corsage purchasing.

The day passed as it always did—in slow motion, with a thousand plaintive glances at the clock. But now it was even more unbearable, because every minute I wasted in school was another minute in which I failed to find her.

My only vaguely interesting class that day was English, when Dr. Holden completely ruined *Moby Dick* for me by incorrectly assuming we'd all read it and talking about Captain Ahab and his obsession with finding and killing this white whale. But it was fun to watch her get more and more excited as she talked. "Ahab's a madman railing against fate. You never see Ahab wanting anything else in this whole novel, do you? He has a singular obsession. And because he is the captain of his ship, no one can stop him. You can argue—indeed, you may argue, if you choose to write about him for your final reaction papers—that Ahab is a fool for being obsessed. But you could also argue that there is something tragically heroic about fighting this battle he is doomed to lose. Is Ahab's hope a kind of insanity, or is it the very definition of humanness?" I wrote down as much as I could of what she said, realizing that I could probably pull off my final reaction paper without actually reading the book. As she talked, it occurred to me that Dr. Holden was unusually good at reading stuff. And she'd said she liked Whitman. So when the bell rang, I took *Leaves of Grass* from my bag and then zipped it back up slowly while everyone raced off either to home or to extracurriculars. I waited behind someone asking for an extension on an already late paper, and then he left.

"It's my favorite Whitman reader," she said.

I forced a smile. "Do you know Margo Roth Spiegelman?" I asked.

She sat down behind her desk and motioned for me to sit. "I never had her in class," Dr. Holden said, "but I've certainly heard of her. I know that she ran away."

"She sort of left me this book of poems before she, uh, disappeared." I handed the book over, and Dr. Holden began paging through it slowly. As she did, I told her, "I've been thinking a lot about the highlighted parts. If you go to the end of 'Song of Myself,' she highlights this stuff about dying. Like, 'If you want me again look for me under your bootsoles.'"

"She left this for you," Dr. Holden said quietly.

"Yeah," I said.

She flipped back and tapped at the green highlighted quote with her fingernail. "What is this about the doorjambs? That's a great moment in the poem, where Whitman—I mean, you can *feel* him shouting at you: 'Open the doors! In fact, remove the doors!'"

"She actually left me something else inside my doorjamb."

Dr. Holden laughed. "Wow. Clever. But it's such a great poem—I hate to see it reduced to such a literal reading. And she seems to have responded very darkly to what is finally a very optimistic poem. The poem is about our connectedness—each of us sharing the same root system like leaves of grass."

"But, I mean, from what she highlighted, it seems kinda like a suicide note," I said. Dr. Holden read the last stanzas again and then looked up at me.

"What a mistake it is to distill this poem into something hopeless. I hope that's not the case, Quentin. If you read the whole poem, I don't see how you can come to any conclusion except that life is sacred and valuable. But—who knows. Maybe she skimmed it for what she was looking for. We often read poems that way. But if so, she completely misunderstood what Whitman was asking of her."

"And what's that?"

She closed the book and looked right at me in a way that made it impossible for me to hold her gaze. "What do you think of it?"

"I don't know," I said, staring at a stack of graded papers on her desk. "I've tried to read it straight through a bunch of times, but I haven't gotten very far. Mostly I just read the parts she highlighted. I'm reading it to try to understand Margo, not to try to understand Whitman."

She picked up a pencil and wrote something on the back of an envelope. "Hold on. I'm writing that down."

"What?"

"What you just said," she explained.

"Why?"

"Because I think that is precisely what Whitman would have wanted. For you to see 'Song of Myself' not just as a poem but as a way into understanding another. But I wonder if maybe you have to read it as a poem, instead of just reading these fragments for quotes and clues. I do think there are some interesting connections between the poet in 'Song of Myself' and Margo

Spiegelman—all that wild charisma and wanderlust. But a poem can't do its work if you only read snippets of it."

"Okay, thanks," I said. I took the book and stood up. I didn't feel much better.

I got a ride home with Ben that afternoon and stayed at his house until he left to go pick up Radar for some pre-prom party being thrown by our friend Jake, whose parents were out of town. Ben asked me to go, but I didn't feel like it.

I walked back to my house, across the park where Margo and I had found the dead guy. I remembered that morning, and I felt something twist at my gut in the remembering of it—not because of the dead guy, but because I remembered that *she* had found him first. Even in my own neighborhood's playground, I'd been unable to find a body on my own—how the hell would I do it now?

I tried to read "Song of Myself" again when I got home that night, but despite Dr. Holden's advice, it still turned into a jumble of nonsensical words.

I woke up early the next morning, just after eight, and went to the computer. Ben was online, so I IM'ed him.

QTHERESURRECTION: How was the party?
ITWASAKIDNEYINFECTION: Lame, of course. Every party I go to is lame.
QTHERESURRECTION: Sorry I missed it. You're up early. Want to come over, play Resurrection?
ITWASAKIDNEYINFECTION: Are you kidding?

QTHERESURRECTION: uh . . . no?
ITWASAKIDNEYINFECTION: Do you know what day it is?
QTHERESURRECTION: Saturday May 15?
ITWASAKIDNEYINFECTION: Bro, prom starts in eleven hours and fourteen minutes. I have to pick Lacey up in less than nine hours. I haven't even washed and waxed RHAPAW yet, which by the way you did a nice job of dirtying up. Then after that I have to shower and shave and trim nasal hairs and wash and wax myself. God, don't even get me started. I have a lot to do. Listen, I'll call you later if I have a chance.

Radar was on, too, so I IM'ed him.

QTHERESURRECTION: What is Ben's problem?
OMNICTIONARIAN96: Whoa there, cowboy.
QTHERESURRECTION: Sorry, I'm just pissed that he thinks prom is oh-so important.
OMNICTIONARIAN96: You're going to be pretty pissed when you hear that the only reason I'm up this early is that I really need to go because I have to pick up my tux, aren't you?
QTHERESURRECTION: Jesus Christ. Seriously?
OMNICTIONARIAN96: Q, tomorrow and the next day and the day after that and all the days for the rest of my life, I am happy to participate in your investigation. But I have a girlfriend. She wants to have a nice prom. I want to have a nice prom. It's not my fault that Margo Roth Spiegelman didn't want us to have a nice prom.

I didn't know what to say. He was right, maybe. Maybe she deserved to be forgotten. But at any rate, *I* couldn't forget her.

My mom and dad were still in bed, watching an old movie on TV. "Can I take the minivan?" I asked.

"Sure, why?"

"Decided to go to prom," I answered hurriedly. The lie occurred to me as I told it. "Gotta pick out a tux and then get over to Ben's. We're both going stag." My mom sat up, smiling.

"Well, I think that's great, hon. It'll be great for you. Will you come back so we can take pictures?"

"Mom, do you really need pictures of me going to prom stag? I mean, hasn't my life been humiliating enough?" She laughed.

"Call before curfew," my dad said, which was midnight.

"Sure thing," I said. It was so easy to lie to them that I found myself wondering why I'd never much done it before that night with Margo.

I took I-4 west toward Kissimmee and the theme parks, and then passed I-Drive where Margo and I had broken into SeaWorld, and then took Highway 27 down toward Haines City. There are a lot of lakes down there, and wherever there are lakes in Florida, there are rich people to congregate around them, so it seemed an unlikely place for a pseudovision. But the Website I'd found had been very specific about there being this huge parcel of oft-foreclosed land that no one had ever managed to develop. I recognized the place immediately, because every other subdivision on the access road was walled in, whereas Quail Hollow was just a plastic sign hammered into the ground. As I turned in, little plastic posters read FOR SALE, PRIME LOCATION, and GREAT DEVELOPMENT OPPORTUNITIE$!

Unlike the previous pseudovisions, someone was keeping up Quail Hollow. No houses had been built, but the lots were marked with surveying stakes, and the grass was freshly mown. All the streets were paved and named with road signs. In the subdivision's center, a perfectly circular lake had been dug and then, for some reason, drained. As I drove up in the minivan, I could see it was about ten feet deep and several hundred feet in diameter. A hose snaked across the bottom of the crater to the middle, where a steel-and-aluminum fountain rose from the bottom to eye level. I found myself feeling thankful the lake was empty, so I wouldn't have to stare into the water and wonder if she was in the bottom somewhere, expecting me to put on scuba gear to find her.

I felt certain Margo could not be in Quail Hollow. It abutted too many subdivisions for it to be a good place to hide, whether you were a person or a body. But I looked anyway, and as I idled down the streets in the minivan, I felt so hopeless. I wanted to be happy that it wasn't here. But if it wasn't Quail Hollow, it would be the next place, or the one after that, or the one after that. Or maybe I'd never find her. Was that the better fate?

I finished my rounds, finding nothing, and headed back toward the highway. I got lunch at a drive-thru and then ate as I drove out west toward the minimall.

12.

As I pulled into the minimall parking lot, I noticed that blue painters' tape had been used to seal our hole in the board. I wondered who could have been there after us.

I drove around to the back and parked the minivan next to a rusted Dumpster that hadn't encountered a garbage truck in decades. I figured I could bust through the painters' tape if I needed to, and I was walking around toward the front when I noticed that the steel back doors to the stores didn't have any visible hinges.

I'd learned a thing or two about hinges thanks to Margo, and I realized why we hadn't had any luck pulling on all those doors: they opened in. I walked up to the door to the mortgage company office and pushed. It opened with no resistance whatsoever. God, we were such idiots. Surely, whoever cared for the building knew about the unlocked door, which made the painters' tape seem even more out of place.

I wiggled out of the backpack I'd packed that morning and pulled out my dad's high-powered Maglite and flashed it around the room. Something sizable in the rafters scurried. I shivered. Little lizards jump-ran through the path of the light.

A single shaft of light from a hole in the ceiling shone in the front corner of the room, and sunlight peeked out from behind the particleboard, but I mostly relied on the flashlight. I walked up and down the rows of desks, looking at the items we'd found in the drawers, which we'd left. It was profoundly creepy to see desktop after desktop with the same unmarked calendar: February 1986. February 1986. February 1986. June 1986. February 1986. I spun around and shone the light on a desk in the very center of the room. The calendar had been changed to June. I leaned in close and looked at the paper of the calendar, hoping to see a jagged edge where previous months had been torn off, or some marks on the page where a pen had pushed through the paper, but there was nothing different from the other calendars, save the date.

With the flashlight crooked between my neck and shoulder, I started to look through desk drawers again, paying special attention to the June desk: some napkins, some still-sharp pencils, memos about mortgages addressed to one Dennis McMahon, an empty pack of Marlboro Lights, and an almost-full bottle of red nail polish.

I took the flashlight in one hand and the nail polish in the other and stared at it closely. So red it was almost black. I'd seen this color before. It had been on the minivan's dash that night. Suddenly, the scurrying in the rafters and the creaking in the building became irrelevant—I felt a perverted euphoria. I couldn't know if it was the same bottle, of course, but it was certainly the same color.

I rotated the bottle around and saw, unambiguously, a tiny smear of blue spray paint on the outside of the bottle. From her spray-painted fingers. I could be sure now. She'd been here *after* we parted ways that morning. Maybe she was still staying here. Maybe she only showed up late at night. Maybe *she* had taped up the particleboard to keep her privacy.

I resolved right then to stay until morning. If Margo had slept here, I could, too. And thus commenced a brief conversation with myself.

Me: But the rats.

Me: Yeah, but they seem to stay in the ceiling.

Me: But the lizards.

Me: Oh, come on. You used to pull their tails off when you were little. You're not scared of lizards.

Me: But the *rats*.

Me: Rats can't really hurt you anyway. They're more scared of you than you are of them.

Me: Okay, but what about the rats?

Me: Shut up.

In the end, the rats didn't matter, not really, because I was in a place where Margo had been alive. I was in a place that saw her after I did, and the warmth of that made the minimall almost comfortable. I mean, I didn't feel like an infant being held by Mommy or anything, but my breath had stopped catching each time I heard a noise. And in becoming comfortable, I found it easier to explore. I knew there was more to find, and now, I felt ready to find it.

I left the office, ducking through a Troll Hole into the room with the labyrinthine shelves. I walked up and down the aisles for a while. At the end of the room I crawled through the next Troll Hole into the empty room. I sat down on the carpet rolled against the far wall. The cracked white paint crunched against my back. I stayed there for a while, long enough that the jagged beam of light coming through a hole in the ceiling crept an inch along the floor as I let myself become accustomed to the sounds.

After a while, I got bored and crawled through the last Troll Hole into the souvenir shop. I rifled through the T-shirts. I pulled the box of tourist brochures out from under the display case and looked through them, looking for some hand-scrawled message from Margo, but I found nothing.

I returned to the room I now found myself calling the library. I thumbed through the *Reader's Digests* and found a stack of *National Geographics* from the 1960s, but the box was covered in so much dust that I knew Margo had never been inside it.

I began to find evidence of human habitation only when I got back to the empty room. On the wall with the rolled-up carpet, I discovered nine thumbtack holes in the cracked and paint-peeled wall. Four of the holes made an approximate square, and then there were five holes inside the square. I thought perhaps Margo had stayed here long enough to hang up some posters, although there were none obviously missing from her room when we searched it.

I unrolled the carpet partway and immediately found something else: a flattened, empty box that had once contained twenty-four nutrition bars. I found myself able to imagine Margo here, leaning against the wall with musty rolled-up carpet for a seat, eating a nutrition bar. She is all alone, with only this to eat. Maybe she drives once a day to a convenience store to buy a sandwich and some Mountain Dew, but most of every day is spent here, on or near this carpet. This image seemed too sad to be true—it all struck me as so lonely and so very *un*Margo. But all the evidence of the past ten days accumulated toward a surprising conclusion: Margo herself was—at least part of the time—very unMargo.

I rolled out the carpet farther and found a blue knit blanket, almost newspaper thin. I grabbed it and held it to my face and there, God, yes. Her smell. The lilac shampoo and the almond in her skin lotion and beneath all of that the faint sweetness of the skin itself.

And I could picture her again: she unravels the carpet halfway each night so her hip isn't against bare concrete as she lies on her side. She crawls beneath the blanket, uses the rest of the carpet as a pillow, and sleeps. But why here? How is this better than home? And if it's so great, why leave? These are the things I cannot imagine, and I realize that I cannot imagine them because I didn't know Margo. I knew how she smelled, and I knew how she acted in front of me, and I knew how she acted in front of others, and I knew that she liked Mountain Dew and adventure and dramatic gestures, and I knew that she was funny and smart and just generally *more* than the rest of us. But I didn't know what brought her here, or what kept her here, or what made her leave. I didn't know why she owned thousands of records but never told anyone she even liked music. I didn't know what she did at night, with the shades down, with the door locked, in the sealed privacy of her room.

And maybe this was what I needed to do above all. I needed to discover what Margo was like when she wasn't being Margo.

I lay there with the her-scented blanket for a while, staring up at the ceiling. I could see a sliver of late-afternoon sky through a crack in the roof, like a jagged canvas painted a bright blue. This would be the perfect place to sleep: one could see stars at night without getting rained on.

I called my parents to check in. My dad answered, and I said we were in the car on the way to meet Radar and Angela, and that I was staying with Ben overnight. He told me not to drink, and I told him I wouldn't, and he said he was proud of me for going to prom, and I wondered if he would be proud of me for doing what I was actually doing.

This place was boring. I mean, once you got past the rodents and the mysterious the-building-is-falling-apart groans in the walls, there wasn't anything to *do*. No Internet, no TV, no music. *I* was bored, so it again confused me that she would pick this place, since Margo always struck me as a person with a very limited tolerance for boredom. Maybe she liked the idea of slumming it? Unlikely. Margo wore designer jeans to break into SeaWorld.

It was the lack of alternative stimuli that led me back to "Song of Myself," the only certain gift I had from her. I moved to a water-stained patch of concrete floor directly beneath the hole in the ceiling, sat down cross-legged, and angled my body so the light shone upon the book. And for some reason, finally, I could read it.

The thing is that the poem starts out really slowly—it's just sort of a long introduction, but around the ninetieth line, Whitman finally starts to tell a bit of a story, and that's where it picked up for me. So Whitman is sitting around (which he calls loafing) on the grass, and then:

> *A child said, What is the grass? fetching it to me with full hands;*
> *How could I answer the child? . . . . . . I do not know what it is any more than he.*

I guess it must be the flag of my disposition, out of hopeful
green stuff woven.

There was the hope Dr. Holden had talked about—the grass was a metaphor for his hope. But that's not all. He continues,

Or I guess it is the handkerchief of the Lord,
A scented gift and remembrancer designedly dropped,

Like grass is a metaphor for God's greatness or something. . . .

Or I guess the grass is itself a child . . . .

And then soon after that,

Or I guess it is a uniform hieroglyphic,
And it means, Sprouting alike in broad zones and narrow
zones,
Growing among black folks as among white.

So maybe the grass is a metaphor for our equality and our essential connectedness, as Dr. Holden had said. And then finally, he says of grass,

And now it seems to me the beautiful uncut hair of graves.

So grass is death, too—it grows out of our buried bodies. The grass was so many different things at once, it was bewildering. So grass is a metaphor for life, and for death, and for equality, and for connectedness, and for children, and for God, and for hope.

I couldn't figure out which of these ideas, if any, was at the core of the poem. But thinking about the grass and all the different ways you can see it made me think about all the ways I'd seen and mis-seen Margo. There was no shortage of ways to see her. I'd been focused on what had become of her, but now with my head trying to understand the multiplicity of grass and her smell from the blanket still in my throat, I realized that the most important question was *who* I was looking for. If "What is the grass?" has such a complicated answer, I thought, so, too, must "Who is Margo Roth Spiegelman?" Like a metaphor rendered incomprehensible by its ubiquity, there was room enough in what she had left me for endless imaginings, for an infinite set of Margos.

I had to narrow her down, and I figured there had to be things here that I was seeing wrong or not seeing. I wanted to tear off the roof and light up the whole place so that I could see it all at once, instead of one flashlight beam at a time. I put aside Margo's blanket and shouted, loud enough for all the rats to hear, "I Am Going To Find Something Here!"

I went through each desk in the office again, but it seemed more and more obvious that Margo had used only the desk with the nail polish in the drawer and the calendar set to June.

I ducked through a Troll Hole and made my way back to the library, walking again through the abandoned metal shelves. On each shelf I looked for dustless shapes that would tell me Margo had used this space for something, but I couldn't find any. But then my darting flashlight happened across something atop the shelf in a corner of the room, right near the boarded-up storefront window. It was the spine of a book.

The book was called *Roadside America: Your Travel Guide*, and had been published in 1998, *after* this place had been abandoned. I flipped through it with the flashlight crooked between neck and shoulder. The book listed hundreds of attractions you could visit, from the world's largest ball of twine in Darwin, Minnesota, to the world's largest ball of stamps in Omaha, Nebraska. Someone had folded down the corners of several seemingly random pages. The book wasn't too dusty. Maybe SeaWorld was only the first stop on some kind of whirlwind adventure. Yes. That made sense. That was Margo. She found out about this place somehow, came here to gather her supplies, spent a night or two, and then hit the road. I could imagine her pinballing among tourist traps.

As the last light fled from the holes in the ceiling, I found more books above other bookshelves. *The Rough Guide to Nepal*; *The Great Sights of Canada*; *America by Car*; *Fodor's Guide to the Bahamas*; *Let's Go Bhutan*. There seemed to be no connection at all among the books, except that they were all about traveling and had all been published after the minimall was abandoned. I tucked the Maglite under my chin, scooped up the books into a stack that extended from my waist to my chest, and carried them into the empty room I was now imagining as the bedroom.

So it turned out that I did spend prom night with Margo, just not quite as I'd dreamed. Instead of busting into prom together, I sat against her rolled-up carpet with her ratty blanket draped over my knees, alternately reading travel guides by flashlight and sitting still in the dark as the cicadas hummed above and around me.

Maybe she had sat here in the cacophonous darkness and felt some kind of desperation take her over, and maybe she found it impossible to unthink the thought of death. I could imagine that, of course.

But I could also imagine this: Margo picking these books up at various garage sales, buying every travel guide she could get her hands on for a quarter or less. And then coming here—even before she disappeared—to read the books away from prying eyes. Reading them, trying to decide on destinations. *Yes.* She would stay on the road and in hiding, a balloon floating through the sky, eating up hundreds of miles a day with the help of a perpetual tailwind. And in this imagining, she was alive. Had she brought me here to give me the clues to piece together an itinerary? Maybe. Of course I was nowhere near an itinerary. Judging from the books, she could be in Jamaica or Namibia, Topeka or Beijing. But I had only just begun to look.

13.

In my dream, her head was on my shoulder as I lay on my back, only the corner of carpet between us and the concrete floors. Her arm was around my rib cage. We were just lying there, sleeping. God help me. The only teenaged guy in America who dreams of sleeping with girls, and *just* sleeping with them. And then my phone rang. It took two more rings before my fumbling hands found the phone lying on the unrolled carpet. It was 3:18 A.M. Ben was calling.

"Good morning, Ben," I said.

"YESSS!!!!!" he answered, screaming, and I could tell right away that now was not the time to try to explain to him all I had learned and imagined about Margo. I could damn near smell the booze on his breath. That one word, in the way it was shouted, contained more exclamation points than anything Ben had ever said to me in his entire life.

"I take it prom is going well?"

"YESSSS! Quentin Jacobsen! The Q! America's greatest Quentin! Yes!" His voice got distant then but I could still hear him. "Everybody, hey, shut up, hold on, shut up—QUENTIN! JACOBSEN! IS INSIDE MY PHONE!" There was a cheer then, and Ben's voice returned. "Yes, Quentin! Yes! Bro, you have got to come over here."

"Where is here?" I asked.

"Becca's! Do you know where it is?"

As it happened, I knew precisely where it was. I'd been in her basement. "I know where it is, but it's the middle of the night, Ben. And I'm in—"

"YESSS!!! You have to come right now. Right now!"

"Ben, there are more important things going on," I answered.

"DESIGNATED DRIVER!"

"What?"

"You're my designated driver! Yes! You are so designated! I love that you answered! That's so awesome! I have to be home by six! And I designate you to get me there! YESSSSSSS!"

"Can't you just spend the night there?" I asked.

"NOOOO! Booooo. Booo on Quentin. Hey, everybody! Boooo Quentin!" And then I was booed. "Everybody's drunk. Ben drunk. Lacey drunk. Radar drunk. Nobody drive. Home by six. Promised Mom. Boo, Sleepy Quentin! Yay, Designated Driver! YESSSS!"

I took a long breath. If Margo were going to show up, she would have showed up by three. "I'll be there in half an hour."

"YES YES YES YES YES YES YES YES YES YES YES YESSSSSS!!!! YES! YES!"

Ben was still making assertions of affirmation when I hung up the phone. I lay there for a moment, telling myself to get up, and then I did. Still half asleep, I crawled through Troll Holes past the library and into the office, then pulled open the back door and got into the minivan.

I turned in to Becca Arrington's subdivision just before four. There were dozens of cars parked along both sides of Becca's street, and I knew there would be more people inside, since many of them had been dropped off via limo. I found a spot a couple cars away from RHAPAW.

I had never seen Ben drunk. In tenth grade, I once drank a bottle of pink "wine" at a band party. It tasted as bad going down as it did coming up. It was Ben who sat with me in Cassie Hiney's Winnie-the-Pooh–themed bathroom while I projectile-vomited pink liquid all over a painting of Eeyore. I think the experience soured both of us on alcoholic pursuits. Until tonight, anyway.

Now, I knew Ben was going to be drunk. I'd heard him on the phone. No sober person says "yes" that many times per minute. Nonetheless, when I pushed past some people smoking cigarettes on Becca's front lawn and opened the door to her house, I did not expect to see Jase Worthington and two other baseball players holding a tuxedo-clad Ben upside down above a keg of beer. The spout of the beer keg was in Ben's mouth, and the entire room was transfixed on him. They were all chanting in unison, "Eighteen, nineteen, twenty," and for a moment, I thought Ben was getting—like—hazed or something. But no, as he sucked on that beer spout like it was mother's milk, little trickles of beer spilled from the sides of his mouth, because he was smiling. "Twenty-three, twenty-four, twenty-five," the people shouted, and you could hear their enthusiasm. Apparently, something remarkable was taking place.

It all seemed so trivial, so embarrassing. It all seemed like paper kids having their paper fun. I made my way through the crowd toward Ben, and was surprised to happen across Radar and Angela.

"What the hell is this?" I asked.

Radar paused from counting and looked over at me. "Yes!" he said. "The Designated Driver cometh! Yes!"

"Why is everyone saying 'yes' so much tonight?"

"Good question," Angela shouted to me. She puffed out her cheeks and sighed. She looked almost as annoyed as I felt.

"Hell yes, it's a good question!" Radar said, holding a red plastic cup full of beer in each hand.

"They're both his," Angela explained to me calmly.

"Why aren't *you* designated driver?" I asked.

"They wanted you," she said. "Thought it would get you here." I rolled my eyes. She rolled hers back, sympathetically.

"You must really like him," I said, nodding toward Radar, who was holding both beers over his head, joining in the counting. Everybody seemed so proud of the fact that they could count.

"Even now he's sort of adorable," she answered.

"Gross," I said.

Radar nudged me with one of the beer cups. "Look at our boy Ben! He's some kind of autistic savant when it comes to keg stands. Apparently he's like setting a world record right now or something."

"What is a keg stand?" I asked.

Angela pointed at Ben. "That," she said.

"Oh," I said. "Well, it's—I mean, how hard can it be to hang upside down?"

"Apparently, the longest keg stand in Winter Park history is sixty-two seconds," she explained. "And it was set by Tony Yorrick," who's this gigantic guy who'd graduated when we were freshmen and now played for the University of Florida football team.

I was all for Ben setting records, but I couldn't bring myself to join in as everyone shouted, "Fifty-eight, fifty-nine, sixty, sixty-one, sixty-two, sixty-three!" And then Ben pulled the spout out of his mouth and screamed, "YESSS! I MUST BE THE GREATEST! I SHOOK UP THE WORLD!" Jase and some baseball players flipped him right-side-up and carried him around on their shoulders. And then Ben caught sight of me, pointed, and let out the loudest and most passionate "YESSSS!!!!!!" I'd ever heard. I mean, soccer players don't get that excited about winning the World Cup.

Ben jumped off the baseball players' shoulders, landing in an awkward crouch, and then swayed a bit on his way to standing. He wrapped his arm around my shoulders. "YES!" he said again. "Quentin is here! The Great Man! Let's hear it for Quentin, the best friend of the fucking keg stand world record holder!" Jase rubbed the top of my head and said, "You're the man, Q!" and then I heard Radar in my ear, "By the way, we are like folk heroes to these people. Angela and I left our afterparty to come here because Ben told me I'd be greeted as a king. I mean, they were chanting my name. Apparently they all think Ben is hilarious or something, and so they like us, too."

To Radar, and also to everyone else, I said, "Wow."

Ben turned away from us, and I watched him grab Cassie Hiney. His hands were on her shoulders, and she put her hands on his shoulders, and he said, "My prom date was almost prom queen," and Cassie said, "I know. That's great," and Ben said, "I've wanted to kiss you every single day for the last three years," and Cassie said, "I think you should," and then Ben said, "YES! That's *awesome*!" But he didn't kiss Cassie. He just turned around to me and said, "Cassie wants to kiss me!" And I said, "Yeah," and he said, "That's so *awesome*." And then he seemed to forget about Cassie and me both, as if the idea of kissing Cassie Hiney felt better than actually kissing her ever could.

Cassie said to me, "This party is so great, isn't it?" and I said, "Yeah," and she said, "This is like the opposite of band parties, huh?" And I said, "Yeah," and she said, "Ben is a spaz, but I love him." And I said, "Yeah." "Plus he's got really green eyes," she added, and I said, "Uh-huh," and then she said, "Everyone says you're cuter, but I like Ben," and I said, "Okay," and she said, "This party is so great, isn't it?" And I said, "Yeah." Talking to a drunk person was like talking to an extremely happy, severely brain-damaged three-year-old.

Chuck Parson walked up to me just as Cassie walked away. "Jacobsen," he said, matter-of-factly.

"Parson," I answered.

"You shaved my fucking eyebrow, didn't you?"

"I didn't shave it, actually," I said. "I used a depilatory cream."

He poked me quite hard in the middle of my chest. "You're a douche," he said, but he was laughing. "That took such big balls, bro. And now you're all puppet master and shit. I mean, maybe I'm just drunk, but I'm feeling a little love for your douchey ass right now."

"Thank you," I said. I felt so detached from all this shit, all this high-school-is-ending-so-we-have-to-reveal-that-deep-down-we-all-love-everybody bullshit. And I imagined her at this party, or at thousands like this one. The life drawn out of her eyes. I imagined her listening to Chuck Parson babble at her and thinking about ways out, about the living ways out and the dead ways out. I could imagine the two paths with equal clarity.

"You want a beer, dicklicker?" Chuck asked. I might have forgotten he was even there, but the smell of booze on his breath made it hard to overlook his presence. I just shook my head, and he wandered off.

I wanted to go home, but I knew I couldn't rush Ben. This was probably the single greatest day of his life. He was entitled to it.

So instead, I found a stairway and headed down to the basement. I'd been in the dark so long I was still craving it, and I just wanted to lie down somewhere halfway quiet and halfway dark and go back to imagining Margo. But as I walked past Becca's bedroom, I heard some muffled noises—specifically, moanish noises—and so I paused outside her door, which was open just a crack.

I could see the top two-thirds of Jase, shirtless, on top of Becca, and she had her legs wrapped around him. Nobody was naked or anything, but they were headed in that direction. And maybe a better person would have turned away, but people like me don't get a lot of chances to see people like Becca Arrington naked, so I stayed there in the doorway, peering into the room. And then they rolled around so Becca was on top of Jason, and she was sighing as she kissed him, and she was reaching down for her shirt. "Do you think I'm hot?" she said.

"God yeah, you are so hot, Margo," Jase said.

"What!?" Becca said, furious, and it became quickly clear to me that I wasn't going to see Becca naked. She started screaming; I backed away from the door; Jase spotted me and screamed, "What's your problem?" And Becca shouted, "Screw him. Who gives a shit about him? What about me?! Why are you thinking about her and not me!"

That seemed like as good a time as any to take my leave of the situation, so I closed the door and went to the bathroom. I did need to pee, but mostly I just needed to be away from the human voice.

It always takes a few seconds for me to start peeing after all the equipment has been properly set up, and so I stood there for a second, waiting, and then I started peeing. I'd just gotten to the full-stream, shudder-of-relief part of peeing when a girl's voice from the general area of the bathtub said, "Who's there?"

And I said, "Uh, Lacey?"

"Quentin? What the hell are you doing here?" I wanted to stop peeing but couldn't, of course. Peeing is like a good book in that it is very, very hard to stop once you start.

"Um, peeing," I said.

"How's it going?" she asked through the curtain.

"Um, fine?" I shook out the last of it, zipped my shorts, and flushed.

"You wanna hang out in the bathtub?" she asked. "That's not a come-on."

After a moment, I said, "Sure." I pulled the shower curtain back. Lacey smiled up at me, and then pulled her knees up to her chest. I sat down across from her, my back against the cold sloping porcelain. Our feet were intertwined. She was wearing shorts and a sleeveless T-shirt and these cute little flip-flops. Her makeup was just a little smeared around her eyes. Her hair was half up, still styled for prom, and her legs were tan. It must be said that Lacey Pemberton was very beautiful. She was not the kind of girl who could make you forget about Margo Roth Spiegelman, but she was the kind of girl who could make you forget about a lot of things.

"How was prom?" I asked.

"Ben is really sweet," she answered. "I had fun. But then Becca and I had a huge fight and she called me a whore and then she stood up on the couch upstairs and she shushed the entire party and then she told everyone I have an STD."

I winced. "God," I said.

"Yeah. I'm sort of ruined. It's just . . . God. It sucks, honestly, because . . . it's just so humiliating, and she knew it would be, and . . . it sucks. So then I went to the bathtub and then Ben came down here and I told him to leave me alone. Nothing against Ben, but he wasn't very good at, like, listening. He's kinda drunk. I don't even have it. I *had* it. It's cured. Whatever. It's just, I'm not a slut. It was one guy. One lame-ass guy. God, I can't believe I ever told her. I should have just told Margo when Becca wasn't around."

"I'm sorry," I said. "The thing is that Becca is just jealous."

"Why would she be jealous? She's prom queen. She's dating Jase. She's the new Margo."

My butt was sore against the porcelain, so I tried to rearrange myself. My knees were touching her knees. "No one will ever be the new Margo," I said. "Anyway, you have what she really wants. People like you. People think you're cuter."

Lacey shrugged bashfully. "Do you think I'm superficial?"

"Well, yeah." I thought of myself standing outside Becca's bedroom, hoping she'd take her shirt off. "But so am I," I added. "So is everyone." I'd often thought, *If only I had the body of Jase Worthington. Walked like I knew how to walk. Kissed like I knew how to kiss.*

"But not in the same way. Ben and I are superficial in the same way. You don't give a shit if people like you."

Which was both true and not. "I care more than I'd like to," I said.

"Everything sucks without Margo," she said. She was drunk, too, but I didn't mind her variety of drunk.

"Yeah," I said.

"I want you to take me to that place," she said. "That strip mall. Ben told me about it."

"Yeah, we can go whenever you want," I said. I told her I'd been there all night, that I'd found Margo's nail polish and her blanket.

Lacey was quiet for a while, breathing through her open mouth. When she finally said it, she almost whispered it. Worded like a question and spoken like a statement: "She's dead, isn't she."

"I don't know, Lacey. I thought so until tonight, but now I don't know."

"She's dead and we're all . . . doing this."

I thought of the highlighted Whitman: "If no other in the world be aware I sit content, / And if each and all be aware I sit content." I said, "Maybe that's what she wanted, for life to go on."

"That doesn't sound like my Margo," she said, and I thought of my Margo, and Lacey's Margo, and Mrs. Spiegelman's Margo, and all of us looking at her reflection in different fun house mirrors. I was going to say something, but Lacey's open mouth became truly slack-jawed, and she leaned her head against the cold gray tile of the bathroom wall, asleep.

It wasn't until after two people had come into the bathroom to pee that I decided to wake her up. It was almost 5 A.M., and I needed to take Ben home.

"Lace, wake up," I said, touching her flip-flop with my shoe.

She shook her head. "I like being called that," she said. "You know that you're, like, currently my best friend?"

"I'm thrilled," I said, even though she was drunk and tired and lying. "So listen, we're going to go upstairs together, and if anybody says anything about you, I will defend your honor."

"Okay," she said. And so we went upstairs together, and the party had thinned out a little, but there were still some baseball players, including Jase, over by the keg. Mostly there were people sleeping in sleeping bags all over the floor; some of them were squeezed onto the pullout couch. Angela and Radar were lying together on a love seat, Radar's legs dangling over the side. They were sleeping over.

Just as I was about to ask the guys by the keg if they'd seen Ben, he ran into the living room. He wore a blue baby bonnet on his head and was wielding a sword made out of eight empty cans of Milwaukee's Best Light, which had, I assumed, been glued together.

"I SEE YOU!" Ben shouted, pointing at me with the sword. "I SPY QUENTIN JACOBSEN! YESSS! Come here! Get on your knees!" he shouted.

"What? Ben, calm down."

"KNEES!"

I obediently knelt, looking up at him.

He lowered the beer sword and tapped me on each shoulder. "By the power of the superglue beer sword, I hereby designate you my driver!"

"Thanks," I said. "Don't puke in the minivan."

"YES!" he shouted. And then when I tried to get up, he pushed me back down with his non-beer-sworded hand, and he tapped me again with the beer sword, and he said, "By the power of the superglue beer sword, I hereby announce that you will be naked under your robe at graduation."

"What?" I stood then.

"YES! Me and you and Radar! Naked under our robes! At graduation! It will be so awesome!"

"Well," I said, "it *will* be really hot."

"YES!" he said. "Swear you will do it! I already made Radar swear. RADAR, DIDN'T YOU SWEAR?"

Radar turned his head ever so slightly, and opened his eyes a slit. "I swore," he mumbled.

"Well then, I swear, too," I said.

"YES!" Then Ben turned to Lacey. "I love you."

"I love you, too, Ben."

"No, *I love you*. Not like a sister loves a brother or like a friend loves a friend. I love you like a really drunk guy loves the best girl ever." She smiled.

I took a step forward, trying to save him from further embarrassment, and placed a hand on his shoulder. "If we're gonna get you home by six, we should be leaving," I said.

"Okay," he said. "I just gotta thank Becca for this awesome party."

So Lacey and I followed Ben downstairs, where he opened the door to Becca's room and said, "Your party kicked so much ass! Even though you suck so much! It's like instead of blood, your heart pumps liquid suck! But thanks for the beer!" Becca was alone, lying on top of her covers, staring at the ceiling. She didn't even glance over at him. She just mumbled, "Oh, go to hell, shitface. I hope your date gives you her crabs."

Without a hint of irony in his voice, Ben answered, "Great talking to you!" and then closed the door. I don't think he had the faintest idea he'd just been insulted.

And then we were upstairs again and getting ready to walk out the door. "Ben," I said, "you're going to have to leave the beer sword here."

"Right," he said, and then I grabbed the sword's tip and tugged, but Ben refused to relinquish it. I was about to start screaming at his drunk ass when I realized he *couldn't* let go of the sword.

Lacey laughed. "Ben, did you glue yourself to the beer sword?"

"No," Ben answered. "I *super*glued. That way no one can steal it from me!"

"Good thinking," Lacey deadpanned.

Lacey and I managed to break off all the beer cans except the one that was superglued directly to Ben's hand. No matter how hard I pulled, Ben's hand just limply followed along, like the beer was the string and his hand the puppet. Finally, Lacey just said, "We gotta go." So we did. We strapped Ben into the backseat of the minivan. Lacey sat next to him, because "I should make sure he doesn't puke or beat himself to death with his beer hand or whatever."

But he was far enough gone for Lacey to feel comfortable talking about him. As I drove down the interstate, she said, "There's something to be said for trying hard, you know? I mean, I know he tries too hard, but why is that such a bad thing? And he's sweet, isn't he?"

"I guess so," I said. Ben's head was lolling around, seemingly unconnected to a spine. He didn't strike me as particularly sweet, but whatever.

I dropped Lacey off first on the other side of Jefferson Park. When Lacey leaned over and pecked him on the mouth, he perked up enough to mumble, "Yes."

She walked up to the driver's-side door on the way to her condo. "Thanks," she said. I just nodded.

I drove across the subdivision. It wasn't night and it wasn't morning. Ben snored quietly in the back. I pulled up in front of his house, got out, opened the sliding door of the minivan, and unfastened his seat belt.

"Time to go home, Benners."

He sniffed and shook his head, then awoke. He reached up to rub his eyes and seemed surprised to find an empty can of Milwaukee's Best Light attached to his right hand. He tried to make a fist and dented the can some, but did not dislodge it. He looked at it for a minute, and then nodded. "The Beast is stuck to me," he noted.

He climbed out of the minivan and staggered up the sidewalk to his house, and when he was standing on the front porch, he turned around, smiling. I waved at him. The beer waved back.

14.

I slept for a few hours and then spent the morning poring over the travel guides I'd discovered the day before. I waited until noon to call Ben and Radar. I called Ben first. "Good morning, Sunshine," I said.

"Oh, God," Ben said, his voice dripping abject misery. "Oh, sweet baby Jesus, come and comfort your little bro Ben. Oh, Lord. Shower me with your mercy."

"There've been a lot of Margo developments," I said excitedly, "so you need to come over. I'm gonna call Radar, too."

Ben seemed not to have heard me. "Hey, when my mom came into my room at nine o'clock this morning, why is it that as I reached up to yawn, she and I both discovered a beer can was stuck to my hand?"

"You superglued a bunch of beers together to make a beer sword, and then you superglued your hand to it."

"Oh, yeah. The beer sword. That rings a bell."

"Ben, come over."

"Bro. I feel like shit."

"Then I'll come over to your house. How soon?"

"Bro, you can't come over here. I have to sleep for ten thousand hours. I have to drink ten thousand gallons of water, and take ten thousand Advils. I'll just see you tomorrow at school."

I took a deep breath and tried not to sound pissed. "I drove across Central Florida in the middle of the night to be sober at the world's drunkest party and drive your soggy ass home, and this is—" I would have kept talking, but I noticed that Ben had hung up. He hung up on me. Asshole.

As time passed, I only got more pissed. It's one thing not to give a shit about Margo. But really, Ben didn't give a shit about me, either. Maybe our friendship had always been about convenience—he didn't have anyone cooler than me to play video games with. And now he didn't have to be nice to me, or care about the things I cared about, because he had Jase Worthington. He had the school keg stand record. He had a hot prom date. He'd jumped at his first opportunity to join the fraternity of vapid asshats.

Five minutes after he hung up on me, I called his cell again. He didn't answer, so I left a message. "You want to be cool like Chuck, Bloody Ben? That's what you always wanted? Well, congratulations. You got it. And you deserve him, because you're also a shitbag. Don't call back."

Then I called Radar. "Hey," I said.

"Hey," he answered. "I just threw up in the shower. Can I call you back?"

"Sure," I said, trying not to sound angry. I just wanted *someone* to help me sort through the world according to Margo. But Radar wasn't Ben; he called back just a couple minutes later.

"It was so disgusting that I puked while cleaning it up, and then while cleaning *that* up, I puked again. It's like a perpetual motion machine. If you just kept feeding me, I could have just kept puking forever."

"Can you come over? Or can I come over to your house?"

"Yeah, of course. What's up?"

"Margo was alive and in the minimall for at least one night after her disappearance."

"I'll come to you. Four minutes."

Radar showed up at my window precisely four minutes later. "You should know I'm having a huge fight with Ben," I said as he climbed in.

"I'm too hungover to mediate," Radar answered quietly. He lay down on the bed, his eyes half closed, and rubbed his buzzed hair. "It's like I got hit by lightning." He sniffed. "Okay, bring me up-to-date." I sat down in the desk chair and told Radar about my evening in Margo's vacation house, trying hard not to leave out any possibly helpful details. I knew Radar was better at puzzles than I, and I was hoping he'd piece together this one.

He waited to talk until I'd said, "And then Ben called me and I left for that party."

"Do you have that book, the one with the turned-down corners?" he asked. I got up and fished for it under the bed, finally pulling it out. Radar held it above his head, squinting through his headache, and flipped through the pages.

"Write this down," he said. "Omaha, Nebraska. Sac City, Iowa. Alexandria, Indiana. Darwin, Minnesota. Hollywood, California. Alliance, Nebraska. Okay. Those are the locations of all the things she—well, or whoever read this book—found interesting." He got up, motioned me out of the chair, and then swiveled to the computer. Radar had an amazing talent for carrying on conversations while typing. "There's a map mash-up that allows you to enter multiple destinations and it will spit out a variety of itineraries. Not that she'd know about this program. But still, I want to see."

"How do you know all this shit?" I asked.

"Um, reminder: I. Spend. My. Entire. Life. On. Omnictionary. In the hour between when I got home this morning and when I hurled in the shower, I completely rewrote the page for the Blue-spotted Anglerfish. I have a *problem*. Okay, look at this," he said. I leaned in and saw several jagged routes drawn onto a map of the United States. All began in Orlando and ended in Hollywood, California.

"Maybe she'll stay in LA?" Radar suggested.

"Maybe," I said. "There's no way to tell her route, though."

"True. Also nothing else points to LA. What she said to Jase points to New York. The 'go to the paper towns and never come back' points to a nearby pseudovision, it seems. The nail polish also points to maybe her still being in the area? I'm just saying we can now add the location of the world's largest ball of popcorn to our list of possible Margo locales."

"The traveling would fit with one of the Whitman quotes: 'I tramp a perpetual journey.'"

Radar stayed hunched over the computer. I went to sit down on the bed. "Hey, will you just print out a map of the U.S. so I can plot the points?" I asked.

"I can just do it online," he said.

"Yeah, but I want to be able to look at it." The printer fired up a few seconds later and I placed the U.S. map next to the one with the pseudovisions on the wall. I put a tack in for each of the six locations she (or someone) had marked in the book. I tried to look at them as a constellation, to see if they formed a shape or a letter—but I couldn't see anything. It was a totally random distribution, like she'd blindfolded herself and thrown darts at the map.

I sighed. "You know what would be nice?" Radar asked. "If we could find some evidence that she was checking her e-mail or anywhere on the Internet. I search for her name every day; I've got a bot that will alert me if she ever logs on to Omnictionary with that username. I track IP addresses of people who search for the phrase 'paper towns.' It's incredibly frustrating."

"I didn't know you were doing all that stuff," I said.

"Yeah, well. Only doing what I'd want someone else to do. I know I wasn't friends with her, but she deserves to be found, you know?"

"Unless she doesn't want to be," I said.

"Yeah, I guess that's possible. It's all still possible." I nodded. "Yeah, so—okay," he said. "Can we brainstorm over video games?"

"I'm not really in the mood."

"Can we call Ben then?"

"No. Ben's an asshole."

Radar looked at me sideways. "Of course he is. You know your problem, Quentin? You keep expecting people not to be themselves. I mean, I could hate you for being massively unpunctual and for never being interested in anything other than Margo Roth Spiegelman, and for, like, never asking me about how it's going with my girlfriend—but I don't give a shit, man, because you're you. My parents have a shit ton of black Santas, but that's okay. They're them. I'm too obsessed with a reference Web site to answer my phone sometimes when my friends call, or my girlfriend. That's okay, too. That's me. You like me anyway. And I like you. You're funny, and you're smart, and you may show up late, but you always show up eventually."

"Thanks."

"Yeah, well, I wasn't complimenting you. Just saying: stop thinking Ben should be you, and he needs to stop thinking you should be him, and y'all just chill the hell out."

"All right," I said finally, and called Ben. The news that Radar was over and wanted to play video games led to a miraculous hangover recovery.

"So," I said after hanging up. "How's Angela?"

Radar laughed. "She's good, man. She's real good. Thanks for asking."

"You still a virgin?" I asked.

"I don't kiss and tell. Although, yes. Oh, and we had our first fight this morning. We had breakfast at Waffle House, and she was going on about how awesome the black Santas are, and how my parents are great people for collecting them because it's important for us not to presume that everybody cool in our culture like God and Santa Claus is white, and how the black Santa empowers the whole African-American community."

"I actually think I kind of agree with her," I said.

"Yeah, well, it's a fine idea, but it happens to be bullshit. They're not trying to spread the black Santa gospel. If they were, they'd *make* black Santas. Instead, they're trying to buy the entire world supply. There's this old guy in Pittsburgh with the second-biggest collection, and they're always trying to buy it off him."

Ben spoke from the doorway. He'd been there a while, apparently. "Radar, your failure to bop that lovely honeybunny is the greatest humanitarian tragedy of our time."

"What's up, Ben?" I said.

"Thanks for the ride last night, bro."

15.

Even though we only had a week before finals, I spent Monday afternoon reading "Song of Myself." I'd wanted to go to the last two pseudovisions, but Ben needed his car. I was no longer looking for clues in the poem so much as I was looking for Margo herself. I'd made it about halfway through "Song of Myself" this time when I stumbled into another section that I found myself reading and rereading.

"I think I will do nothing for a long time but listen," Whitman writes. And then for two pages, he's just hearing: hearing a steam whistle, hearing people's voices, hearing an opera. He sits on the grass and lets the sound pour through him. And this is what I was trying to do, too, I guess: to listen to all the little sounds of her, because before any of it could make sense, it had to be heard. For so long, I hadn't really *heard* Margo—I'd seen her screaming and thought her laughing—that now I figured it was my job. To try, even at this great remove, to hear the opera of her.

If I couldn't hear Margo, I could at least listen to what she once heard, so I downloaded the album of Woody Guthrie covers. I sat at the computer, my eyes closed, elbows against the desk, and listened to a voice singing in a minor key. I tried to hear, inside a song I'd never heard before, the voice I had trouble remembering after twelve days.

I was still listening—but now to another of her favorites, Bob

Dylan—when my mom got home. "Dad's gonna be late," she said through the closed door. "I thought I might make turkey burgers?"

"Sounds good," I answered, and then closed my eyes again and listened to the music. I didn't sit up again until Dad called me for dinner an album and a half later.

At dinner, Mom and Dad were talking about politics in the Middle East. Even though they completely agreed with each other, they still managed to yell about it, saying that so-and-so was a liar, and so-and-so was a liar *and* a thief, and that the lot of them should resign. I focused on the turkey burger, which was excellent, dripping with ketchup and smothered with grilled onions.

"Okay, enough," my mom said after a while. "Quentin, how was your day?"

"Fine," I said. "Getting ready for finals, I guess."

"I can't believe this is your last week of classes," Dad said. "It really does just seem like yesterday . . ."

"It does," Mom said. A voice in my head was like: WARNING NOSTALGIA ALERT WARNING WARNING WARNING. Great people, my parents, but prone to bouts of crippling sentimentality.

"We're just very proud of you," she said. "But, God, we'll miss you next fall."

"Yeah, well, don't speak too soon. I could still fail English."

My mom laughed, and then said, "Oh, guess who I saw at the YMCA yesterday? Betty Parson. She said Chuck was going to the University of Georgia next fall. I was pleased for him; he's always struggled."

"He's an asshole," I said.

"Well," my dad said, "he was a bully. And his behavior was deplorable." This was typical of my parents: in their minds, no one was just an asshole. There was always something wrong with people other than just sucking: they had socialization disorders, or borderline personality syndrome, or whatever.

My mom picked up the thread. "But Chuck has learning difficulties. He has all kinds of problems—just like anyone. I know it's impossible for you to see peers this way, but when you're older, you start to see them—the bad kids and the good kids and all kids—as people. They're just people, who deserve to be cared for. Varying degrees of sick, varying degrees of neurotic, varying degrees of self-actualized. But you know, I always liked Betty, and I always had hopes for Chuck. So it's good that he's going to college, don't you think?"

"Honestly, Mom, I don't really care about him one way or another." But I did think, if everyone is such a person, how come Mom and Dad still hated all the politicians in Israel and Palestine? They didn't talk about *them* like they were people.

My dad finished chewing something and then put his fork down and looked at me. "The longer I do my job," he said, "the more I realize that humans lack good mirrors. It's so hard for anyone to show us how we look, and so hard for us to show anyone how we feel."

"That is really lovely," my mom said. I liked that they liked each other. "But isn't it also that on some fundamental level we find it difficult to understand that other people are human beings in the same way that we are? We idealize them as gods or dismiss them as animals."

"True. Consciousness makes for poor windows, too. I don't think I'd ever thought about it quite that way."

I was sitting back. I was listening. And I was hearing something about her and about windows and mirrors. Chuck Parson was a person. Like me. Margo Roth Spiegelman was a person, too. And I had never quite thought of her that way, not really; it was a failure of all my previous imaginings. All along—not only since she left, but for a decade before—I had been imagining her without listening, without knowing that she made as poor a window as I did. And so I could not imagine her as a person who could feel fear, who could feel isolated in a roomful of people, who could be shy about her record collection because it was too personal to share. Someone who might read travel books to escape having to live in the town that so many people escape to. Someone who—because no one thought she was a person—had no one to really talk to.

And all at once I knew how Margo Roth Spiegelman felt when she wasn't being Margo Roth Spiegelman: she felt empty. She felt the unscaleable wall surrounding her. I thought of her asleep on the carpet with only that jagged sliver of sky above her. Maybe Margo felt comfortable there because Margo the person lived like that all the time: in an abandoned room with blocked-out windows, the only light pouring in through holes in the roof. *Yes.* The fundamental mistake I had always made—and that she had, in fairness, always led me to make—was this: Margo was not a miracle. She was not an adventure. She was not a fine and precious thing. She was a girl.

16.

The clock was always punishing, but feeling like I was closer to unraveling the knots made time seem to stop entirely on Tuesday. We'd all decided to go to the minimall right after school, and the waiting was unbearable. When the bell finally rang for the end of English, I raced downstairs and was almost out the door when I realized we couldn't leave until Ben and Radar finished band practice. I sat down outside the band room and took a personal pizza wrapped in napkins from my backpack, where I'd had it since lunch. I was through the first quarter when Lacey Pemberton sat down next to me. I offered her a piece. She declined.

We talked about Margo, of course. The hole we had in common. "What I need to figure out," I said, rubbing pizza grease onto my jeans, "is a place. But I don't even know if I'm close with the pseudovisions. Sometimes I think we're just entirely off track."

"Yeah, I don't know. Honestly, everything else aside, I like finding stuff out about her. I mean, that I didn't know before. I had no idea who she really was. I honestly never thought of her as anything but my crazy beautiful friend who does all the crazy beautiful things."

"Right, but she didn't come up with these things *on the fly,*" I said. "I mean, all of her adventures had a certain . . . I don't know."

"Elegance," Lacey said. "She is the only person I know who's not, like, grown up who has total elegance."

"Yeah."

"So it's hard to imagine her in some gross unlit dusty room."

"Yeah," I said. "With rats."

Lacey pulled her knees to her chest and assumed the fetal position. "Ick. That's *so* not Margo."

Somehow Lacey got shotgun, although she was the shortest of us. Ben was driving. I sighed quite loudly as Radar, seated next to me, pulled out his handheld and started working on Omnictionary.

"Just deleting vandalism on the Chuck Norris page," he said. "For instance, while I do think Chuck Norris specializes in the roundhouse kick, I don't think it's accurate to say, 'Chuck Norris's tears can cure cancer, but unfortunately he has never cried.' Anyway, vandalism-deletion only takes like four percent of my brain."

I understood Radar was trying to make me laugh, but I only wanted to talk about one thing. "I'm not convinced she's in a pseudovision. Maybe that's not even what she meant by 'paper towns,' you know? There are so many place hints, but nothing *specific*."

Radar looked up for a second and then back down at the screen. "Personally, I think she's far away, doing some ridiculous roadside attraction tour that she wrongly thinks she left enough clues to explain. So I think she's currently in, like, Omaha, Nebraska, visiting the world's largest ball of stamps, or in Minnesota checking out the world's largest ball of twine."

With a glance into the rearview mirror, Ben said, "So you think that Margo is on a national tour in search of various World's Largest Balls?" Radar nodded.

"Well," Ben went on, "someone should just tell her to come on home, because she can find the world's largest balls right here in Orlando, Florida. They're located in a special display case known as 'my scrotum.'"

Radar laughed, and Ben continued. "I mean, seriously. My balls are so big that when you order french fries from McDonald's, you can choose one of four sizes: small, medium, large, and my balls."

Lacey cut her eyes at Ben and said, "Not. Appropriate."

"Sorry," Ben mumbled. "I think she's in Orlando," he said. "Watching us look. And watching her parents not look."

"I'm still for New York," Lacey said.

"All still possible," I said. A Margo for each of us—and each more mirror than window.

The minimall looked as it had a couple days before. Ben parked, and I took them through the push-open door to the office. Once everyone was inside, I said softly, "Don't turn on the flashlight yet. Give your eyes a chance to adjust." I felt fingernails dig at my forearm. I whispered, "It's okay, Lace."

"Whoops," she said. "Wrong arm." She'd been searching, I realized, for Ben.

Slowly, the room came into a hazy gray focus. I could see the desks lined up, still waiting for workers. I turned on my flashlight, and then everyone else turned theirs on as well. Ben and Lacey stayed together, walking toward the Troll Hole to explore the other rooms. Radar walked with me to Margo's desk. He knelt down to look closely at the paper calendar frozen on June.

I was leaning in next to him when I heard fast footsteps coming toward us.

"*People*," Ben whispered urgently. He ducked down behind Margo's desk, pulling Lacey with him.

"What? Where?"

"Next room!" he said. "Wearing masks. Official-looking. Gotta go."

Radar shone his flashlight in the direction of the Troll Hole but Ben knocked it down forcefully. "We. Have. To. Get. Out. Of. Here." Lacey was looking up at me, big-eyed and probably a little bit pissed off that I'd falsely promised her safety.

"Okay," I whispered. "Okay, everybody out, through the door. Very cool, very quick." I had just started to walk when I heard a booming voice shout, "WHO GOES THERE!"

Shit. "Um," I said, "we're just visiting." What an outlandishly lame thing to say. Through the Troll Hole, a white light blinded me. It might have been God Himself.

"What are your intentions?" The voice had a slight faked Britishness to it.

I watched Ben stand up next to me. It felt good not to be alone. "We're here investigating a disappearance," he said with great confidence. "We weren't going to break anything." The light snapped off, and I blinked away the blindness until I saw three figures, each wearing jeans, a T-shirt, and a mask with two circular filters. One of them pulled the mask up to his forehead and looked at us. I recognized the goatee and flat, wide mouth.

"Gus?" asked Lacey. She stood up. The SunTrust security guard.

"Lacey Pemberton. Jesus. What are you doing here? With no mask? This place has a ton of asbestos."

"What are *you* doing here?"

"Exploring," he said. Somehow Ben was emboldened with enough confidence to walk up to the other guys and offer handshakes. They introduced themselves as Ace and the Carpenter. I would venture to guess that these were pseudonyms.

We pulled around some rolling desk chairs and sat in an approximate circle. "Did you guys break the particleboard?" Gus asked.

"Well, I did," Ben explained.

"We taped that up because we didn't want anyone else in. If people can see a way in from the road, you get a lot of people coming in who don't know shit about exploring. Bums and crack addicts and everything."

I stepped forward toward them and said, "So, you, uh, knew that Margo came here?"

Before Gus answered, Ace spoke through the mask. His voice was slightly modulated but easy to understand. "Man, Margo was here all the damned time. We only come here a few times a year; it's got asbestos, and anyway, it's not even that good. But we probably saw her, like, what, like more than half the time we came here in the last couple years. She was hot, huh?"

"Was?" asked Lacey pointedly.

"She ran away, right?"

"What do you know about that?" Lacey asked.

"Nothing, Jesus. I saw Margo with him," Gus said, nodding toward me, "a couple weeks ago. And then I heard that she ran away. It occurred to me a few days later she might be here, so we visited."

"I never got why she liked this place so much. There's not much here," said the Carpenter. "It's not great exploring."

"What do you mean *exploring*?" Lacey asked Gus.

"Urban exploring. We enter abandoned buildings, explore them, photograph them. We take nothing; we leave nothing. We're just observers."

"It's a hobby," said Ace. "Gus used to let Margo tag along on exploring trips when we were still in school."

"She had a great eye, even though she was only, like, thirteen," Gus said. "She could figure a way into anywhere. It was just occasional back then, but now we go out like three times a week. There's places all over. There's an abandoned mental hospital over in Clearwater. It's amazing. You can see where they strapped down the crazies and gave them electroshock. And there's an old jail out west of here. But she wasn't really into it. She liked to break into the places, but then she just wanted to *stay*."

"Yeah, God that was annoying," added Ace.

The Carpenter said, "She wouldn't even, like, take pictures. Or run around and find stuff. She just wanted to go inside and, like, sit. Remember, she had that black notebook? And she would just sit in the corner and write, like she was in her house, doing homework or something."

"Honestly," Gus said, "she never really got what it's all about. The adventure. She seemed pretty depressed, actually."

I wanted to let them keep talking, because I figured everything they said would help me imagine Margo. But all of a sudden, Lacey stood up and kicked her chair behind her. "And you never thought to ask her about how she was pretty depressed actually? Or why she hung out in these sketch-ass places? That never bothered you?" She was standing above him now, shouting, and he stood up, too, half a foot taller than her, and then the Carpenter said, "Jesus, somebody calm that bitch down."

"Oh no you didn't!" Ben yelled, and before I even knew what was going on, Ben tackled the Carpenter, who fell awkwardly out of his chair onto his shoulder. Ben straddled the guy and started pounding on him, furiously and awkwardly smacking and punching his mask, shouting, "SHE'S NOT THE BITCH, YOU ARE!" I scrambled up and grabbed one of Ben's arms as Radar grabbed the other. We pulled him away, but he was still shouting, "I have a lot of anger right now! I was enjoying punching the guy! I want to go back to punching him!"

"Ben," I said, trying to sound calm, trying to sound like my mom. "Ben, it's okay. You made your point."

Gus and Ace picked up the Carpenter, and Gus said, "Jesus Christ, we're getting out of here, okay? It's all yours."

Ace picked up their camera equipment, and they hustled out the back door. Lacey started to explain to me how she knew him, saying, "He was a senior when we were fr—." But I waved it off. None of it mattered anyway.

Radar knew what mattered. He returned immediately to the calendar, his eyes an inch away from the paper. "I don't think anything was written on the May page," he says. "The paper is pretty thin and I can't see any marks. But it's impossible to say for sure." He went off to search for more clues, and I saw Lacey's and Ben's flashlights dipping as they went through a Troll Hole, but I just stood there in the office, imagining her. I thought of her following these guys, four years older than her, into abandoned buildings. That was Margo as I'd seen her. But then, inside the buildings, she is not the Margo I'd always imagined. While everyone else walks off to explore and take pictures and bounce around the walls, Margo sits on the floor, writing something.

From next door, Ben shouted, "Q! We got something!"

I wiped sweat from my face with both sleeves and used Margo's desk to pull myself up. I walked across the room, ducked through the Troll Hole, and headed toward the three flashlights scanning the wall above the rolled-up carpet.

"Look," Ben said, using the beam to draw a square on the wall. "You know those little holes you mentioned?"

"Yeah?"

"They had to have been mementos tacked up there. Postcards or pictures, we think, from the spacing of the holes. Which maybe she took with her," Ben said.

"Yeah, maybe," I said. "I wish we could find that notebook Gus was talking about."

"Yeah, when he said that, I remembered that notebook," Lacey said, the beam of my flashlight lighting up only her legs. "She had one with her all the time. I never saw her write in it, but I just figured it was like a day planner or whatever. God, I never asked about it. I get pissed at Gus, who wasn't even her friend. But what did I ever ask her?"

"She wouldn't have answered anyway," I said. It was dishonest to act like Margo hadn't participated in her own obfuscation.

We walked around for another hour, and just when I felt sure the trip had been a waste, my flashlight happened over the subdivision brochures that had been built into a house of cards when we first came here. One of the brochures was for Grovepoint Acres. My breath caught as I spread out the other brochures. I jogged to my backpack by the door and came back with a pen and a notebook and wrote down the names of all the advertised subdivisions. I recognized one immediately: Collier Farms—one of the two pseudovisions on my list I hadn't yet visited. I finished copying the subdivision names and returned my notebook to my backpack. Call me selfish, but if I found her, I wanted it to be alone.

17.

The moment Mom got home from work on Friday, I told her that I was going to a concert with Radar and then proceeded to drive out to rural Seminole County to see Collier Farms. All the other subdivisions from the brochures turned out to exist—most of them on the north side of town, which had been totally developed a long time ago.

I only recognized the turnoff for Collier Farms because I'd become something of an expert in hard-to-see dirt access roads. But Collier Farms was like none of the other pseudovisions I'd seen, because it was wildly overgrown, as if it had been abandoned for fifty years. I didn't know if it was older than the other pseudovisions, or if the low-lying, swamp-wet land made everything grow faster, but the Collier Farms access road became impassable just after I turned in because a thick grove of brambly brush had sprouted across the entire road.

I got out and walked. The overgrown grass scraped at my shins, and my sneakers sunk into the mud with each step. I couldn't help but hope she had a tent pitched out here somewhere on some little piece of land two feet higher than everything else, keeping the rain off. I walked slowly, because there was more to see than at any of the others, more places to hide, and because I knew this pseudovision had a direct connection to the minimall. The ground was so thick I had to walk slowly as I let myself take in each new landscape, checking each place big enough to fit a person. At the end of the street I saw a blue-and-white cardboard box in the mud, and for a second it looked like the same nutrition bars I'd found in the minimall. But, no. A rotting container for a twelve-pack of beer. I trudged back to the minivan and headed for a place called Logan Pines farther to the north.

It took an hour to get there, and by now I was up near the Ocala National Forest, not really even the Orlando metro area anymore. I was a few miles away when Ben called.

"What's up?"

"You hittin' those paper towns?" he asked.

"Yeah, I'm almost to the last one I know of. Nothing yet."

"So listen, bro, Radar's parents had to leave town real suddenly."

"Is everything okay?" I asked. I knew Radar's grandparents were really old and lived in a nursing home down in Miami.

"Yeah, get this: you know the guy in Pittsburgh with the world's second-largest collection of black Santas?"

"Yeah?"

"He just bit it."

"You're kidding."

"Bro, I don't kid about the demise of black Santa collectors. This guy had an aneurysm, and so Radar's folks are flying to Pennsylvania to try to buy his entire collection. So we're having a few people over."

"Who's we?"

"You and me and Radar. We're the hosts."

"I don't know," I said.

There was a pause, and then Ben used my full name. "Quentin," he said, "I know you want to find her. I know she is the most important thing to you. And that's cool. But we graduate in, like, a week. I'm not asking you to abandon the search. I'm asking you to come to a party with your two best friends who you have known for half your life. I'm asking you to spend two to three hours drinking sugary wine coolers like the pretty little girl you are, and then another two to three hours vomiting the aforementioned wine coolers through your nose. And then you can go back to poking around abandoned housing projects."

It bothered me that Ben only wanted to talk about Margo when it involved an adventure that appealed to him, that he thought there was something wrong with me for focusing on her over my friends, even though she was missing and they weren't. But Ben was Ben, like Radar said. And I had nothing left to search after Logan Pines anyway. "I've got to go to this last place and then I'll be over."

Because Logan Pines was the last pseudovision in Central Florida—or at least the last one I knew about—I had placed so much hope in it. But as I walked around its single dead-end street with a flashlight, I saw no tent. No campfire. No food wrappers. No sign of people. No Margo. At the end of the road, I found a single concrete foundation dug into the dirt. But there was nothing built atop it, just the hole cut into the earth like a dead mouth agape, tangles of briars and waist-high grass growing up all around. If she'd wanted me to see these places, I could not understand why. And if Margo had gone to the pseudovisions never to come back, she knew about a place I hadn't uncovered in all my research.

It took an hour and a half to drive back to Jefferson Park. I parked the minivan at home, changed into a polo shirt and my only nice pair of jeans, and walked down Jefferson Way to Jefferson Court, and then took a right onto Jefferson Road. A few cars were already lined up on both sides of Jefferson Place, Radar's street. It was only eight-forty-five.

I opened the door and was greeted by Radar, who had an armful of plaster black Santas. "Gotta put away all of the nice ones," he said. "God forbid one of them breaks."

"Need any help?" I asked. Radar nodded toward the living room, where the tables on either side of the couch held three sets of unnested black Santa nesting dolls. As I renested them, I couldn't help but notice that they were really very beautiful—hand-painted and extraordinarily detailed. I didn't say this to Radar, though, for fear that he would beat me to death with the black Santa lamp in the living room.

I carried the matryoshka dolls into the guest bedroom, where Radar was carefully stashing Santas into a dresser. "You know, when you see them all together, it really does make you question the way we imagine our myths."

Radar rolled his eyes. "Yeah, I always find myself questioning the way I imagine my myths when I'm eating my Lucky Charms every morning with a goddamned black Santa spoon."

I felt a hand on my shoulder spinning me around. It was Ben, his feet fidgeting in fast-motion like he needed to pee or something. "We kissed. Like, she kissed me. About ten minutes ago. On Radar's parents' bed."

"That's disgusting," Radar said. "Don't make out in my parents' bed."

"Wow, I figured you'd already gotten past that," I said. "What with you being such a pimp and everything."

"Shut up, bro. I'm freaked out," he said, looking at me, his eyes almost crossed. "I don't think I'm very good."

"At what?"

"At kissing. And, I mean, she's done a lot more kissing than me over the years. I don't want to suck so bad she dumps me. Girls dig you," he said to me, which was at best true only if you defined the word *girls* as "girls in the marching band." "Bro, I'm asking for advice."

I was tempted to bring up all Ben's endless blather about the various ways in which he would rock various bodies, but I just said, "As far as I can tell, there are two basic rules: 1. Don't bite anything without permission, and 2. The human tongue is like wasabi: it's very powerful, and should be used sparingly."

Ben's eyes suddenly grew bright with panic. I winced, and said, "She's standing behind me, isn't she?"

"'The human tongue is like wasabi,'" Lacey mimicked in a deep, goofy voice that I hoped didn't really resemble mine. I wheeled around. "I actually think Ben's tongue is like sunscreen," she said. "It's good for your health and should be applied liberally."

"I just threw up in my mouth," Radar said.

"Lacey, you just kind of took away my will to go on," I added.

"I wish I could stop imagining that," Radar said.

I said, "The very idea is so offensive that it's actually illegal to say the words 'Ben Starling's tongue' on television."

"The penalty for violating that law is either ten years in prison or one Ben Starling tongue bath," Radar said.

"Everyone," I said.

"Chooses," Radar said, smiling.

"Prison," we finished together.

And then Lacey kissed Ben in front of us. "Oh God," Radar said, waving his arms in front of his face. "Oh, God. I'm blind. I'm blind."

"Please stop," I said. "You're upsetting the black Santas."

The party ended up in the formal living room on the second floor of Radar's house, all twenty of us. I leaned against a wall, my head inches from a black Santa portrait painted on velvet. Radar had one of those sectional couches, and everyone was crowded onto it. There was beer in a cooler by the TV, but no one was drinking. Instead, they were telling stories about one another. I'd heard most of them before—band camp stories and Ben Starling stories and first kiss stories—but Lacey hadn't heard any of them, and anyway, they were still entertaining. I stayed mostly out of it until Ben said, "Q, how are we going to graduate?"

I smirked. "Naked but for our robes," I said.

"Yes!" Ben sipped a Dr Pepper.

"I'm not even *bringing* clothes, so I don't wuss out," Radar said.

"Me neither! Q, swear not to bring clothes."

I smiled. "Duly sworn," I said.

"I'm in!" said our friend Frank. And then more and more of the guys got behind the idea. The girls, for some reason, were resistant.

Radar said to Angela, "Your refusal to do this makes me question the whole foundation of our love."

"You don't get it," Lacey said. "It's not that we're *afraid*. It's just that we already have our dresses picked out."

Angela pointed at Lacey. "*Exactly*." Angela added, "Y'all better hope it's not windy."

"I hope it *is* windy," Ben said. "The world's largest balls benefit from fresh air."

Lacey put a hand to her face, ashamed. "You're a challenging boyfriend," she said. "Rewarding, but challenging." We laughed.

This was what I liked most about my friends: just sitting around and telling stories. Window stories and mirror stories. I only listened—the stories on my mind weren't that funny.

I couldn't help but think about school and everything else ending. I liked standing just outside the couches and watching them—it was a kind of sad I didn't mind, and so I just listened, letting all the happiness and the sadness of this ending swirl around in me, each sharpening the other. For the longest time, it felt kind of like my chest was cracking open, but not precisely in an unpleasant way.

I left just before midnight. Some people were staying later, but it was my curfew, and plus I didn't feel like staying. Mom was half asleep on the couch, but she perked up when she saw me. "Did you have fun?"

"Yeah," I said. "It was pretty chill."

"Just like you," she said, smiling. This sentiment struck me as hilarious, but I didn't say anything. She stood up and pulled me into her, kissing me on the cheek. "I really like being your mom," she said.

"Thanks," I said.

I went to bed with the Whitman, flipping to the part I'd liked before, where he spends all the time hearing the opera and the people.

After all that hearing, he writes, "I am exposed . . . . cut by bitter and poisoned hail." That was perfect, I thought: you listen to people so that you can imagine them, and you hear all the terrible and wonderful things people do to themselves and to one another, but in the end the listening exposes *you* even more than it exposes the people you're trying to listen to.

Walking through pseudovisions and trying to listen to her does not crack the Margo Roth Spiegelman case so much as it cracks me. Pages later—hearing and exposed—Whitman starts to write about all the travel he can do by imagining, and lists all the places he can visit while loafing on the grass. "My palms cover continents," he writes.

I kept thinking about maps, like the way sometimes when I was a kid I would look at atlases, and just the looking was kind of like being somewhere else. This is what I had to do. I had to hear and imagine my way into *her* map.

But hadn't I been trying to do that? I looked up at the maps above my computer. I had tried to plot her possible travels, but just as the grass stood for too much, so Margo stood for too much. It seemed impossible to pin her down with maps. She was too small and the space covered by the maps too big. They were more than a waste of time—they were the physical representation of the total fruitlessness of all of it, my absolute inability to develop the kinds of palms that cover continents, to have the kind of mind that correctly imagines.

I got up and walked over to the maps and tore them off the wall, the pins and tacks flying out with the paper and falling to the ground. I balled up the maps and threw them in the garbage can. On my way back to bed I stepped on a tack, like an idiot, and even though I was annoyed and exhausted and out of pseudovisions and ideas, I had to pick up all the thumbtacks scattered around the carpet so I didn't step on them later. I just wanted to punch the wall, but I had to pick up those stupid goddamned thumbtacks. When I finished, I got back into bed and socked my pillow, my teeth clenched.

I started trying to read the Whitman again, but between it and thinking of Margo, I felt exposed enough for this night. So finally I put the book down. I couldn't be bothered to get up and turn off the light. I just stared at the wall, my blinks growing longer. And every time I opened my eyes, I saw where each map had been—the four holes marking the rectangle, and the pinholes seemingly randomly distributed inside the rectangle. I'd seen a similar pattern before. In the empty room above the rolled-up carpet.

A map. With plotted points.

18.

I woke up with the sunlight just before seven on Saturday morning. Amazingly, Radar was online.

QTHERESURRECTION: I thought you'd be sleeping for sure.
OMNICTIONARIAN96: Nah, man. I've been up since six, expanding the article on this Malaysian pop singer. Angela's still in bed, though.
QTHERESURRECTION: Ooh she stayed over?
OMNICTIONARIAN96: Yeah but my purity is still intact. Graduation night, though . . . I think maybe.
QTHERESURRECTION: Hey, I thought of something last night. The little holes in that wall in the strip mall—maybe a map that plotted points with thumbtacks?
OMNICTIONARIAN96: Like a route.
QTHERESURRECTION: Exactly.
OMNICTIONARIAN96: Wanna go over? I have to wait till Ange gets up, though.
QTHERESURRECTION: Sounds good.

He called at ten. I picked him up in the minivan and then we drove to Ben's house, figuring that a surprise attack would be the only way to wake him up. But even singing "You Are My

Sunshine" outside his window only resulted in him opening the window and spitting at us. "I'm not doing anything until noon," he said authoritatively.

So it was just Radar and me on the drive out. He talked a little about Angela and how much he liked her and how weird it was to fall in love just a few months before they would leave for different colleges, but I found it hard to listen very well. I wanted that map. I wanted to see the places she'd pinpointed. I wanted to get those tacks back into the wall.

We walked in through the office, hustled through the library, paused briefly to examine the holes in the bedroom wall, and entered the souvenir shop. The place didn't scare me at all anymore. Once we'd been in each room and established we were alone, I felt as safe as I did at home. Beneath a display counter, I found the box of maps and brochures I'd rifled through on prom night. I lifted it out and balanced it on the corners of a broken glass counter. Radar sorted through them initially, looking for anything with a map, and then I unfolded them, scanning for pinholes.

We were getting near the bottom of the box when Radar pulled out a black-and-white brochure entitled FIVE THOUSAND AMERICAN CITIES. It was copyrighted 1972 by the Esso company. As I carefully unfolded the map, trying to smooth the creases, I saw a pinhole in a corner. "This is it," I said, my voice rising. There was a small rip around the pinhole, like it'd been torn off the wall. It was a yellowing, brittle, classroom-size map of the United States printed thick with potential destinations. The rips in the map told me that she had not intended this as a clue—Margo was too precise and assured with her clues to muddy the waters. Somehow or another, we'd stumbled into something she *hadn't* planned, and in seeing what she hadn't planned, I thought again of how much she *had* planned. And maybe, I thought, that's what she did in the quiet dark here. Traveling while loafing, like Whitman had, as she prepared for the real thing.

I ran all the way back to the office and found a bunch of thumbtacks in a desk adjacent to Margo's, before Radar and I carefully carried the unfurled map back to Margo's room. I held it up against the wall while Radar tried to get the tacks into the corners, but three of the four corners had ripped, as had three of the five locations, presumably when the map was taken off the wall. "Higher and to the left," he said. "No, down. Yeah. Don't move." Finally we got the map on the wall, and then we started lining up the holes in the map with the ones on the wall. We got all five pins in pretty easily. But some of these pinholes were also ripped, so it was impossible to tell their EXACT location. And exact location mattered in a map blackened with the names of five thousand places. The lettering was so small and exact that I had to stand up on the carpet and put my bare eyeballs inches away from the map even to guess each location. As I suggested town names, Radar pulled out his handheld and looked them up on Omnictionary.

There were two unripped dots: one looked like Los Angeles, although there were a bunch of towns clustered so close together in Southern California that the type overlapped. The other unripped hole was over Chicago. There was a ripped one in New York that, judging from the location of the hole in the wall, was one of the five boroughs of New York City.

"That makes sense with what we know."

"Yeah," I said. "But God, *where* in New York? That's the question."

"We're missing something," he says. "Some locational hint. What're the other dots?"

"There's another in New York State, but not near the city. I mean, look, all the towns are tiny. It might be Poughkeepsie or Woodstock or the Catskill Park."

"Woodstock," Radar said. "That'd be interesting. She's not much of a hippie, but she has that whole free-spirit vibe."

"I don't know," I said. "The last one is either Washington, D.C., or else maybe Annapolis or Chesapeake Bay. That one could be a bunch of things, actually."

"It'd be helpful if there was only one point on the map," Radar said sullenly.

"But she's probably going from place to place," I said. Tramping her perpetual journey.

I sat on the carpet for a while as Radar read to me more about New York, about the Catskill Mountains, about the nation's capital, about the concert at Woodstock in 1969. Nothing seemed to help. I felt as if we'd played out the string and found nothing.

After I dropped Radar off that afternoon, I sat around the house reading "Song of Myself" and halfheartedly studying for finals. I had calc and Latin on Monday, probably my two toughest subjects, and I couldn't afford to ignore them completely. I studied most of Saturday night and throughout the day Sunday, but then a Margo idea popped into my head just after dinner, so I took a break from practicing Ovid translations and logged onto IM. I saw Lacey online. I'd only just gotten her screen name from Ben, but I figured I knew her well enough to IM her.

QTHERESURRECTION: Hey, it's Q.
SACKCLOTHANDASHES: Hi!
QTHERESURRECTION: Did you ever think about how much time Margo must have spent planning everything?
SACKCLOTHANDASHES: Yeah, like leaving the letters in the alphabet soup before Mississippi and leading you to the minimall, you mean?
QTHERESURRECTION: Yeah, these aren't things you think up in ten minutes.
SACKCLOTHANDASHES: Maybe the notebook.
QTHERESURRECTION: *Exactly.*
SACKCLOTHANDASHES: Yeah. I was thinking about it today because I remembered one time when we were shopping, she kept sticking the notebook into purses she liked, to make sure it fit.
QTHERESURRECTION: I wish I had that notebook.
SACKCLOTHANDASHES: Yeah, probably with her, though.
QTHERESURRECTION: Yeah. It wasn't in her locker?
SACKCLOTHANDASHES: No, just textbooks, stacked neat like they always were.

I studied at my desk and waited for other people to come online. Ben did after a while, and I invited him into a chat room with me and Lacey. They did most of the talking—I was still sort of translating—until Radar logged in and joined the room. Then I put down my pencil for the night.

OMNICTIONARIAN96: Someone from New York City searched Omnictionary for Margo Roth Spiegelman today.
ITWASAKIDNEYINFECTION: Can you tell *where* in New York City?
OMNICTIONARIAN96: Unfortunately, no.
SACKCLOTHANDASHES: Also there are still some posters up in record stores there. It was probably just someone trying to find out about her.
OMNICTIONARIAN96: Oh, right. I forgot about that. Suck.
QTHERESURRECTION: Hey, I'm in and out because I'm using that site Radar showed me to map routes between the places she pinholed.
ITWASAKIDNEYINFECTION: Link?
QTHERESURRECTION: thelongwayround.com
OMNICTIONARIAN96: I have a new theory. She's going to show up for graduation, sitting in the audience.
ITWASAKIDNEYINFECTION: I have an old theory, that she is somewhere in Orlando, screwing with us and making sure that she's the center of our universe.
SACKCLOTHANDASHES: Ben!
ITWASAKIDNEYINFECTION: Sorry, but I'm totally right.

They went on like that, talking about their Margos, as I tried to map her route. If she hadn't intended the map as a clue—and the ripped tack holes told me she hadn't—I figured we'd gotten all the clues she'd intended for us and now much more. Surely I had what I needed, then. But I still felt very far away from her.

19.

After three long hours alone with eight hundred words from Ovid on Monday morning, I walked through the halls feeling as if my brain might drip out of my ears. But I'd done okay. We had an hour and a half for lunch, to give our minds time to firm back up before the second exam period of the day. Radar was waiting for me at my locker.

"I just bombed me some Spanish," Radar said.

"I'm sure you did okay." He was going to Dartmouth on a huge scholarship. He was plenty smart.

"Dude, I don't know. I kept falling asleep during the oral part. But listen, I was up half the night building this program. It's so awesome. What it does is it allows you to enter a category—it can be a geographical area or like a family in the animal kingdom—and then you can read the first sentences of up to a hundred Omnictionary articles about your topic on a single page. So, like, say you are trying to find a particular kind of rabbit but can't remember its name. You can read an introduction to all twenty-one species of rabbits on the same page in, like, three minutes."

"You did this the night before finals?" I asked.

"Yeah, I know, right? Anyway I'll e-mail it to you. It's nerdtastic."

Ben showed up then. "I swear to God, Q, Lacey and I were up

on IM until two o'clock in the morning playing on that site, the-longwayround? And having now plotted every single possible trip that Margo could have taken between Orlando and those five points, I realize I was wrong all this time. She's not in Orlando. Radar's right. She's coming back here for graduation day."

"Why?"

"The timing is *perfect*. To drive from Orlando to New York to the mountains to Chicago to Los Angeles back to Orlando is like *exactly* a twenty-three-day trip. Plus, it's a totally retarded joke, but it's a Margo joke. You make everyone think you offed yourself. Surround yourself with an air of mystery so that everyone pays attention. And then right as all the attention starts to go away, you show up at graduation."

"No," I said. "No way." I knew Margo better than that by now. She did want attention. I believed that. But Margo didn't play life for laughs. She didn't get off on mere trickery.

"I'm telling you, bro. Look for her at graduation. She's gonna be there." I just shook my head. Since everyone had the same lunch period, the cafeteria was beyond packed, so we exercised our rights as seniors and drove to Wendy's. I tried to stay focused on my coming calc exam, but I was starting to feel like maybe there was more string to the story. If Ben was right about the twenty-three-day trip, that was very interesting, indeed. Maybe that's what she'd been planning in her black notebook, a long and lonesome road trip. It didn't explain everything, but it did fit with Margo as a planner. Not that this brought me closer to her. As hard as it is to pinpoint a dot inside a ripped segment of a map, it only becomes harder when the dot is moving.

After a long day of finals, returning to the comfortable impenetrability of "Song of Myself" was almost a relief. I had reached a weird part of the poem—after all this time listening and hearing people, and then traveling alongside them, Whitman stops hearing and he stops visiting, and he starts to *become* other people. Like, actually inhabit them. He tells the story of a ship's captain who saved everyone on his boat except himself. The poet can tell the story, he argues, because he has become the captain. As he writes, "I am the man . . . . I suffered . . . . I was there." A few lines later, it becomes even more clear that Whitman no longer needs to listen to become another: "I do not ask the wounded person how he feels . . . . I myself become the wounded person."

I put the book down and lay on my side, staring out the window that had always been between us. It is not enough just to see her or hear her. To find Margo Roth Spiegelman, you must become Margo Roth Spiegelman.

And I had done many of the things she might have done: I had engineered a most unlikely prom coupling. I had quieted the hounds of caste warfare. I had come to feel comfortable inside the rat-infested haunted house where she did her best thinking. I had seen. I had listened. But I could not yet become the wounded person.

I limped through my physics and government finals the next day and then stayed up till 2 A.M. on Tuesday finishing my final reaction paper for English about *Moby Dick*. Ahab was a hero, I decided. I had no particular reason for having decided this—particularly given that I hadn't read the book—but I decided it and reacted thusly.

The abbreviated exam week meant that Wednesday was the

last day of school for us. And all day long, it was hard not to walk around, thinking about the lastness of it all: The last time I stand in a circle outside the band room in the shade of this oak tree that has protected generations of band geeks. The last time I eat pizza in the cafeteria with Ben. The last time I sit in this school scrawling an essay with a cramped hand into a blue book. The last time I glance up at the clock. The last time I see Chuck Parson prowling the halls, his smile half a sneer. God. I was becoming nostalgic for Chuck Parson. Something sick was happening inside of me.

It must have been like this for Margo, too. With all the planning she'd done, she must have known she was leaving, and even she couldn't have been totally immune to the feeling. She'd had good days here. And on the last day, the bad days become so difficult to recall, because one way or another, she had made a life here, just as I had. The town was paper, but the memories were not. All the things I'd done here, all the love and pity and compassion and violence and spite, kept welling up inside me. These whitewashed cinder-block walls. My white walls. Margo's white walls. We'd been captive in them for so long, stuck in their belly like Jonah.

Throughout the day, I found myself thinking that maybe this feeling was why she'd planned everything so intricately and precisely: even if you want to leave, it is so hard. It took preparation, and maybe sitting in that minimall scrawling her plans was both intellectual and emotional practice—Margo's way of imagining herself into her fate.

Ben and Radar both had a marathon band practice to make sure they would rock "Pomp and Circumstance" at graduation. Lacey offered me a ride, but I decided to clean out my locker, because I didn't really want to come back here and again have to feel like my lungs were drowning in this perverse nostalgia.

My locker was an unadulterated crap hole—half trash can, half book storage. Her locker had been neatly stacked with textbooks when Lacey opened it, I remembered, as if she intended to come to school the next day. I pulled a garbage can over to the bank of lockers and opened mine up. I began by pulling off a picture of Radar and Ben and me goofing off. I put it inside my backpack and then started the disgusting process of picking through a year's worth of accumulated filth—gum wrapped in scraps of notebook paper, pens out of ink, greasy napkins—and scraping it all into the garbage. All along, I kept thinking, *I will never do this again, I will never be here again, this will never be my locker again, Radar and I will never write notes in calculus again, I will never see Margo across the hall again.* This was the first time in my life that so many things would never happen again.

And finally it was too much. I could not talk myself down from the feeling, and the feeling became unbearable. I reached in deep to the recesses of my locker. I pushed everything—photographs and notes and books—into the trash can. I left the locker open and walked away. As I walked past the band room, I could hear through the walls the muffled sounds of "Pomp and Circumstance." I kept walking. It was hot outside, but not as hot as usual. It was bearable. *There are sidewalks most of the way home,* I thought. So I kept walking.

And as paralyzing and upsetting as all the never agains were, the final leaving felt perfect. Pure. The most distilled possible form of liberation. Everything that mattered except one lousy picture was in the trash, but it felt so great. I started jogging, wanting to put even more distance between myself and school.

It is so hard to leave—until you leave. And then it is the easiest goddamned thing in the world.

As I ran, I felt myself for the first time becoming Margo. I knew: *she is not in Orlando. She is not in Florida.* Leaving feels too good, once you leave. If I'd been in a car, and not on foot, I might have kept going, too. She was gone and not coming back for graduation or anything else. I felt sure of that now.

I leave, and the leaving is so exhilarating I know I can never go back. But then what? Do I just keep leaving places, and leaving them, and leaving them, tramping a perpetual journey?

Ben and Radar drove past me a quarter mile from Jefferson Park, and Ben brought RHAPAW to a screeching halt right on Lakemont in spite of traffic everywhere, and I ran up to the car and got in. They wanted to play Resurrection at my house, but I had to tell them no, because I was closer than I'd ever been before.

20.

All night Wednesday, and all day Thursday, I tried to use my new understanding of her to figure out some meaning to the clues I had—some relationship between the map and the travel books, or else some link between the Whitman and the map that would allow me to understand her travelogue. But increasingly I felt like maybe she had become too enthralled with the pleasure of leaving to construct a proper bread crumb trail. And if that were the case, the map she had never intended for us to see might be our best chance to find her. But no site on the map was adequately specific. Even the Catskill Park dot, which interested me because it was the only location not in or near a big city, was far too big and populous to find a single person. "Song of Myself" made references to places in New York City, but there were too many locations to track them all down. How do you pinpoint a spot on the map when the spot seems to be moving from metropolis to metropolis?

I was already up and paging through travel guides when my parents came into my room on Friday morning. They rarely both entered the room at the same time, and I felt a ripple of nausea—maybe they had bad news about Margo—before I remembered it was my graduation day.

"Ready, bud?"

"Yeah. I mean, it's not that big of a deal, but it'll be fun."

"You only graduate from high school once," Mom said.

"Yeah," I said. They sat down on the bed across from me. I noticed them share a glance and giggle. "What?" I asked.

"Well, we want to give you your graduation present," Mom said. "We're really proud of you, Quentin. You're the greatest accomplishment of our lives, and this is just such a great day for you, and we're— You're just a great young man."

I smiled and looked down. And then my dad produced a very small gift wrapped in blue wrapping paper.

"No," I said, snatching it from him.

"Go ahead and open it."

"No way," I said, staring at it. It was the size of a key. It was the weight of a key. When I shook the box, it rattled like a key.

"Just open it, sweetie," my mom urged.

I tore off the wrapping paper. A KEY! I examined it closely. A Ford key! Neither of our cars was a Ford. "You got me a car?!"

"We did," my dad said. "It's not brand-new—but only two years old and just twenty thousand miles on it." I jumped up and hugged both of them.

"It's mine?"

"Yeah!" my mom almost shouted. I had a car! A car! Of my own!

I disentangled myself from my parents and shouted "*thank you thank you thank you thank you thank you thank you*" as I raced through the living room, and yanked open the front door wearing only an old T-shirt and boxer shorts. There, parked in the driveway with a huge blue bow on it, was a Ford minivan.

They'd given me a minivan. They could have picked any car, and they picked a minivan. A minivan. O God of Vehicular Justice, why dost thou mock me? Minivan, you albatross around my neck! You mark of Cain! You wretched beast of high ceilings and few horsepower!

I put on a brave face when I turned around. "Thank you thank you thank you!" I said, although surely I didn't sound quite as effusive now that I was completely faking it.

"Well, we just knew how much you loved driving mine," Mom said. She and Dad were beaming—clearly convinced they'd landed me the transportation of my dreams. "It's great for getting around with your friends!" added my dad. And to think: these people specialize in the analysis and understanding of the human psyche.

"Listen," Dad said, "we should get going pretty soon if we want to get good seats."

I hadn't showered or dressed or anything. Well, not that I would technically be *dressing*, but still. "I don't have to be there until twelve-thirty," I said. "I need to, like, get ready."

Dad frowned. "Well, I really want to have a good sight line so I can take some pic— "

I interrupted him. "I can just take MY CAR," I said. "I can drive MYSELF in MY CAR." I smiled broadly.

"I know!" my mom said excitedly. And what the hell—a car's a car, after all. Driving my own minivan was surely a step up from driving someone else's.

I went back to my computer then and informed Radar and Lacey (Ben wasn't online) about the minivan.

OMNICTIONARIAN96: Actually that's really good news. Can I stop by and put a cooler in your trunk? I gotta drive my parents to graduation and don't want them to see.

QTHERESURRECTION: Sure, it's unlocked. Cooler for what?

OMNICTIONARIAN96: Well, since no one drank at my party, there were 212 beers left over, and we're taking them over to Lacey's for her party tonight.

QTHERESURRECTION: 212 beers?

OMNICTIONARIAN96: It's a big cooler.

Ben came online then, SHOUTING about how he was already showered and naked and just needed to put on the cap and gown. We were all talking back and forth about our naked graduation. After everyone logged off to get ready, I got in the shower and stood up straight so that the water shot directly at my face, and I started thinking as the water pounded away at me. New York or California? Chicago or D.C.? I could go now, too, I thought. I had a car just as much as she did. I could go to the five spots on the map, and even if I didn't find her, it would be more fun than another boiling summer in Orlando. But no. It's like breaking into SeaWorld. It takes an immaculate plan, and then you execute it brilliantly, and then—nothing. And then it's just SeaWorld, except darker. She'd told me: the pleasure isn't in doing the thing; the pleasure is in planning it.

And that's what I thought about as I stood beneath the showerhead: the planning. She sits in the minimall with her notebook, planning. Maybe she's planning a road trip, using the map to imagine routes. She reads the Whitman and highlights "I tramp a perpetual journey," because that's the kind of thing she likes to imagine herself doing, the kind of thing she likes to plan.

But is it the kind of thing she likes to actually *do*? No. Because Margo knows the secret of leaving, the secret I have only just now learned: leaving feels good and pure only when you leave something important, something that mattered to you. Pulling life out by the roots. But you can't do that until your life has grown roots.

And so when she left, she left for good. But I could not believe she had left for a perpetual journey. She had, I felt sure, left for a place—a place where she could stay long enough for it to matter, long enough for the next leaving to feel as good as the last one had. *There is a corner of the world somewhere far away from here where no one knows what "Margo Roth Spiegelman" means. And Margo is sitting in that corner, scrawling in her black notebook.*

The water began to get cold. I hadn't so much as touched a bar of soap, but I got out, wrapped a towel around my waist, and sat down at the computer.

I dug up Radar's e-mail about his Omnictionary program and downloaded the plug-in. It really was pretty cool. First, I entered a zip code in downtown Chicago, clicked "location," and asked for a radius of twenty miles. It spit back a hundred responses, from Navy Pier to Deerfield. The first sentence of each entry came up on my screen, and I read through them in about five minutes. Nothing stood out. Then I tried a zip code near the Catskill Park in New York. Fewer responses this time, eighty-two, organized by the date on which the Omnictionary page had been created. I started to read.

> *Woodstock, New York*, is a town in Ulster County, New York, perhaps best known for the eponymous Woodstock concert [see *Woodstock Concert*] in 1969, a three-day event featur-

ing acts from Jimi Hendrix to Janis Joplin, which actually occurred in a nearby town.

Lake Katrine is a small lake in Ulster County, New York, often visited by Henry David Thoreau.

The Catskill Park comprises 700,000 acres of land in the Catskill Mountains owned jointly by state and local governments, including a 5 percent share held by New York City, which gets much of its water from reservoirs partly inside the park.

Roscoe, New York, is a hamlet in New York State, which according to a recent census contains 261 households.

Agloe, New York, is a fictitious village created by the Esso company in the early 1930s and inserted into tourist maps as a copyright trap, or paper town.

I clicked on the link and it took me to the full article, which continued:

Located at the intersection of two dirt roads just north of Roscoe, NY, Agloe was the creation of mapmakers Otto G. Lindberg and Ernest Alpers, who invented the town name by anagramming their initials. Copyright traps have featured in mapmaking for centuries. Cartographers create fictional landmarks, streets, and municipalities and place them obscurely into their maps. If the fictional entry is found on another cartographer's map, it becomes clear a

> map has been plagiarized. Copyright traps are also sometimes known as key traps, paper streets, and paper towns [see also *fictitious entries*]. Although few cartographic corporations acknowledge their existence, copyright traps remain a common feature even in contemporary maps.
>
> In the 1940s, Agloe, New York, began appearing on maps created by other companies. Esso suspected copyright infringement and prepared several lawsuits, but in fact, an unknown resident had built "The Agloe General Store" at the intersection that appeared on the Esso map.
>
> The building, which still stands [*needs citation*], is the only structure in Agloe, which continues to appear on many maps and is traditionally recorded as having a population of zero.

Every Omnictionary entry contains subpages where you can view all the edits ever made to the page and any discussion by Omnictionary members about it. The Agloe page hadn't been edited by anyone in almost a year, but there was one recent comment on the talk page by an anonymous user:

> fyi, whoever Edits this—the Population of agloe Will actually be One until may 29th at Noon.

I recognized the capitalization immediately. *The rules of capitalization are so unfair to words in the middle of a sentence.* My throat tightened, but I forced myself to calm down. The comment had been left fifteen days ago. It had been sitting there all that time, waiting for me. I looked at the clock on the computer. I had just under twenty-four hours.

For the first time in weeks, she seemed completely and undeniably alive to me. She was alive. For one more day at least, she was alive. I had focused on her whereabouts for so long in an attempt to keep me from obsessively wondering whether she was alive that I had no idea how terrified I'd been until now, but oh, my God. She was alive.

I jumped up, let the towel drop, and called Radar. I cradled the phone in the crook of my neck while pulling on boxers and then shorts. "I know what paper towns means! Do you have your handheld?"

"Yeah. You should really be here, dude. They're about to make us line up."

I heard Ben shout into the phone, "Tell him he better be naked!"

"Radar," I said, trying to convey the importance of it. "Look up the page for Agloe, New York. Got it?"

"Yes. Reading. Hold on. Wow. Wow. This could be the Catskills spot on the map?"

"Yes, I think so. It's pretty close. Go to the discussion page."

". . ."

"Radar?"

"Jesus Christ."

"I know, I know!" I shouted. I didn't hear his response because I was pulling my shirt on, but when the phone got back to my ear, I could hear him talking to Ben. I just hung up.

Online, I searched for driving directions from Orlando to Agloe, but the map system had never heard of Agloe, so instead I searched for Roscoe. Averaging sixty-five miles per hour, the computer said it would be a nineteen-hour-and-four-minute trip. It was two-fifteen. I had twenty-one hours and forty-five minutes to get there. I printed the directions, grabbed the keys to the minivan, and locked the front door behind me.

"It's nineteen hours and four minutes away," I said into the cell phone. It was Radar's cell phone, but Ben had answered it.

"So what are you going to do?" he asked. "Are you flying there?"

"No, I don't have enough money, and anyway it's like eight hours away from New York City. So I'm driving."

Suddenly Radar had the phone back. "How long is the trip?"

"Nineteen hours and four minutes."

"According to who?"

"Google maps."

"Crap," Radar said. "None of those map programs calculate for traffic. I'll call you back. And hurry. We've got to line up like right now!"

"I'm not going. Can't risk the time," I said, but I was talking to dead air. Radar called back a minute later. "If you average sixty-five miles per hour, don't stop, and account for average traffic patterns, it's going to take you twenty-three hours and nine minutes. Which puts you there just after one P.M., so you're going to have to make up time when you can."

"What? But the—"

Radar said, "I don't want to criticize, but maybe on this particular topic, the person who is chronically late needs to listen to the person who is always punctual. But you gotta come here at least for a second because otherwise your parents will freak out when you don't show when your name is called, and also, not that it is the most important consideration or anything, but I'm just saying—you have all our beer in there."

"I obviously don't have time," I answered.

Ben leaned into the phone. "Don't be an asshat. It'll cost you five minutes."

"Okay, fine." I hooked a right on red and gunned the minivan—it had better pickup than Mom's but only just barely—toward school. I made it to the gym parking lot in three minutes. I did not park the minivan so much as I stopped it in the middle of the parking lot and jumped out. As I sprinted toward the gym I saw three robed individuals running toward me. I could see Radar's spindly dark legs as his robe blew up around him, and next to him Ben, wearing sneakers without socks. Lacey was just behind them.

"You get the beer," I said as I ran past them. "I gotta talk to my parents."

The families of graduates were spread out across the bleachers, and I ran back and forth across the basketball court a couple times before I spotted Mom and Dad about halfway up. They were waving at me. I ran up the stairs two at a time, and so was a little out of breath when I knelt down next to them and said, "Okay, so I'm not going [breath] to walk, because I [breath] think I found Margo and [breath] I just have to go, and I'll have my cell phone on [breath] and please don't be pissed at me and thank you again for the car."

And my mom wrapped her hand around my wrist and said, "What? Quentin, what are you talking about? Slow down."

I said, "I'm going to Agloe, New York, and I have to go *right now.* That's the whole story. Okay, I gotta go. I'm crunched for time here. I have my cell. Okay, love you."

I had to pull free from her light grasp. Before they could say anything, I bounded down the stairs and took off, sprinting back toward the minivan. I was inside and had the thing in gear and was starting to move when I looked over and saw Ben sitting in the passenger's seat.

"Get the beer and get out of the car!" I shouted.

"We're coming with," he said. "You'd fall asleep if you tried to drive for that long anyway."

I turned back, and Lacey and Radar were both holding cell phones to their ears. "Gotta tell my parents," Lacey explained, tapping the phone. "C'mon, Q. Go go go go go go."

PART THREE

The Vessel

The First Hour

It takes a little while for everyone to explain to their parents that 1. We're all going to miss graduation, and 2. We're driving to New York, to 3. See a town that may or may not technically exist, and hopefully 4. Intercept the Omnictionary poster, who according to the Randomly capitalized Evidence is 5. Margo Roth Spiegelman.

Radar is the last to get off the phone, and when he finally does, he says, "I'd like to make an announcement. My parents are very annoyed that I'm missing graduation. My girlfriend is also annoyed, because we were scheduled to do something *very* special in about eight hours. I don't want to get into details about it, but this had better be one fun road trip."

"Your ability to not lose your virginity is an inspiration to us all," Ben says next to me.

I glance at Radar through the rearview mirror. "WOOHOO ROAD TRIP!" I tell him. In spite of himself, a smile creeps across his face. The pleasure of leaving.

By now we are on I-4, and traffic is fairly light, which in and of itself is borderline miraculous. I'm in the far left lane driving eight miles an hour over the fifty-five-miles-per-hour speed limit, because I heard once that you don't get pulled over until you're going nine miles an hour over the speed limit.

Very quickly, we all settle into our roles.

In the wayback, Lacey is the provisioner. She lists aloud everything we currently have for the trip: the half of a Snickers that Ben was eating when I called about Margo; the 212 beers in the back; the directions I printed out; and the following items from her purse: eight sticks of wintergreen gum, a pencil, some tissue, three tampons, one pair of sunglasses, some ChapStick, her house keys, a YMCA membership card, a library card, some receipts, thirty-five dollars, and a BP card.

From the back, Lacey says, "This is exciting! We're like underprovisioned pioneers! I wish we had more money, though."

"At least we have the BP card," I say. "We can get gas and food."

I look up into the rearview mirror and see Radar, wearing his graduation gown, looking over into Lacey's purse. The graduation gown has a bit of a low-cut neck, so I can see some curled chest hairs. "You got any boxers in there?" he asks.

"Seriously, we better be stopping at the Gap," Ben adds.

Radar's job, which he begins with the calculator on his handheld, is Research and Calculations. He's alone in the row of seats behind me, with the directions and the minivan's owner's manual spread out next to him. He's figuring out how fast we need to travel in order to make it by noon tomorrow, how many times we'll need to stop in order to keep the car from running out of gas, the locations of BP stations on our route and how long each stop will be, and how much time we'll lose in the process of slowing down to exit.

"We gotta stop four times for gas. The stops will have to be very very short. Six minutes at the most off-highway. We're looking at three long areas of construction, plus traffic in Jacksonville, Washington, D.C., and Philadelphia, although it will help that we're driving through D.C. around three in the morning. According to my calculations, our average cruising speed should be around seventy-two. How fast are you going?"

"Sixty-three," I say. "The speed limit is fifty-five."

"Go seventy-two," he says.

"I can't; it's dangerous, and I'll get a ticket."

"Go seventy-two," he says again. I press my foot down hard on the gas. The difficulty is partly that I am hesitant to go seventy-two and partly that the minivan itself is hesitant to go seventy-two. It begins to shake in a way that implies it might fall apart. I stay in the far left lane, even though I'm still not the fastest car on the road, and I feel bad that people are passing me on the right, but I need clear road ahead, because unlike everyone else on this road, I can't slow down. And this is my role: my role is to drive, and to be nervous. It occurs to me that I have played this role before.

And Ben? Ben's role is to need to pee. At first it seems like his main role is going to be complaining about how we don't have any CDs and that all the radio stations in Orlando suck except for the college radio station, which is already out of range. But soon enough, he abandons that role for his true and faithful calling: needing to pee.

"I need to pee," he says at 3:06. We've been on the road for forty-three minutes. We have approximately a day left in our drive.

"Well," says Radar, "the good news is that we will be stopping. The bad news is that it won't be for another four hours and thirty minutes."

"I think I can hold it," Ben says. At 3:10, he announces, "Actually, I really need to pee. Really."

The chorus responds, "Hold it." He says, "But I—" And the chorus responds again, "Hold it!" It is fun, for now, Ben needing to pee and us needing him to hold it. He is laughing, and complaining that laughing makes him need to pee more. Lacey jumps forward and leans in behind him and starts tickling at his sides. He laughs and whines and I laugh, too, keeping the speedometer on seventy-two. I wonder if she created this journey for us on purpose or by accident—regardless, it's the most fun I've had since the last time I spent hours behind the wheel of a minivan.

Hour Two

I'm still driving. We turn north, onto I-95, snaking our way up Florida, near the coast but not quite on it. It is all pine trees here, too skinny for their height, built like I am. But there is mostly just the road, passing cars and occasionally being passed by them, always having to remember who is in front of you and who behind, who is approaching and who is drifting away.

Lacey and Ben are sitting together on the bench seat now, and Radar is in the wayback, and they're all playing a retarded version of I Spy in which they are only allowed to spy things that cannot physically be seen.

"I Spy with my little eye something tragically hip," Radar says.

"Is it the way Ben smiles mostly with the right side of his mouth?" asks Lacey.

"No," says Radar. "Also don't be so gooey about Ben. It's gross."

"Is it the idea of wearing nothing under your graduation gown and then having to drive to New York while all the people in passing cars assume you're wearing a dress?"

"No," says Radar. "That's just tragic."

Lacey smiles. "You'll learn to like dresses. You get to enjoy the breeze."

"Oh, I know!" I say from the front. "You spy a twenty-four-hour road trip in a minivan. Hip because road trips always are; tragic because the gas we're guzzling will destroy the planet."

Radar says no, and they keep guessing. I am driving and going seventy-two and praying not to get a ticket and playing Metaphysical I Spy. The tragically hip thing turns out to be failing to turn in your rented graduation robes on time. I blow past a cop parked on the grass median. I grip the steering wheel hard with both hands, feeling sure he'll race up to pull us over. But he doesn't. Maybe he knows I'm only speeding because I have to.

Hour Three

Ben is sitting shotgun again. I'm still driving. We're all hungry. Lacey distributes one piece of wintergreen gum to each of us, but it's cold comfort. She's writing a gigantic list of everything we're going to buy at the BP when we stop for the first time. This had better be one extraordinarily well-stocked BP station, because we are going to clear the bitch out.

Ben keeps bouncing his legs up and down.

"Will you stop that?"

"I've had to pee for three hours."

"You've mentioned that."

"I can feel the pee all the way up to my rib cage," he says. "I am honestly full of pee. Bro, right now, seventy percent of my body weight is pee."

"Uh-huh," I say, barely cracking a smile. It's funny and all, but I'm tired.

"I feel like I might start crying, and that I'm going to cry pee."

That gets me. I laugh a little.

The next time I glance over, a few minutes later, Ben has a hand tight around his crotch, the fabric of the gown bunched up.

"What the hell?" I ask.

"Dude, I have to *go*. I'm pinching off the flow." He turns around then. "Radar, how long till we stop?"

"We have to go at least a hundred forty-three more miles in order to keep it down to four stops, which means about one hour and fifty-eight-point-five minutes if Q keeps pace."

"I'm keeping up!" I shout. We are just north of Jacksonville, getting close to Georgia.

"I can't make it, Radar. Get me something to pee in."

The chorus erupts: NO. Absolutely not. Just hold it like a man. Hold it like a Victorian lady holds on to her maidenhead. Hold it with dignity and grace, like the president of the United States is supposed to hold the fate of the free world.

"GIVE ME SOMETHING OR I WILL PEE ON THIS SEAT. AND HURRY!"

"Oh, Christ," Radar says as he unbuckles his seat belt. He climbs into the wayback, and then reaches down and opens the cooler. He returns to his seat, leans forward, and hands Ben a beer.

"Thank God it's a twist off," Ben says, gathering a handful of robe and then opening the bottle. Ben rolls down the window, and I watch out the side-view mirror as the beer floats past the car and splashes onto the interstate. Ben manages to get the bottle underneath his robe without showing us the world's purportedly largest balls, and then we all sit and wait, too disgusted to look.

Lacey is just saying, "Can't you just hold it," when we all hear it. I have never heard the sound before, but I recognize it anyway: it is the sound of pee hitting the bottom of a beer bottle. It sounds almost like music. Revolting music with a very fast beat. I glance over and I can see the relief in Ben's eyes. He is smiling, staring into the middle distance.

"The longer you wait, the better it feels," he says. The sound soon changes from the clinking of pee-on-bottle to the blopping of pee-on-pee. And then, slowly, Ben's smile fades.

"Bro, I think I need another bottle," he says suddenly.

"Another bottle STAT," I shout.

"Another bottle coming up!" In a flash, I can see Radar bent over the backseat, his head in the cooler, digging a bottle out of the ice. He opens it with his bare hand, cracks one of the back windows open, and pours the beer out through the crack. Then he leaps to the front, his head between Ben and me, and holds the bottle out for Ben, whose eyes are darting around in panic.

"The, uh, exchange is going to be, uh, complicated," Ben says. There's a lot of fumbling going on beneath that robe, and I'm trying not to imagine what's happening when out from underneath a robe comes a Miller Lite bottle filled with pee (which looks astoundingly similar to Miller Lite). Ben deposits the full bottle in the cup holder, grabs the new one from Radar, and then sighs with relief.

The rest of us, meanwhile, are left to contemplate the pee in the cup holder. The road is not particularly bumpy, but the shocks on the minivan leave something to be desired, so the pee swishes back and forth at the top of the bottle.

"Ben, if you get pee in my brand-new car, I am going to cut your balls off."

Still peeing, Ben looks over at me, smirking. "You're gonna need a hell of a big knife, bro." And then finally I hear the stream slow. He's soon finished, and then in one swift motion he throws the new bottle out the window. The full one follows.

Lacey is fake-gagging—or maybe really gagging. Radar says, "God, did you wake up this morning and drink eighteen gallons of water?"

But Ben is beaming. He is holding his fists in the air, triumphant, and he is shouting, "Not a drop on the seat! I'm Ben Starling. First clarinet, WPHS Marching Band. Keg Stand Record Holder. Pee-in-the-car champion. I shook up the world! I must be the greatest!"

Thirty-five minutes later, as our third hour comes to a close, he asks in a small voice, "When are we stopping again?"

"One hour and three minutes, if Q keeps pace," Radar answers.

"Okay," Ben says. "Okay. Good. Because I have to pee."

Hour Four

For the first time, Lacey asks, "Are we there yet?" We laugh. We *are*, however, in Georgia, a state I love and adore for this reason and this reason only: the speed limit here is seventy, which means I can up my speed to seventy-seven. Aside from that, Georgia reminds me of Florida.

We spend the hour preparing for our first stop. This is an important stop, because I am very, very, very, very hungry and dehydrated. For some reason, talking about the food we'll buy at the BP eases the pangs. Lacey prepares a grocery list for each of us, written in small letters on the backs of receipts she found in her purse. She makes Ben lean out the passenger-side window to see which side the gas cap is on. She forces us to memorize our grocery lists and then quizzes us. We talk through our visit to the gas station several times; it needs to be as well-executed as a stock car pit stop.

"One more time," Lacey says.

"I'm the gas man," Radar says. "After I start the fill-up, I run inside while the pump is pumping even though I'm supposed to stay near the pump at all times, and I give you the card. Then I return to the gas."

"I take the card to the guy behind the counter," Lacey says.

"Or girl," I add.

"Not relevant," Lacey answers.

"I'm just saying—don't be so sexist."

"Oh whatever, Q. I take the card to the person behind the counter. I tell her or him to ring up everything we bring. Then I pee."

I add, "Meanwhile, I'm getting everything on my list and bringing it up to the front."

Ben says, "And I'm peeing. Then when I finish peeing, I'll get the stuff on my list."

"Most importantly shirts," Radar says. "People keep looking at me funny."

Lacey says, "I sign the receipt when I get out of the bathroom."

"And then the moment the tank is full, I'm going to get in the minivan and drive away, so y'all had better be in there. I will seriously leave your asses. You have six minutes," Radar says.

"Six minutes," I say, nodding my head. And Lacey and Ben repeat it also. "Six minutes." "Six minutes." At 5:35 P.M., with nine hundred miles to go, Radar informs us that, according to his handheld, the next exit will have a BP.

As I pull into the gas station, Lacey and Radar are crouched behind the sliding door in the back. Ben, seat belt unbuckled, has one hand on the passenger-door handle and the other on the dashboard. I maintain as much speed as I can for as long as I can, and then slam on the brakes right in front of the gas tank. The minivan jolts to a halt, and we fly out the doors. Radar and I cross in front of the car; I toss him the keys and then run all out to the food mart. Lacey and Ben have beat me to the doors, but only just barely. While Ben bolts for the bathroom, Lacey explains to the gray-haired woman (it *is* a woman!) that we're going to be buying a lot of stuff, and that we're in a huge hurry, and that she should just ring items up as we deliver them and that it will all go on her BP card, and the woman seems a little bewildered but agrees. Radar runs in, his robe aflutter, and hands Lacey the card.

Meanwhile, I'm running through the aisles getting everything on my list. Lacey's on liquids; Ben's on nonperishable supplies; I'm on food. I sweep through the place like I'm a cheetah and the tortilla chips are injured gazelles. I run an armful of chips and beef jerky and peanuts to the front counter, then jog to the candy aisle. A handful of Mentos, a handful of Snickers, and—Oh, it's not on the list, but screw it, I love Nerds, so I add three packages of Nerds. I run back and then head over to the "deli" counter, which consists of ancient turkey sandwiches wherein the turkey strongly resembles ham. I grab two of those. On my way back to the cash register, I stop for a couple Starbursts, a package of Twinkies, and an indeterminate number of GoFast nutrition bars. I run back. Ben's standing there in his graduation gown, handing the woman T-shirts and four-dollar sunglasses. Lacey runs up with gallons of soda, energy drinks, and bottles of water. Big bottles, the kind of bottles that even Ben's pee can't fill.

"ONE MINUTE!" Lacey shouts, and I panic. I'm turning in circles, my eyes darting around the store, trying to remember what I'm forgetting. I glance down at my list. I seem to have everything, but I feel like there's something important I've forgotten. Something. *Come on, Jacobsen.* Chips, candy, turkey-that-looks-like-ham, pbj, and—what? What are the other food groups? Meat, chips, candy, and, and, and, and cheese! "CRACKERS!" I say, much too loud, and then I dart to the crackers, grabbing cheese crackers and peanut butter crackers and some of Grandma's peanut butter cookies for good measure, and then I run back and toss them across the counter. The woman has already bagged up four plastic bags of groceries. Almost a hundred dollars total, not even counting gas; I'll be paying back Lacey's parents all summer.

There's only one moment of pause, and it's after the woman behind the counter swipes Lacey's BP card. I glance at my watch. We're supposed to leave in twenty seconds. Finally, I hear the receipt printing. The woman tears it out of the machine, Lacey scribbles her name, and then Ben and I grab the bags and dash for the car. Radar revs the engine as if to say *hustle,* and we are running through the parking lot, Ben's robe flowing in the wind so that he looks vaguely like a dark wizard, except that his pale skinny legs are visible, and his arms hug plastic bags. I can see the back of Lacey's legs beneath her dress, her calves tight in midstride. I don't know how I look, but I know how I feel: Young. Goofy. Infinite. I watch as Lacey and Ben pile in through the open sliding door. I follow, landing on plastic bags and Lacey's torso. Radar guns the car as I slam the sliding door shut, and then he peels out of the parking lot, marking the first time in the long and storied history of the minivan that anyone anywhere has ever used one to burn rubber. Radar turns left onto the highway at a somewhat unsafe speed, and then merges back onto the interstate. We're four seconds ahead of schedule. And just like with the NASCAR pit stops, we share high-fives and backslaps. We are well supplied. Ben has plenty of containers into which he can urinate. I have adequate beef jerky rations. Lacey has her Mentos. Radar and Ben have T-shirts to wear over their robes. The minivan has become a biosphere—give us gas, and we can keep going forever.

Hour Five

Okay, maybe we are not that well provisioned after all. In the rush of the moment, it turns out that Ben and I made some moderate (although not fatal) mistakes. With Radar alone up front, Ben and I sit in the first bench, unpacking each bag and handing the items to Lacey in the wayback. Lacey, in turn, is sorting items into piles based on an organizational schema only she understands.

"Why is the NyQuil not in the same pile as the NoDoz?" I ask. "Shouldn't all the medicines be together?"

"Q. Sweetie. You're a boy. You don't know how to do these things. The NoDoz is with the chocolate and the Mountain Dew, because those things all contain caffeine and help you stay *up*. The NyQuil is with the beef jerky because eating meat makes you feel tired."

"Fascinating," I say. After I've handed Lacey the last of the food from my bags, Lacey asks, "Q, where is the food that is—you know—good?"

"Huh?"

Lacey produces a copy of the grocery list she wrote for me and reads from it. "Bananas. Apples. Dried cranberries. Raisins."

"Oh." I say. "Oh, right. The fourth food group *wasn't* crackers."

"Q!" she says, furious. "I can't eat any of this!"

Ben puts a hand on her elbow. "Well, but you can eat Grandma's cookies. They're not bad for you. They were made by *Grandma*. Grandma wouldn't hurt you."

Lacey blows a strand of hair out of her face. She seems genuinely annoyed. "Plus," I tell her, "there are GoFast bars. They're fortified with vitamins!"

"Yeah, vitamins and like thirty grams of fat," she says.

From the front Radar announces, "Don't you go talking bad about GoFast bars. Do you want me to stop this car?"

"Whenever I eat a GoFast bar," Ben says, "I'm always like, 'So this is what blood tastes like to mosquitoes.'"

I half unwrap a fudge brownie GoFast bar and hold it in front of Lacey's mouth. "Just smell it," I say. "Smell the vitaminy deliciousness."

"You're going to make me fat."

"Also zitty," Ben said. "Don't forget zitty."

Lacey takes the bar from me and reluctantly bites into it. She has to close her eyes to hide the orgasmic pleasure inherent in GoFast-tasting. "Oh. My. God. That tastes like hope feels."

Finally, we unpack the last bag. It contains two large T-shirts, which Radar and Ben are very excited about, because it means they can be guys-wearing-gigantic-shirts-over-silly-robes instead of just guys-wearing-silly-robes.

But when Ben unfurls the T-shirts, there are two small problems. First, it turns out that a large T-shirt in a Georgia gas station is not the same size as a large T-shirt at, say, Old Navy. The gas station shirt is gigantic—more garbage bag than shirt. It is smaller than the graduation robes, but not by much. But this problem rather pales in comparison to the other problem, which is that both T-shirts are embossed with huge Confederate flags. Printed over the flag are the words HERITAGE NOT HATE.

"Oh no you didn't," Radar says when I show him why we're laughing. "Ben Starling, you better not have bought your token black friend a racist shirt."

"I just grabbed the first shirts I saw, bro."

"Don't bro me right now," Radar says, but he's shaking his head and laughing. I hand him his shirt and he wiggles into it while driving with his knees. "I hope I get pulled over," he says. "I'd like to see how the cop responds to a black man wearing a Confederate T-shirt over a black dress."

Hour Six

For some reason, the stretch of I-95 just south of Florence, South Carolina, is *the* place to drive a car on a Friday evening.

We get bogged down in traffic for several miles, and even though Radar is desperate to violate the speed limit, he's lucky when he can go thirty. Radar and I sit up front, and we try to keep from worrying by playing a game we've just invented called That Guy Is a Gigolo. In the game, you imagine the lives of people in the cars around you.

We're driving alongside a Hispanic woman in a beat-up old Toyota Corolla. I watch her through the early darkness. "Left her family to move here," I say. "Illegal. Sends money back home on the third Tuesday of every month. She's got two little kids—her husband is a migrant. He's in Ohio right now—he only spends three or four months a year at home, but they still get along really well."

Radar leans in front of me and glances over at her for half a second. "Christ, Q, it's not so melodratragic as that. She's a secretary at a law firm—look how she's dressed. It has taken her five years, but she's now close to getting a law degree of her own. And she doesn't have kids, or a husband. She's got a boyfriend, though. He's a little flighty. Scared of commitment. White guy, a little nervous about the Jungle Fever angle of the whole thing."

"She's wearing a wedding ring," I point out. In Radar's defense, I've been able to stare at her. She is to my right, just below me. I can see through her tinted windows, and I watch as she sings along to some song, her unblinking eyes on the road. There are so many people. It is easy to forget how full the world is of people, full to bursting, and each of them imaginable and consistently misimagined. I feel like this is an important idea, one of those ideas that your brain must wrap itself around slowly, the way pythons eat, but before I can get any further, Radar speaks.

"She's just wearing that so pervs like you don't come on to her," Radar explains.

"Maybe." I smile, pick up the half-finished GoFast bar sitting on my lap, and take a bite. It's quiet again for a while, and I am thinking about the way you can and cannot see people, about the tinted windows between me and this woman who is still driving right beside us, both of us in cars with all these windows and mirrors everywhere, as she crawls along with us on this packed highway. When Radar starts talking again, I realize that he has been thinking, too.

"The thing about That Guy Is a Gigolo," Radar says, "I mean, the thing about it as a game, is that in the end it reveals a lot more about the person doing the imagining than it does about the person being imagined."

"Yeah," I say. "I was just thinking that." And I can't help but feel that Whitman, for all his blustering beauty, might have been just a bit too optimistic. We can hear others, and we can travel to them without moving, and we can imagine them, and we are all connected one to the other by a crazy root system like so many leaves of grass—but the game makes me wonder whether we can really ever fully *become* another.

Hour Seven

We finally pass a jackknifed truck and get back up to speed, but Radar calculates in his head that we'll need to average seventy-seven from here to Agloe. It has been one entire hour since Ben announced that he needed to pee, and the reason for this is simple: he is sleeping. At six o'clock exactly, he took NyQuil.

He lay down in the wayback, and then Lacey and I strapped both seat belts around him. This made him even more uncomfortable, but 1. It was for his own good, and 2. We all knew that in twenty minutes, no discomfort would matter to him at all, because he would be dead asleep. And so he is now. He will be awoken at midnight. I have just put Lacey to bed now, at 9 P.M., in the same position in the backseat. We will wake her at 2 A.M. The idea is that everybody sleeps for a shift so we won't be taping our eyelids open by tomorrow morning, when we come rolling into Agloe.

The minivan has become a kind of very small house: I am sitting in the passenger seat, which is the den. This is, I think, the best room in the house: there is plenty of space, and the chair is quite comfortable.

Scattered about the carpet beneath the passenger seat is the office, which contains a map of the United States Ben got at the BP, the directions I printed out, and the scrap paper onto which Radar has scrawled his calculations about speed and distance.

Radar sits in the driver's seat. The living room. It is a lot like the den, only you can't be as relaxed when you're there. Also, it's cleaner.

Between the living room and the den, we have the center console, or kitchen. Here we keep a plentiful supply of beef jerky and GoFast bars and this magical energy drink called Bluefin, which Lacey put on the shopping list. Bluefin comes in small, fancily contoured glass bottles, and it tastes like blue cotton candy. It also keeps you awake better than anything in all of human history, although it makes you a bit twitchy. Radar and I have agreed to keep drinking it until two hours before our rest periods. Mine starts at midnight, when Ben gets up.

This first bench seat is the first bedroom. It's the less desirable bedroom, because it is close to the kitchen and the living room, where people are awake and talking, and sometimes there is music on the radio.

Behind that is the second bedroom, which is darker and quieter and altogether superior to the first bedroom.

And behind that is the refrigerator, or cooler, which currently contains the 210 beers that Ben has not yet peed into, the turkey-that-looks-like-ham sandwiches, and some Coke.

There is much to recommend this house. It is carpeted throughout. It has central air-conditioning and heating. The whole place is wired for surround sound. Admittedly, it contains only fifty-five square feet of living space. But you can't beat the open floor plan.

Hour Eight

Just after we pass into South Carolina, I catch Radar yawning and insist upon a driver switch. I like driving, anyway—this vehicle may be a minivan, but it's *my* minivan. Radar scoots out of his seat and into the first bedroom, while I grab the steering wheel and hold it steady, quickly stepping over the kitchen and into the driver's seat.

Traveling, I am finding, teaches you a lot of things about yourself. For instance, I never thought myself to be the kind of person who pees into a mostly empty bottle of Bluefin energy drink while driving through South Carolina at seventy-seven miles per hour—but in fact I am that kind of person. Also, I never previously knew that if you mix a lot of pee with a little Bluefin energy drink, the result is this amazing incandescent turquoise color. It looks so pretty that I want to put the cap on the bottle and leave it in the cup holder so Lacey and Ben can see it when they wake up.

But Radar feels differently. "If you don't throw that shit out the window right now, I'm ending our eleven-year friendship," he says.

"It's not *shit*," I say. "It's *pee*."

"Out," he says. And so I litter. In the side-view mirror, I can see the bottle hit the asphalt and burst open like a water balloon. Radar sees it, too.

"Oh, my God," Radar says. "I hope that's like one of those traumatic events that is so damaging to my psyche that I just forget it ever happened."

Hour Nine

I never previously knew that it is possible to become tired of eating GoFast nutrition bars. But it *is* possible. I'm only two bites into my fourth of the day when my stomach turns. I pull open the center console and stick it back inside. We refer to this part of the kitchen as the pantry.

"I wish we had some apples," Radar said. "God, wouldn't an apple taste good right now?"

I sigh. Stupid fourth food group. Also, even though I stopped drinking Bluefin a few hours ago, I still feel exceedingly twitchy.

"I still feel kinda twitchy," I say.

"Yeah," Radar says. "I can't stop tapping my fingers." I look down. He is drumming his fingers silently against his knees. "I mean," he says, "I actually cannot stop."

"Okay, yeah I'm not tired, so we'll stay up till four and then we'll get them up and we'll sleep till eight."

"Okay," he says. There is a pause. The road has emptied out now; there is only me and the semitrucks, and I feel like my brain is processing information at eleven thousand times its usual pace, and it occurs to me that what I'm doing is very easy, that driving on the interstate is the easiest and most pleasant thing in the world: all I have to do is stay in between the lines and make sure that no one is too close to me and I am not too close to anyone and keep leaving. Maybe it felt like this for her, too, but I could never feel like this alone.

Radar breaks the silence. "Well, if we're not going to sleep until four . . ."

I finish his sentence. "Yeah, then we should probably just open another bottle of Bluefin."

And so we do.

Hour Ten

It is time for our second stop. It is 12:13 in the morning. My fingers do not feel like they are made of fingers; they feel like they are made of motion. I am tickling the steering wheel as I drive.

After Radar finds the nearest BP on his handheld, we decide to wake up Lacey and Ben.

I say, "Hey, guys, we're about to stop." No reaction.

Radar turns around and puts a hand on Lacey's shoulder. "Lace, time to get up." Nothing.

I turn on the radio. I find an oldies station. It's the Beatles. The song is "Good Morning." I turn it up some. No response. So Radar turns it up more. And then more. And then the chorus comes, and he starts singing along. And then I start singing along. I think it is finally my atonal screeching that awakes them.

"MAKE IT STOP!" Ben shouts. We turn down the music.

"Ben, we're stopping. Do you have to pee?"

He pauses, and there's a kerfuffle in the darkness back there, and I wonder if he has some physical strategy for checking the fullness of his bladder. "I think I'm okay, actually," he says.

"Okay, then you're on gas."

"As the only boy who has not yet peed inside this car, I call first bathroom," says Radar.

"Shhh," mumbles Lacey. "Shhh. Everybody stop talking."

"Lacey, you have to get up and pee," Radar says. "We're stopping."

"You can buy apples," I tell her.

"Apples," she mumbles happily in a cute little girl voice. "I likey the apples."

"And then after that you get to *drive*," Radar says. "So you really gotta wake up."

She sits up, and in her regular Lacey voice, she says, "I don't so much likey that."

We take the exit and it's .9 miles to the BP, which doesn't seem like much but Radar says that it's probably going to cost us four minutes, and the South Carolina traffic hurt us, so it could be real trouble with the construction Radar says is an hour ahead of us. But I am not allowed to worry. Lacey and Ben have now shaken off their sleep well enough to line up together by the sliding door, just like last time, and when we come to a stop in front of the pump, everybody flies out, and I flip the keys to Ben, who catches them in midair.

As Radar and I walk briskly past the white man behind the counter, Radar stops when he notices the guy is staring. "Yes," Radar says without embarrassment. "I'm wearing a HERITAGE NOT HATE shirt over my graduation gown," he says. "By the way, do you sell pants here?"

The guy looks nonplussed. "We got some camo pants over by the motor oil."

"Excellent," Radar says. And then he turns to me and says, "Be a dear and pick me out some camo pants. And maybe a better T-shirt?"

"Done and done," I answer. Camo pants, it turns out, do not come in regular numbered sizes. They come in medium and large. I grab a pair of medium pants, and then a large pink T-shirt that reads WORLD'S BEST GRANDMA. I also grab three bottles of Bluefin.

I hand everything to Lacey when she comes out of the bathroom and then walk into the girls' room, since Radar is still in the guys'. I don't know that I've ever been inside a girls' bathroom in a gas station before.

Differences:
No condom machine
Less graffiti
No urinal

The smell is more or less the same, which is rather disappointing.

When I come out, Lacey is paying and Ben is honking the horn, and after a moment of confusion, I jog toward the car.

"We lost a minute," Ben says from the passenger seat. Lacey is turning onto the road that will take us back to the interstate.

"Sorry," Radar answers from the back, where he is sitting next to me, wiggling into his new camo pants beneath his robe. "On the upside, I got pants. And a new T-shirt. Where's the shirt, Q?" Lacey hands it to him. "Very funny." He pulls off the robe and replaces it with the grandma shirt while Ben complains that no one got *him* any pants. His ass itches, he says. And on second thought, he kind of does need to pee.

Hour Eleven

We hit the construction. The highway narrows to one lane, and we're stuck behind a tractor-trailer driving the *precise* road-work speed limit of thirty-five mph. Lacey is the right driver for the situation; I'd be pounding the steering wheel, but she's just amiably chatting with Ben until she turns half around and says, "Q, I really need to go to the bathroom, and we're losing time behind this truck anyway."

I just nod. I can't blame her. I would have forced us to stop long ago had it been impossible for me to pee in a bottle. It was heroic of her to make it as long as she did.

She pulls into an all-night gas station, and I get out to stretch my rubbery legs. When Lacey comes racing back to the minivan, I'm sitting in the driver's seat. I don't even really know how I came to be sitting in the driver's seat, why I end up there and not Lacey. She comes around to the front door, and she sees me there, and the window is open, and I say to her, "I can drive." It's my car, after all, and my mission. And she says, "Really, you're sure?" and I say, "Yeah, yeah, I'm good to go," and she just throws open the sliding door and lies down in the first row.

Hour Twelve

It is 2:40 in the morning. Lacey is sleeping. Radar is sleeping. I drive. The road is deserted. Even most of the truck drivers have gone to bed. We go minutes without seeing headlights coming in the opposite direction. Ben keeps me awake, chattering next to me. We are talking about Margo.

"Have you given any thought to how we will actually, like, *find* Agloe?" he asks me.

"Uh, I have an approximate idea of the intersection," I say. "And it's nothing but an intersection."

"And she's just gonna be sitting at the corner on the trunk of her car, chin in her hands, waiting for you?"

"That would certainly be helpful," I answered.

"Bro, I gotta say I'm a little worried that you might, like—if it doesn't go as you're planning it—you might be really disappointed."

"I just want to find her," I say, because I do. I want her to be safe, alive, found. The string played out. The rest is secondary.

"Yeah, but— I don't know," Ben says. I can feel him looking over at me, being Serious Ben. "Just— Just remember that sometimes, the way you think about a person isn't the way they actually are. Like, I always thought Lacey was so hot and so awesome and so cool, but now when it actually comes to being with her . . .

it's not the exact same. People are different when you can smell them and see them up close, you know?"

"I know that," I say. I know how long, and how badly, I wrongly imagined her.

"I'm just saying that it was easy for me to like Lacey before. It's easy to like someone from a distance. But when she stopped being this amazing unattainable thing or whatever, and started being, like, just a regular girl with a weird relationship with food and frequent crankiness who's kinda bossy—then I had to basically start liking a whole different person."

I can feel my cheeks warming. "You're saying I don't *really* like Margo? After all this—I'm twelve hours inside this car already and you don't think I care about her because I don't— " I cut myself off. "You think that since you have a girlfriend you can stand atop the lofty mountain and lecture me? You can be such a—"

I stop talking because I see in the outer reaches of the headlights the thing that will shortly kill me.

Two cows stand oblivious in the highway. They come into view all at once, a spotted cow in the left lane, and in our lane an immense creature, the entire width of our car, standing stock-still, her head turned back as she appraises us with blank eyes. The cow is flawlessly white, a great white wall of cow that cannot be climbed or ducked or dodged. It can only be hit. I know that Ben sees it, too, because I hear his breath stop.

They say that your life flashes before your eyes, but for me that is not the case. Nothing flashes before my eyes except this impossibly vast expanse of snowy fur, now only a second from us. I don't know what to do. No, that's not the problem. The problem is that there is nothing to do, except to hit this white wall and kill it and us, both. I slam on the brakes, but out of habit not expectation: there is absolutely no avoiding this. I raise my hands off the steering wheel. I do not know why I am doing this, but I raise my hands up, as if I am surrendering. I'm thinking the most banal thing in the world: I am thinking that I don't want this to happen. I don't want to die. I don't want my friends to die. And to be honest, as the time slows down and my hands are in the air, I am afforded the chance to think one more thought, and I think about her. I blame her for this ridiculous, fatal chase—for putting us at risk, for making me into the kind of jackass who would stay up all night and drive too fast. I would not be dying were it not for her. I would have stayed home, as I have always stayed home, and I would have been safe, and I would have done the one thing I have always wanted to do, which is to grow up.

Having surrendered control of the vessel, I am surprised to see a hand on the steering wheel. We are turning before I realize why we are turning, and then I realize that Ben is pulling the wheel toward him, turning us in a hopeless attempt to miss the cow, and then we are on the shoulder and then on the grass. I can hear the tires spinning as Ben turns the wheel hard and fast in the opposite direction. I stop watching. I don't know if my eyes close or if they just cease to see. My stomach and my lungs meet in the middle and crush each other. Something sharp hits my cheek. We stop.

I don't know why, but I touch my face. I pull my hand back and there is a streak of blood. I touch my arms with my hands, hugging my arms to myself, but I am only checking to make sure that they are there, and they are. I look at my legs. They are there. There is some glass. I look around. Bottles are broken.

Ben is looking at me. Ben is touching his face. He looks okay. He holds himself as I held myself. His body still works. He is just looking at me. In the rearview mirror, I can see the cow. And now, belatedly, Ben screams. He is staring at me and screaming, his mouth all the way open, the scream low and guttural and terrified. He stops screaming. Something is wrong with me. I feel faint. My chest is burning. And then I gulp air. I had forgotten to breathe. I had been holding my breath the whole time. I feel much better when I start up again. *In through the nose, out through the mouth.*

"Who is hurt?!" Lacey shouts. She's unbuckled herself from her sleeping position and she's leaning into the wayback. When I turn around, I can see that the back door has popped open, and for a moment I think that Radar has been thrown from the car, but then he sits up. He is running his hands over his face, and he says, "I'm okay. I'm okay. Is everyone okay?"

Lacey doesn't even respond; she just jumps forward, between Ben and me. She is leaning over the apartment's kitchen, and she looks at Ben. She says, "Sweetie, where are you hurt?" Her eyes are overfull of water like a swimming pool on a rainy day. And Ben says, "I'mfineI'mfineQisbleeding."

She turns to me, and I shouldn't cry but I do, not because it hurts, but because I am scared, and I raised my hands, and Ben saved us, and now there is this girl looking at me, and she looks at me kind of the way a mom does, and that shouldn't crack me open, but it does. I know the cut on my cheek isn't bad, and I'm trying to say so, but I keep crying. Lacey is pressing against the cut with her fingers, thin and soft, and shouting at Ben for something to use as a bandage, and then I've got a small swath of the Confederate flag pressed against my cheek just to the right of my nose. She says, "Just hold it there tight; you're fine does anything else hurt?" and I say no. That's when I realize that the car is still running, and still in gear, stopped only because I'm still standing on the brakes. I put it into park and turn it off. When I turn it off, I can hear liquid leaking—not dripping so much as pouring.

"We should probably get out," Radar says. I hold the Confederate flag to my face. The sound of liquid pouring out of the car continues.

"It's gas! It's gonna blow!" Ben shouts. He throws open the passenger door and takes off, running in a panic. He hurdles a split-rail fence and tears across a hay field. I get out as well, but not in quite the same hurry. Radar is outside, too, and as Ben hauls ass, Radar is laughing. "It's the beer," he says.

"What?"

"The beers all broke," he says again, and nods toward the split-open cooler, gallons of foamy liquid pouring out from inside it.

We try to call Ben but he can't hear us because he's too busy screaming, "IT'S GONNA BLOW!" as he races across the field. His graduation robe flies up in the gray dawn, his bony bare ass exposed.

I turn and look out at the highway as I hear a car coming. The white beast and her spotted friend have successfully ambled to the safety of the opposite shoulder, still impassive. Turning back, I realize the minivan is against the fence.

I'm assessing damage when Ben finally schleps back to the car. As we spun, we must have grazed the fence, because there is a deep gouge on the sliding door, deep enough that if you look closely, you can just see inside the van. But other than that, it looks immaculate. No other dents. No windows broken. No flat tires. I walk around to close the back door and appraise the 210 broken bottles of beer, still bubbling. Lacey finds me and puts an arm around me. We are both staring at the rivulet of foaming beer flowing into the drainage ditch beneath us. "What happened?" she asks.

I tell her: we were dead, and then Ben managed to spin the car in just the right way, like some kind of brilliant vehicular ballerina.

Ben and Radar have crawled underneath the minivan. Neither of them knows shit about cars, but I suppose it makes them feel better. The hem of Ben's robe and his naked calves peek out.

"Dude," Radar shouts. "It looks, like, *fine*."

"Radar," I say, "the car spun around like eight times. Surely it's not *fine*."

"Well it *seems* fine," Radar says.

"Hey," I say, grabbing at Ben's New Balances. "Hey, come out here." He scoots his way out, and I offer him my hand and help him up. His hands are black with car gunk. I grab him and hug him. If I had not ceded control of the wheel, and if he had not assumed control of the vessel so deftly, I'm sure I'd be dead. "Thank you," I say, pounding his back probably too hard. "That was the best damned passenger-seat driving I've ever seen in my life."

He pats my uninjured cheek with a greasy hand. "I did it to save myself, not you," he says. "Believe me when I say that you did not once cross my mind."

I laugh. "Nor you mine," I say.

Ben looks at me, his mouth on the edge of smiling, and then says, "I mean, that was a big damned cow. It wasn't even a cow so much as it was a land whale." I laugh.

Radar scoots out then. "Dude, I really think it's fine. I mean, we've only lost like five minutes. We don't even have to push up the cruising speed."

Lacey is looking at the gouge in the minivan, her lips pursed. "What do you think?" I ask her.

"Go," she says.

"Go," Radar votes.

Ben puffs out his cheeks and exhales. "Mostly because I'm prone to peer pressure: go."

"Go," I say. "But I'm sure as hell not driving anymore."

Ben takes the keys from me. We get into the minivan. Radar guides us up a slow-sloping embankment and back onto the interstate. We're 542 miles from Agloe.

Hour Thirteen

Every couple minutes, Radar says, "Do you guys remember that time when we were all definitely going to die and then Ben grabbed the steering wheel and dodged a ginormous freaking cow and spun the car like the teacups at Disney World and we didn't die?"

Lacey leans across the kitchen, her hand on Ben's knee, and says, "I mean, you are a *hero*, do you realize that? They give out *medals* for this stuff."

"I've said it before and I'll say it again: I wasn't thinking about none of y'all. I. Wanted. To. Save. My. Ass."

"You liar. You heroic, adorable liar," she says, and then plants a kiss on his cheek.

Radar says, "Hey guys, do you remember that time I was double-seat-belted in the wayback and the door flew open and the beer fell out but I survived completely uninjured? How is that even *possible*?"

"Let's play metaphysical I Spy," Lacey says. "I Spy with my little eye a hero's heart, a heart that beats not for itself but for all humanity."

"I'M NOT BEING MODEST. I JUST DIDN'T WANT TO DIE," Ben exclaims.

"Do you guys remember that one time, in the minivan, twenty minutes ago, that we somehow didn't die?"

Hour Fourteen

Once the initial shock passes, we clean. We try to shepherd as much glass from the broken Bluefin bottles as possible onto pieces of paper and then gather them into a single bag for later disposal. The minivan's carpet is soaked with sticky Mountain Dew and Bluefin and Diet Coke, and we try to sop it up with the few napkins we've collected. But this will require a serious car wash, at the very least, and there's no time for that before Agloe. Radar has looked up the side panel replacement I'll need: $300 plus paint. The cost of this trip keeps going up, but I'll make it back this summer working in my dad's office, and anyway, it's a small ransom to pay for Margo.

The sun is rising to our right. My cheek is still bleeding. The Confederate flag is stuck to the wound now, so I no longer need to hold it there.

Hour Fifteen

A thin stand of oak trees obscures the cornfields that stretch out to the horizon. The landscape changes, but nothing else. Big interstates like this one make the country into a single place: McDonald's, BP, Wendy's. I know I should probably hate that about interstates and yearn for the halcyon days of yore, back when you could be drenched in local color at every turn—but whatever. I like this. I like the consistency. I like that I can drive fifteen hours from home without the world changing too much. Lacey double-belts me down in the wayback. "You need the rest," she says. "You've been through a lot." It's amazing that no one has yet blamed me for not being more proactive in the battle against the cow.

As I trail off, I hear them making one another laugh—not the words exactly, but the cadence, the rising and falling pitches of banter. I like just listening, just loafing on the grass. And I decide that if we get there on time but don't find her, that's what we'll do: we'll drive around the Catskills and find a place to sit around and hang out, loafing on the grass, talking, telling jokes. Maybe the sure knowledge that she is alive makes all of that possible again—even if I never see proof of it. I can almost imagine a happiness without her, the ability to let her go, to feel our roots are connected even if I never see that leaf of grass again.

Hour Sixteen

I sleep.

Hour Seventeen

I sleep.

Hour Eighteen

I sleep.

Hour Nineteen

When I wake up, Radar and Ben are loudly debating the name of the car. Ben would like to name it Muhammad Ali, because, just like Muhammad Ali, the minivan takes a punch and keeps going. Radar says you can't name a car after a historical figure. He thinks the car ought to be called Lurlene, because it sounds right.

"You want to name it *Lurlene*?" Ben asks, his voice rising with the horror of it all. "Hasn't this poor vehicle been through enough?!"

I unbuckle one seat belt and sit up. Lacey turns around to me. "Good morning," she says. "Welcome to the great state of New York."

"What time is it?"

"Nine-forty-two." Her hair is pulled back in a ponytail, but the shorter strands have strayed. "How's it going?" she asks.

I tell her. "I'm scared."

Lacey smiles at me and nods. "Yeah, me, too. It's like there's too many things that could happen to prepare for all of them."

"Yeah," I say.

"I hope you and me stay friends this summer," she says. And that helps, for some reason. You can never tell what is going to help.

Radar is now saying that the car should be called the Gray Goose. I lean forward a little so everyone can hear me and say, "The Dreidel. The harder you spin it, the better it performs."

Ben nods. Radar turns around. "I think you should be the official stuff-namer."

Hour Twenty

I'm sitting in the first bedroom with Lacey. Ben drives. Radar's navigating. I was asleep when they last stopped, but they picked up a map of New York. Agloe isn't marked, but there are only five or six intersections north of Roscoe. I always thought of New York as being a sprawling and endless metropolis, but here it is just lush rolling hills that the minivan heroically strains its way up. When there's a lull in the conversation and Ben reaches for the radio knob, I say, "Metaphysical I Spy!"

Ben starts. "I Spy with my little eye something I really like."

"Oh, I know," Radar says. "It's the taste of balls."

"No."

"Is it the taste of penises?" I guess.

"No, dumbass," Ben says.

"Hmm," says Radar. "Is it the *smell* of balls?"

"The *texture* of balls?" I guess.

"Come on, asshats, it has nothing to do with genitalia. Lace?"

"Um, is it the feeling of knowing you just saved three lives?"

"No. And I think you guys are out of guesses."

"Okay, what is it?"

"Lacey," he says, and I can see him looking at her through the rearview.

"Dumbass," I say, "it's supposed to be *meta*physical I Spy. It has to be things that can't be seen."

"And it is," he says. "That's what I really like—Lacey but not the visible Lacey."

"Oh, hurl," Radar says, but Lacey unbuckles her seat belt and leans forward over the kitchen to whisper something in his ear. Ben blushes in response.

"Okay, I promise not to be a cheese ball," Radar says. "I Spy with my little eye something we're all feeling."

I guess, "Extraordinary fatigue?"

"No, although excellent guess."

Lacey says, "Is it that weird feeling you get from so much caffeine that, like, your heart isn't beating so much as your whole body is beating?"

"No. Ben?"

"Um, are we feeling the need to pee, or is that just me?"

"That is, as usual, just you. More guesses?" We are silent. "The correct answer is that we are all feeling like we will be happier after an a cappella rendition of 'Blister in the Sun.'"

And so it is. Tone deaf as I may be, I sing as loud as anybody. And when we finish, I say, "I Spy with my little eye a great story."

No one says anything for a while. There's just the sound of the Dreidel devouring the blacktop as she speeds downhill. And then after a while Ben says, "It's this, isn't it?"

I nod.

"Yeah," Radar says. "As long as we don't die, this is gonna be one hell of a story."

It will help if we can find her, I think, but I don't say anything. Ben turns on the radio finally and finds a rock station with ballads we can sing along to.

Hour Twenty-one

After more than 1,100 miles on interstates, it's finally time to exit. It's entirely impossible to drive seventy-seven miles per hour on the two-lane state highway that takes us farther north, up toward the Catskills. But we'll be okay. Radar, ever the brilliant tactician, has banked an extra thirty minutes without telling us. It's beautiful up here, the late-morning sunlight pouring down on old-growth forest. Even the brick buildings in the ramshackle little downtowns we drive past seem crisp in this light.

Lacey and I are telling Ben and Radar everything we can think of in hopes of helping them find Margo. Reminding them of her. Reminding ourselves of her. Her silver Honda Civic. Her chestnut hair, stick straight. Her fascination with abandoned buildings.

"She has a black notebook with her," I say.

Ben wheels around to me. "Okay, Q. If I see a girl who looks exactly like Margo in Agloe, New York, I'm not going to do anything. Unless she has a *notebook.* That'll be the giveaway."

I shrug him off. I just want to remember her. One last time, I want to remember her while still hoping to see her again.

Agloe

The speed limit drops from fifty-five to forty-five and then to thirty-five. We cross some railroad tracks, and we're in Roscoe. We drive slowly through a sleepy downtown with a café, a clothing store, a dollar store, and a couple boarded-up storefronts.

I lean forward and say, "I can imagine her in there."

"Yeah," Ben allows. "Man, I really don't want to break into buildings. I don't think I would do well in New York prisons."

The thought of exploring these buildings doesn't strike me as particularly scary, though, since the whole town seems deserted. Nothing's open here. Past downtown, a single road bisects the highway, and on that road sits Roscoe's lone neighborhood and an elementary school. Modest wood-frame houses are dwarfed by the trees, which grow thick and tall here.

We turn onto a different highway, and the speed limit goes back up incrementally, but Radar is driving slowly anyway. We haven't gone a mile when we see a dirt road on our left with no street sign to tell us its name.

"This may be it," I say.

"That's a *driveway*," Ben answers, but Radar turns in anyway. But it *does* seem to be a driveway, actually, cut into the hard-packed dirt. To our left, uncut grass grows as high as the tires; I don't see anything, although I worry that it'd be easy for a person to hide anywhere in that field. We drive for a while and the road dead-ends into a Victorian farmhouse. We turn around and head back up the two-lane highway, farther north. The highway turns into Cat Hollow Road, and we drive until we see a dirt road identical to the previous one, this time on the right side of the street, leading to a crumbling barnlike structure with grayed wood. Huge cylindrical bales of hay line the fields on either side of us, but the grass has begun to grow up again. Radar drives no faster than five miles an hour. We are looking for something unusual. Some crack in the perfectly idyllic landscape.

"Do you think that could have been the Agloe General Store?" I ask.

"That barn?"

"Yeah."

"I dunno," Radar says. "Did general stores look like barns?"

I blow a long breath from between pursed lips. "Dunno."

"Is that—shit, that's her car!" Lacey shouts next to me. "Yes yes yes yes yes her car her car!"

Radar stops the minivan as I follow Lacey's finger back across the field, behind the building. A glint of silver. Leaning down so my face is next to hers, I can see the arc of the car's roof. God knows how it got there, since no road leads in that direction.

Radar pulls over, and I jump out and run back toward her car. Empty. Unlocked. I pop the trunk. Empty, too, except for an open and empty suitcase. I look around, and take off toward what I now believe to be the remnants of Agloe's General Store. Ben and Radar pass me as I run through the mown field. We enter the barn not through a door but through one of several gaping holes where the wooden wall has simply fallen away.

Inside the building, the sun lights up segments of the rotting wooden floor through the many holes in the roof. As I look for her, I register things: the soggy floorboards. The smell of almonds, like her. An old claw-footed bathtub in a corner. So many holes everywhere that this place is simultaneously inside and outside.

I feel someone pull hard on my shirt. I spin my head and see Ben, his eyes shooting back and forth between me and a corner of the room. I have to look past a wide beam of bright white light shining down from the ceiling, but I can see into that corner. Two long panes of chest-high, dirty, gray-tinted Plexiglas lean against each other at an acute angle, held up on the other side by the wooden wall. It's a triangular cubicle, if such a thing is possible.

And here's the thing about tinted windows: the light still gets through. So I can see the jarring scene, albeit in gray scale: Margo Roth Spiegelman sits in a black leather office chair, hunched over a school desk, writing. Her hair is much shorter—she has choppy bangs above her eyebrows and everything is mussed-up, as if to emphasize the asymmetry—but it is her. She is alive. She has relocated her offices from an abandoned mini-mall in Florida to an abandoned barn in New York, and I have found her.

We walk toward Margo, all four of us, but she doesn't seem to see us. She just keeps writing. Finally, someone—Radar, maybe—says, "Margo. Margo?"

She stands up on her tiptoes, her hands resting atop the make-shift cubicle's walls. If she is surprised to see us, her eyes do not give it away. Here is Margo Roth Spiegelman, five feet away from me, her lips chapped to cracking, makeup-less, dirt in her finger-nails, her eyes silent. I've never seen her eyes dead like that, but then again, maybe I've never seen her eyes before. She stares at me. I feel certain she is staring at me and not at Lacey or Ben or Radar. I haven't felt so stared at since Robert Joyner's dead eyes watched me in Jefferson Park.

She stands there in silence for a long time, and I am too scared of her eyes to keep walking forward. "I and this mystery here we stand," Whitman wrote.

Finally, she says, "Give me like five minutes," and then sits back down and resumes her writing.

I watch her write. Except for being a little grimy, she looks like she has always looked. I don't know why, but I always thought she would look different. Older. That I would barely recognize her when I finally saw her again. But there she is, and I am watching her through the Plexiglas, and she looks like Margo Roth Spiegelman, this girl I have known since I was two—this girl who was an idea that I loved.

And it is only now, when she closes her notebook and places it inside a backpack next to her and then stands up and walks toward us, that I realize that the idea is not only wrong but dangerous. What a treacherous thing it is to believe that a person is more than a person.

"Hey," she says to Lacey, smiling. She hugs Lacey first, then shakes Ben's hand, then Radar's. She raises her eyebrows and says, "Hi, Q," and then hugs me, quickly and not hard. I want to hold on. I want an event. I want to feel her heaving sobs against my chest, tears running down her dusty cheeks onto my shirt. But she just hugs me quickly and sits down on the floor. I sit down across from her, with Ben and Radar and Lacey following in a line, so that we are all facing Margo.

"It's good to see you," I say after a while, feeling like I'm breaking a silent prayer.

She pushes her bangs to the side. She seems to be deciding exactly what to say before she says it. "I, uh. Uh. I'm rarely at a loss for words, huh? Not much talking to people lately. Um. I guess maybe we should start with, what the hell are you doing here?"

"Margo," Lacey says. "Christ, we were so worried."

"No need to worry," Margo answers cheerfully. "I'm good." She gives us two thumbs-up. "I am A-OK."

"You could have called us and let us know that," Ben says, his voice tinged with frustration. "Saved us a hell of a drive."

"In my experience, Bloody Ben, when you leave a place, it's best to *leave*. Why are you wearing a dress, by the way?"

Ben blushes. "Don't call him that," Lacey snaps.

Margo cuts a look at Lacey. "Oh, my God, are you *hooking up* with him?" Lacey says nothing. "You're not *actually* hooking up with him," Margo says.

"Actually, yes," Lacey says. "And actually he's great. And actually you're a bitch. And actually, I'm leaving. It's nice to see you again, Margo. Thanks for terrifying me and making me feel like shit for the entire last month of my senior year, and then being a bitch when we track you down to make sure you're okay. It's been a real pleasure knowing you."

"You, too. I mean, without you, how would I have ever known how fat I was?" Lacey gets up and stomps off, her footfalls vibrating through the crumbling floor. Ben follows. I look over, and Radar has stood up, too.

"I never knew you until I got to know you through your clues," he says. "I like the clues more than I like you."

"What the hell is he talking about?" Margo asks me. Radar doesn't answer. He just leaves.

I should, too, of course. They're my friends—more than Margo, certainly. But I have questions. As Margo stands and starts to walk back toward her cubicle, I start with the obvious one. "Why are you acting like such a brat?"

She spins around and grabs a fistful of my shirt and shouts

into my face, "Where do you get off showing up here without any kind of warning?!"

"How could I have warned you when you completely dropped off the face of the planet?!" I see a long blink and know she has no response for this, so I keep going. I'm so pissed at her. For . . . for, I don't know. Not being the Margo I had expected her to be. Not being the Margo I thought I had finally imagined correctly. "I thought for sure there was a good reason why you never got in touch with anyone after that night. And . . . this is your good reason? So you can live like a bum?"

She lets go of my shirt and pushes away from me. "Now who's being a brat? I left the only way you can leave. You pull your life off all at once—like a Band-Aid. And then you get to be you and Lace gets to be Lace and everybody gets to be everybody and I get to be me."

"Except I didn't get to be me, Margo, because I thought you were *dead*. For the longest time. So I had to do all kinds of crap that I would never do."

She screams at me now, pulling herself up by my shirt so she can get in my face. "Oh, bullshit. You didn't come here to make sure I was okay. You came here because you wanted to save poor little Margo from her troubled little self, so that I would be oh-so-thankful to my knight in shining armor that I would strip my clothes off and beg you to ravage my body."

"Bullshit!" I shout, which it mostly is. "You were just playing with us, weren't you? You just wanted to make sure that even after you left to go have your fun, you were still the axis we spun around."

She's screaming back, louder than I thought possible. "You're not even pissed at me, Q! You're pissed at this idea of me you keep inside your brain from when we were little!"

She tries to turn away from me, but I grab her shoulders and hold her in front of me and say, "Did you ever even think about what your leaving meant? About Ruthie? About me or Lacey or any of the other people who cared about you? No. Of course you didn't. Because if it doesn't happen to you, it doesn't happen at all. Isn't that it, Margo? Isn't it?"

She doesn't fight me now. She just slumps her shoulders, turns, and walks back to her office. She kicks down both of the Plexiglas walls, and they clamor against the desk and chair before sliding onto the ground. "SHUT UP SHUT UP YOU ASSHOLE."

"Okay," I say. Something about Margo completely losing her temper allows me to regain mine. I try to talk like my mom. "I'll shut up. We're both upset. Lots of, uh, unresolved issues on my side."

She sits down in the desk chair, her feet on what had been the wall of her office. She's looking into a corner of the barn. At least ten feet between us. "How the hell did you even find me?"

"I thought you wanted us to," I answer. My voice is so small I'm surprised she even hears me, but she spins the chair to glare at me.

"I sure as shit did not."

"'Song of Myself,'" I say. "Guthrie took me to Whitman. Whitman took me to the door. The door took me to the mini-mall. We figured out how to read the painted-over graffiti. I didn't understand 'paper towns'; it can also mean subdivisions that never got built, and so I thought you had gone to one and were never coming back. I thought you were dead in one of these places, that you had killed yourself and wanted me to find you for whatever reason. So I went to a bunch of them, looking for you. But then I matched the map in the gift shop to the thumbtack holes. I started reading the poem more closely, figured out you weren't running probably, just holed up, planning. Writing in that notebook. I found Agloe from the map, saw your comment on the talk page of Omnictionary, skipped graduation, and drove here."

She brushes her hair down, but it isn't long enough to fall over her face anymore. "I hate this haircut," she says. "I wanted to look different, but—it looks ridiculous."

"I like it," I say. "It frames your face nicely."

"I'm sorry I was being so bitchy," she says. "You just have to understand—I mean, you guys walk in here out of nowhere and you scare the shit out of me—"

"You could have just said, like, 'Guys, you are scaring the shit out of me,'" I said.

She scoffs. "Yeah, right, 'cause that's the Margo Roth Spiegelman everybody knows and loves." Margo is quiet for a moment, and then says, "I knew I shouldn't have said that on Omnictionary. I just thought it would be funny for them to find it later. I thought the cops might trace it somehow, but not soon enough. There's like a billion pages on Omnictionary or whatever. I never thought . . ."

"What?"

"I thought about you a lot, to answer your question. And Ruthie. And my parents. Of course, okay? Maybe I am the most horribly self-centered person in the history of the world. But God, do you think I would have done it if I didn't *need* to?" She shakes her head. Now, finally, she leans toward me, elbows on knees, and we are talking. At a distance, but still. "I couldn't figure out any other way that I could leave without getting dragged back."

"I'm happy you're not dead," I say to her.

"Yeah. Me, too," she says. She smirks, and it's the first time I've seen that smile I have spent so much time missing. "That's why I had to leave. As much as life can suck, it always beats the alternative."

My phone rings. It's Ben. I answer it.

"Lacey wants to talk to Margo," he tells me.

I walk over to Margo, hand her the phone, and linger there as she sits with her shoulders hunched, listening. I can hear the noises coming through the phone, and then I hear Margo cut her off and say, "Listen, I'm really sorry. I was just so scared." And then silence. Lacey starts talking again finally, and Margo laughs, and says something. I feel like they should have some privacy, so I do some exploring. Against the same wall as the office, but in the opposite corner of the barn, Margo has set up a kind of bed—four forklift pallets beneath an orange air mattress. Her small, neatly folded collection of clothes sits next to the bed on a pallet of its own. There's a toothbrush and toothpaste, along with a large plastic cup from Subway. Those items sit atop two books: *The Bell Jar* by Sylvia Plath and *Slaughterhouse-Five* by Kurt Vonnegut. I can't believe she's been living like this, this irreconcilable mix of tidy suburbanality and creepy decay. But then again, I can't believe how much time I wasted believing she was living any other way.

"They're staying at a motel in the park. Lace said to tell you they're leaving in the morning, with or without you," Margo says from behind me. It is when she says *you* and not *us* that I think for the first time of what comes after this.

"I'm mostly self-sufficient," she says, standing next to me now. "There's an outhouse here, but it's not in great shape, so I usually go to the bathroom at this truck stop east of Roscoe. They have showers there, too, and the girls' shower is pretty clean because there aren't a lot of female truckers. Plus, they have Internet there. It's like this is my house, and the truck stop is my beach house." I laugh.

She walks past me and kneels down, looking inside the pallets beneath the bed. She pulls out a flashlight and a square, thin piece of plastic. "These are the only two things I've purchased in the whole month except gas and food. I've only spent about three hundred dollars." I take the square thing from her and finally realize that it's a battery-powered record player. "I brought a couple albums," she says. "I'm gonna get more in the City, though."

"The City?"

"Yeah. I'm leaving for New York City today. Hence the Omnictionary thing. I'm going to start really traveling. Originally, this was the day I was going to leave Orlando—I was going to go to graduation and then do all of these elaborate pranks on graduation night with you, and then I was going to leave the next morning. But I just couldn't take it anymore. I seriously could not take it for one more hour. And when I heard about Jase—I was like, 'I have it all planned; I'm just changing the day.' I'm sorry I scared you, though. I was trying *not* to scare you, but that last part was so rushed. Not my best work."

As dashed-together escape plans replete with clues go, I thought it was pretty impressive. But mostly I was surprised that she'd wanted me involved in her original plan, too. "Maybe you'll fill me in," I said, managing a smile. "I have, you know, been wondering. What was planned and what wasn't? What meant what?

Why the clues went to me, why you left, that kind of thing."

"Um, okay. Okay. For that story, we have to start with a different story." She gets up and I follow her footsteps as she nimbly avoids the rotting patches of floor. Returning to her office, she digs into the backpack and pulls out the black moleskin notebook. She sits down on the floor, her legs crossed, and pats a patch of wood next to her. I sit. She taps the closed book. "So this," she says, "this goes back a long way. When I was in, like, fourth grade, I started writing a story in this notebook. It was kind of a detective story."

I think that if I grab this book from her, I can use it as blackmail. I can use it to get her back to Orlando, and she can get a summer job and live in an apartment till college starts, and at least we'll have the summer. But I just listen.

"I mean, I don't like to brag, but this is an unusually brilliant piece of literature. Just kidding. It's the retarded wish-fulfilling magical-thinking ramblings of ten-year-old me. It stars this girl, named Margo Spiegelman, who is just like ten-year-old me in every way except her parents are nice and rich and buy her anything she wants. Margo has a crush on this boy named Quentin, who is just like you in every way except all fearless and heroic and willing to die to protect me and everything. Also, it stars Myrna Mountweazel, who is exactly like Myrna Mountweazel except with magical powers. Like, for example, in the story, anyone who pets Myrna Mountweazel finds it impossible to tell a lie for ten minutes. Also, she can talk. Of course she can talk. Has a ten-year-old ever written a book about a dog that *can't* talk?"

I laugh, but I'm still thinking about ten-year-old Margo having a crush on ten-year-old me.

"So, in the story," she continues, "Quentin and Margo and

Myrna Mountweazel are investigating the death of Robert Joyner, whose death is exactly like his real-life death except instead of having obviously shot himself in the face, *someone else* shot him in the face. And the story is about us finding out who did it."

"Who did it?"

She laughs. "You want me to spoil the entire story for you?"

"Well," I say, "I'd rather read it." She pulls open the book and shows me a page. The writing is indecipherable, not because Margo's handwriting is bad, but because on top of the horizontal lines of text, writing also goes vertically down the page. "I write crosshatch," she says. "Very hard for non-Margo readers to decode. So, okay, I'm going to spoil the story for you, but first you have to promise not to get mad."

"Promise," I say.

"It turns out that the crime was committed by Robert Joyner's alcoholic ex-wife's sister's brother, who was insane because he'd been possessed by the spirit of an evil ancient Egyptian house cat. Like I said, really top-notch storytelling. But anyway, in the story, you and me and Myrna Mountweazel go and confront the killer, and he tries to shoot me, but you jump in front of the bullet, and you die very heroically in my arms."

I laugh. "Great. This story was all promising with the beautiful girl who has a crush on me and the mystery and the intrigue, and then I get whacked."

"Well, yeah." She smiles. "But I had to kill you, because the only other possible ending was us doing it, which I wasn't really emotionally ready to write about at ten."

"Fair enough," I say. "But in the revision, I want to get some action."

"After you get shot up by the bad guy, maybe. A kiss before dying."

"How kind of you." I could stand up and go to her and kiss her. I could. But there is still too much to be ruined.

"So anyway, I finished this story in fifth grade. A few years later, I decide I'm going to run away to Mississippi. And then I write all my plans for this epic event into this notebook on top of the old story, and then I finally do it—take Mom's car and put a thousand miles on it and leave these clues in the soup. I didn't even *like* the road trip, really—it was incredibly lonely—but I love having done it, right? So I start crosshatching more schemes—pranks and ideas for matching up certain girls with certain guys and huge TPing campaigns and more secret road trips and whatever else. The notebook is half full by the start of junior year, and that's when I decide that I'm going to do one more thing, one big thing, and then leave."

She's about to start talking again, but I have to stop her. "I guess I'm wondering if it was the place or the people. Like, what if the people around you had been different?"

"How can you separate those things, though? The people are the place is the people. And anyway, I didn't think there *was* anybody else to be friends with. I thought everyone was either scared, like you, or oblivious, like Lacey. And th—"

"I'm not as scared as you think," I say. Which is true. I only realize it's true after saying it. But still.

"I'm *getting* to that," she says, almost whiningly. "So when I'm a freshman, Gus takes me to the Osprey—" I tilt my head, confused. "The minimall. And I start going there by myself all the time, just hanging out and writing plans. And by last year, all the plans started to be about this last escape. And I don't know if it's because I was reading my old story as I went, but I put you into the plans early on. The idea was that we were going to do all these things together—like break into SeaWorld, that was in the original plan—and I was going to push you toward being a badass. This one night would, like, liberate you. And then I could disappear and you'd always remember me for that.

"So this plan eventually gets like seventy pages long, and then it's about to happen, and the plan has come together really well. But then I find out about Jase, and I just decide to leave. Immediately. I don't need to graduate. What's the point of graduating? But first I have to tie up loose ends. So all that day in school I have my notebook out, and I'm trying like crazy to adapt the plan to Becca and Jase and Lacey and everyone who wasn't a friend to me like I thought they were, trying to come up with ideas for letting everyone know just how pissed off I am before I ditch them forever.

"But I still wanted to do it with you; I still liked that idea of maybe being able to create in you at least an echo of the kick-ass hero of my little-kid story.

"And then you surprise me," she says. "You had been a paper boy to me all these years—two dimensions as a character on the page and two different, but still flat, dimensions as a person. But that night you turned out to be real. And it ends up being so odd and fun and magical that I go back to my room in the morning and I just *miss* you. I want to come over and hang out and talk, but I've already decided to leave, so I have to leave. And then at the last second, I have this idea to will you the Osprey. To leave it for you so that it can help you make even further progress in the field of not-being-such-a-scaredy-cat.

"So, yeah. That's it. I come up with something real quick. Tape the Woody poster to the back of the blinds, circle the song on the record, highlight those two lines from "Song of Myself" in a different color than I'd highlighted stuff when I was actually reading it. Then after you leave for school, I climb in through your window and put the scrap of newspaper in your door. Then I go to the Osprey that morning, partly because I just don't feel ready to leave yet, and partly because I want to clean the place up for you. I mean, the thing is, I *didn't* want you to worry. That's why I painted over the graffiti; I didn't know you'd be able to see through it. I ripped off the pages of the desk calendar I'd been using, and I took down the map, too, which I'd had up there ever since I saw that it contained Agloe. Then because I'm tired and don't have anyplace to go, I sleep there. I end up there for two nights, actually, just trying to get my courage up, I guess. And also, I don't know, I thought maybe you would find it really quickly somehow. Then I go. Took two days to get here. I've been here since."

She seemed finished, but I had one more question. "And why here of all places?"

"A paper town for a paper girl," she says. "I read about Agloe in this book of 'amazing facts' when I was ten or eleven. And I never stopped thinking about it. The truth is that whenever I went up to the top of the SunTrust Building—including that last time with you—I didn't really look down and think about how everything was made of paper. I looked down and thought about how *I* was made of paper. I was the flimsy-foldable person, not everyone else. And here's the thing about it. People love the idea of a paper girl. They always have. And the worst thing is that *I* loved it, too. I cultivated it, you know?

"Because it's kind of great, being an idea that everybody likes. But I could never be the idea to myself, not all the way. And Agloe is a place where a paper creation became real. A dot on the map became a real place, more real than the people who created the dot could ever have imagined. I thought maybe the paper cutout of a girl could start becoming real here also. And it seemed like a way to tell that paper girl who cared about popularity and clothes and everything else: 'You are going to the paper towns. And you are *never* coming back.'"

"That graffiti," I said. "God, Margo, I walked through so many of those abandoned subdivisions looking for your body. I really thought—I really thought you were dead."

She gets up and searches around her backpack for a moment, and then reaches over and grabs *The Bell Jar,* and reads to me. "'But when it came right down to it, the skin of my wrist looked so white and defenseless that I couldn't do it. It was as if what I wanted to kill wasn't in that skin or the thin blue pulse that jumped under my thumb, but somewhere else, deeper, more secret, and a whole lot harder to get at.'" She sits back down next to me, close, facing me, the fabric of our jeans touching without our knees actually touching. Margo says, "I know what she's talking about. The something deeper and more secret. It's like cracks inside of you. Like there are these fault lines where things don't meet up right."

"I like that," I say. "Or it's like cracks in the hull of a ship."

"Right, right."

"Brings you down eventually."

"Exactly," she says. We're talking back and forth so fast now.

"I can't believe you didn't want me to find you."

"Sorry. If it makes you feel any better, I'm impressed. Also, it's nice to have you here. You're a good traveling companion."

"Is that a proposal?" I ask.

"Maybe." She smiles.

My heart has been fluttering around my chest for so long now that this variety of intoxication almost seems sustainable—but only almost. "Margo, if you just come home for the summer—my parents said you can live with us, or you can get a job and an apartment for the summer, and then school will start, and you'll never have to live with your parents again."

"It's not just them. I'd get sucked right back in," she says, "and I'd never get out. It's not just the gossip and the parties and all that crap, but the whole allure of a life rightly lived—college and job and husband and babies and all that bullshit."

The thing is that I *do* believe in college, and jobs, and maybe even babies one day. I believe in the future. Maybe it's a character flaw, but for me it is a congenital one. "But college expands your opportunities," I say finally. "It doesn't limit them."

She smirks. "Thank you, College Counselor Jacobsen," she says, and then changes the subject. "I kept thinking about you inside the Osprey. Whether you would get used to it. Stop worrying about the rats."

"I did," I say. "I started to like it there. I spent prom night there, actually."

She smiles. "Awesome. I imagined you would like it eventually. It never got boring in the Osprey, but that was because I had to go home at some point. When I got here, I did get bored. There's nothing to do; I've read so much since I got here. I got more and more nervous here, too, not knowing anybody. And I kept waiting for that loneliness and nervousness to make me want to go back. But it never did. It's the one thing I can't do, Q."

I nod. I understand this. I imagine it is hard to go back once you've felt the continents in your palm. But I still try one more time. "But what about after the summer? What about college? What about the rest of your life?"

She shrugged. "What about it?"

"Aren't you worried about, like, *forever*?"

"Forever is composed of nows," she says. I have nothing to say to that; I am just chewing through it when Margo says, "Emily Dickinson. Like I said, I'm doing a lot of reading."

I think the future deserves our faith. But it is hard to argue with Emily Dickinson. Margo stands up, slings her backpack over one shoulder, and reaches her hand down for me. "Let's take a walk." As we're walking outside, Margo asks for my phone. She punches in a number, and I start to walk away to let her talk, but she grabs my forearm and keeps me with her. So I walk beside her out into the field as she talks to her parents.

"Hey, it's Margo. . . . I'm in Agloe, New York, with Quentin. . . . Uh. . . . well, no, Mom, I'm just trying to think of a way to answer your question honestly. . . . Mom, come on. . . . I don't know, Mom . . . I decided to move to a fictitious place. That's what happened. . . . Yeah, well, I don't think I'm headed that way, regardless. . . . Can I talk to Ruthie? . . . Hey, buddy. . . . Yeah, well, I loved you first. . . . Yeah, I'm sorry. It was a mistake. I thought—I don't know what I thought, Ruthie, but anyway it was a mistake and I'll call now. I may not call Mom, but I'll call you. . . . Wednesdays? . . . You're busy on Wednesdays. Hmm. Okay. What's a good day for you? . . . Tuesday it is. . . . Yeah, every Tuesday. . . . Yeah, including this Tuesday." Margo closes her eyes tight, her teeth clenched. "Okay, Ruthers, can you put

Mom back on? . . . I love you, Mom. I'll be okay. I swear. . . . Yeah, okay, you, too. Bye."

She stops walking and closes the phone but holds it a minute. I can see her fingertips pinkening with the tightness of her grip, and then she drops it onto the ground. Her scream is short but deafening, and in its wake I am aware for the first time of Agloe's abject silence. "It's like she thinks my job is to please her, and that should be my dearest wish, and when I don't please her—I get shut out. She changed the locks. That's the first thing she said. Jesus."

"Sorry," I say, pushing aside some knee-high yellow-green grass to pick up the phone. "Nice to talk to Ruthie, though?"

"Yeah, she's pretty adorable. I kind of hate myself for—you know—not talking to her."

"Yeah," I say. She shoves me playfully.

"You're supposed to make me feel better, not worse!" she says. "That's your whole gig!"

"I didn't realize my job was to please you, Mrs. Spiegelman."

She laughs. "Ooh, the Mom comparison. What a burn. But fair enough. So how have you been? If Ben is dating Lacey, surely you are having nightly orgies with dozens of cheerleaders."

We walk slowly through the uneven dirt of this field. It doesn't look big, but as we walk, I realize that we do not seem to be getting closer to the stand of trees in the distance. I tell her about leaving graduation, about the miraculous spinning of the Dreidel. I tell her about prom, Lacey's fight with Becca, and my night in the Osprey. "That was the night I really knew you'd definitely been there," I tell her. "That blanket still smelled like you."

And when I say that her hand brushes up against mine, and I just grab hers because it feels like there is less to ruin now. She looks at me. "I had to leave. I didn't have to scare you and that was stupid and I should have done a better job leaving, but I did have to leave. Do you see that yet?"

"Yeah," I say, "but I think you can come back now. I really do."

"No, you don't," she answers, and she's right. She can see it in my face—I understand now that I can't be her and she can't be me. Maybe Whitman had a gift I don't have. But as for me: I must ask the wounded man where he is hurt, because I cannot become the wounded man. The only wounded man I can be is me.

I stomp down some grass and sit. She lies down next to me, her backpack a pillow. I lay back, too. She digs a couple of books out of her backpack and hands them to me so I can have a pillow, too. *Selected Poems of Emily Dickinson* and *Leaves of Grass*. "I had two copies," she says, smiling.

"It's a hell of a good poem," I tell her. "You couldn't have picked a better one."

"Really, it was an impulse decision that morning. I remembered the bit about the doors and thought that was perfect. But then when I got here I reread it. I hadn't read it since sophomore English, and yeah, I liked it. I tried to read a bunch of poetry. I was trying to figure out—like, what was it that surprised me about you that night? And for a long time I thought it was when you quoted T. S. Eliot."

"But it wasn't," I say. "You were surprised by the size of my biceps and my graceful window-exiting."

She smirks. "Shut up and let me compliment you, dillhole. It wasn't the poetry or your biceps. What surprised me was that, in spite of your anxiety attacks and everything, you *were* like the

Quentin in my story. I mean, I've been crosshatching over that story for years now, and whenever I write over it, I also read that page, and I would always laugh, like—don't get offended, but, like, 'God I can't believe I used to think *Quentin Jacobsen* was like a superhot, superloyal defender of justice.' But then—you know—you kind of *were*."

I could turn on my side, and she might turn on her side, too. And then we could kiss. But what's the point of kissing her now, anyway? It won't go anywhere. We are both staring at the cloudless sky. "Nothing ever happens like you imagine it will," she says.

The sky is like a monochromatic contemporary painting, drawing me in with its illusion of depth, pulling me up. "Yeah, that's true," I say. But then after I think about it for a second, I add, "But then again, if you don't imagine, nothing ever happens at all." Imagining isn't perfect. You can't get all the way inside someone else. I could never have imagined Margo's anger at being found, or the story she was writing over. But imagining being someone else, or the world being something else, is the only way in. It is the machine that kills fascists.

She turns over toward me and puts her head onto my shoulder, and we lie there, as I long ago imagined lying on the grass at SeaWorld. It has taken us thousands of miles and many days, but here we are: her head on my shoulder, her breath on my neck, the fatigue thick inside both of us. We are now as I wished we could be then.

When I wake up, the dying light of the day makes everything seem to matter, from the yellowing sky to the stalks of grass above my head, waving in slow motion like a beauty queen. I roll onto my side and see Margo Roth Spiegelman on her hands and knees a few feet from me, the jeans tight against her legs. It takes me a moment to realize that she is digging. I crawl over to her and start to dig beside her, the dirt beneath the grass dry as dust in my fingers. She smiles at me. My heart beats at the speed of sound.

"What are we digging to?" I ask her.

"That's not the right question," she says. "The question is, Who are we digging for?"

"Okay, then. Who are we digging for?"

"We are digging graves for Little Margo and Little Quentin and puppy Myrna Mountweazel and poor dead Robert Joyner," she says.

"I can get behind those burials, I think," I say. The dirt is clumpy and dry, drilled through with the paths of insects like an abandoned ant farm. We dig our bare hands into the ground over and over again, each fistful of earth accompanied by a little cloud of dust. We dig the hole wide and deep. This grave must be proper. Soon I'm reaching in as deep as my elbows. The sleeve of my shirt gets dusty when I wipe the sweat from my cheek. Margo's cheeks are reddening. I can smell her, and she smells like that night right before we jumped into the moat at SeaWorld.

"I never really thought of him as a real person," she says.

When she speaks, I take the opportunity to take a break, and sit back on my haunches. "Who, Robert Joyner?"

She keeps digging. "Yeah. I mean, he was something that happened to *me*, you know? But before he was this minor figure in the drama of my life, he was—you know, the central figure in the drama of his own life."

I have never really thought of him as a person, either. A guy who played in the dirt like me. A guy who fell in love like me. A guy whose strings were broken, who didn't feel the root of his leaf of grass connected to the field, a guy who was cracked. Like me.

"Yeah," I say after a while as I return to digging. "He was always just a body to me."

"I wish we could have done something," she says. "I wish we could have proven how heroic we were."

"Yeah," I say. "It would have been nice to tell him that, whatever it was, that it didn't have to be the end of the world."

"Yeah, although in the end *something* kills you."

I shrug. "Yeah, I know. I'm not saying that everything is survivable. Just that everything except the last thing is." I dig my hand in again, the dirt here so much blacker than back home. I toss a handful into the pile behind us, and sit back. I feel on the edge of an idea, and I try to talk my way into it. I have never spoken this many words in a row to Margo in our long and storied relationship, but here it is, my last play for her.

"When I've thought about him dying—which admittedly isn't that much—I always thought of it like you said, that all the strings inside him broke. But there are a thousand ways to look at it: maybe the strings break, or maybe our ships sink, or maybe we're grass—our roots so interdependent that no one is dead as long as someone is still alive. We don't suffer from a shortage of metaphors, is what I mean. But you have to be careful which metaphor you choose, because it matters. If you choose the strings, then you're imagining a world in which you can become irreparably broken. If you choose the grass, you're saying that we are all infinitely interconnected, that we can use these root systems not only to understand one another but to become one another. The metaphors have implications. Do you know what I mean?"

She nods.

"I like the strings. I always have. Because that's how it *feels*. But the strings make pain seem more fatal than it is, I think. We're not as frail as the strings would make us believe. And I like the grass, too. The grass got me to you, helped me to imagine you as an actual person. But we're not different sprouts from the same plant. I can't be you. You can't be me. You can imagine another well—but never quite perfectly, you know?

"Maybe it's more like you said before, all of us being cracked open. Like, each of us starts out as a watertight vessel. And these things happen—these people leave us, or don't love us, or don't get us, or we don't get them, and we lose and fail and hurt one another. And the vessel starts to crack open in places. And I mean, yeah, once the vessel cracks open, the end becomes inevitable. Once it starts to rain inside the Osprey, it will never be remodeled. But there is all this time between when the cracks start to open up and when we finally fall apart. And it's only in that time that we can see one another, because we see out of ourselves through our cracks and into others through theirs. When did we see each other face-to-face? Not until you saw into my cracks and I saw into yours. Before that, we were just looking at ideas of each other, like looking at your window shade but never seeing inside. But once the vessel cracks, the light can get in. The light can get out."

She raises her fingers to her lips, as if concentrating, or as if hiding her mouth from me, or as if to feel the words she speaks. "You're pretty something," she says finally. She stares at me, my eyes and her eyes and nothing between them. I have nothing to gain from kissing her. But I am no longer looking to gain anything. "There's something I have to do," I say, and she nods very slightly, as if she knows the something, and I kiss her.

It ends quite a while later when she says, "You can come to New York. It will be fun. It will be like kissing."

And I say, "Kissing is pretty something."

And she says, "You're saying no."

And I say, "Margo, I have a whole life there, and I'm not you, and I—" But I can't say anything because she kisses me again, and it's in the moment that she kisses me that I know without question that we're headed in different directions. She stands up and walks over to where we were sleeping, to her backpack. She pulls out the moleskin notebook, walks back to the grave, and places it in the ground.

"I'll miss you," she whispers, and I don't know if she's talking to me or to the notebook. Nor do I know to whom I'm talking when I say, "As will I."

"Godspeed, Robert Joyner," I say, and drop a handful of dirt onto the notebook.

"Godspeed, young and heroic Quentin Jacobsen," she says, tossing in dirt of her own.

Another handful as I say, "Godspeed, fearless Orlandoan Margo Roth Spiegelman."

And another as she says, "Godspeed, magical puppy Myrna Mountweazel." We shove the dirt over the book, tamping down the disturbed soil. The grass will grow back soon enough. It will be for us the beautiful uncut hair of graves.

We hold hands rough with dirt as we walk back to the Agloe General Store. I help Margo carry her belongings—an armful of clothes, her toiletries, and the desk chair—to her car. The preciousness of the moment, which should make it easier to talk, makes it harder.

We're standing outside in the parking lot of a single-story motel when the good-byes become unavoidable. "I'm gonna get a cell, and I'll call you," she says. "And e-mail. And post mysterious statements on Omnictionary's Paper Towns talk page."

I smile. "I'll e-mail you when we get home," I say, "and I expect a response."

"You have my word. And I'll see you. We're not done seeing each other."

"At the end of the summer, maybe, I can meet you somewhere before school," I say.

"Yeah," she says. "Yeah, that's a good idea." I smile and nod. She turns away, and I am wondering if she means any of it when I see her shoulders collapse. She is crying.

"I'll see you then. And I'll write in the meantime," I say.

"Yes," she says without turning around, her voice thick. "I'll write you, too."

It is saying these things that keeps us from falling apart. And maybe by imagining these futures we can make them real, and maybe not, but either way we must imagine them. The light rushes out and floods in.

I stand in this parking lot, realizing that I've never been this far from home, and here is this girl I love and cannot follow. I hope this is the hero's errand, because not following her is the hardest thing I've ever done.

I keep thinking she will get into the car, but she doesn't, and she finally turns around to me and I see her soaked eyes. The physical space between us evaporates. We play the broken strings of our instruments one last time.

I feel her hands on my back. And it is dark as I kiss her, but I have my eyes open and so does Margo. She is close enough to me that I can see her, because even now there is the outward sign of the invisible light, even at night in this parking lot on the outskirts of Agloe. After we kiss, our foreheads touch as we stare at each other. Yes, I can see her almost perfectly in this cracked darkness.

AUTHOR'S NOTE

I learned about paper towns by coming across one during a road trip my junior year of college. My traveling companion and I kept driving up and down the same desolate stretch of highway in South Dakota, searching for this town the map promised existed—as I recall, the town was called Holen. Finally, we pulled into a driveway and knocked on a door. The friendly woman who answered had been asked the question before. She explained that the town we were seeking existed only on the map.

The story of Agloe, New York—as outlined in this book—is mostly true. Agloe began as a paper town created to protect against copyright infringement. But then people with those old Esso maps kept looking for it, and so someone built a store, making Agloe real. The business of cartography has changed a lot since Otto G. Lindberg and Ernest Alpers invented Agloe. But many mapmakers still include paper towns as copyright traps, as my bewildering experience in South Dakota attests.

The store that was Agloe no longer stands. But I believe that if we were to put it back on our maps, someone would eventually rebuild it.

ACKNOWLEDGMENTS

I would like to thank:

—My parents, Sydney and Mike Green. I never thought I would say this, but: thank you for raising me in Florida.

—My brother and favorite collaborator, Hank Green.

—My mentor, Ilene Cooper.

—Everyone at Dutton, but particularly my incomparable editor, Julie Strauss-Gabel, Lisa Yoskowitz, Sarah Shumway, Stephanie Owens Lurie, Christian Fuenfhausen, Rosanne Lauer, Irene Vandervoort, and Steve Meltzer.

—My delightfully tenacious agent, Jodi Reamer.

—The Nerdfighters, who have taught me so much about the meaning of awesome.

—My writing partners Emily Jenkins, Scott Westerfeld, Justine Larbalestier, and Maureen Johnson.

—Two particularly helpful books I read about disappearance while researching *Paper Towns*: William Dear's *The Dungeon Master* and Jon Krakauer's *Into the Wild*. I am also grateful to Cecil Adams, the big brain behind "The Straight Dope," whose short article on copyright traps is—so far as I know—the definitive resource on the subject.

—My grandparents: Henry and Billie Grace Goodrich, and William and Jo Green.

—Emily Johnson, whose readings of this book were invaluable; Joellen Hosler, the best therapist a writer could ask for; cousins-in-law Blake and Phyllis Johnson; Brian Lipson and Lis Rowinski at Endeavor; Katie Else; Emily Blejwas, who joined me on that trip to the paper town; Levin O'Connor, who taught me most of what I know about funny; Tobin Anderson and Sean, who took me urban exploring in Detroit; school librarian Susan Hunt and all those who risk their jobs to stand against censorship; Shannon James; Markus Zusak; John Mauldin and my wonderful parents-in-law, Connie and Marshall Urist.

—Sarah Urist Green, my first reader and first editor and best friend and favorite teammate.

DISCUSSION QUESTIONS

- When Margo and Quentin are nine, they make a horrible discovery and respond in very different ways. Quentin says, "As I took those two steps back, Margo took two equally small and quiet steps forward." Do these descriptions still apply to the characters when they reach high school? When the story ends?

- Describe Q's best friends. Where do they fit into the social strata of Winter Park High? If you had to choose one of these characters as your best friend who would you pick? Why?

- How does Quentin struggle at times with Ben? How does Q learn to accept Ben for who he is? How does this relate to Q's changing understanding of Margo?

- Why do you think Margo picks Q as her accomplice?

- Do you think the characters Margo targets for revenge get what they deserve? Does Lacey deserve to be included?

- When Margo disappears after her outing with Q, it's not the first time she seems to have vanished for a long period. What makes her disappearance after her night with Q different from the others?

- When Margo disappears, she's always been known to leave "a bit of a bread crumb trail." What clues does Margo leave for Quentin? How are these different from past clues?

- Do you think Margo wants to be found? Do you think Margo wants to be found by Q?

- Q visits several abandoned subdivisions on his quest to find Margo. How are they different? How might these differences parallel the evolution of Q's search?

- How does Q's visit to the abandoned minimall shift the story? What does it reveal about Margo? About Q?

- How does the road trip to find Margo mirror the adventure she and Q had in the beginning of the book? How is it different?

- How does Margo's reaction to being found, and seeing her friends, make you feel? Do you believe that she didn't want Q to come after her?

- Why does Q decide to turn down Margo's invitation at the end of the book? Do you agree with his decision?

- The definition of a "paper town" changes many times in the book. How does its meaning evolve? How does it relate to the mystery? To the themes of the book?

- With which character's version of the "real" Margo do you most agree?

- Do you think that Margo meant to give her friends a false impression of her true self?

- Q's parents describe people as "mirrors" and "windows." What does this mean? Do you agree with this metaphor?

- Q comes to this conclusion: "Margo was not a miracle. She was not an adventure. She was not a fine and precious thing. She was a girl." Discuss.

- The book is divided into three sections: The Strings; The Grass; and The Vessel. What is the connection between the sections/titles and the content within those sections? How do the sections/titles connect to the themes of the book?

- Which philosophy of life do you most agree with: Margo's Strings? Whitman's Grass? Or Q's Cracked Vessel? Why?

- At different times, both Margo and Q use lines of poetry without considering the context of the whole poem. How do you think this changes the meaning?

- Q is reading *Moby Dick* in English class. How does it appear elsewhere in Q's story?

- Q's interpretation and understanding of Walt Whitman's "Song of Myself" changes as the mystery progresses. What are the different phases of his understanding? Do you agree with his final conclusion about the poem's meaning?

- The book opens with two epigraphs, a poem and a song. Why do you think the author chose these? Why do you think he chose to use them together?

- Discuss the last line of the book, how it relates to the rest of the story, and what it ultimately says about Margo and Q's relationship.

- How does the last line of the book relate to the rest of the story? What does it say about Margo and Q's relationship?

ONE

AT THE TIME I FIRST REALIZED I might be fictional, my weekdays were spent at a publicly funded institution on the north side of Indianapolis called White River High School, where I was required to eat lunch at a particular time—between 12:37 P.M. and 1:14 P.M.—by forces so much larger than myself that I couldn't even begin to identify them. If those forces had given me a different lunch period, or if the tablemates who helped author my fate had chosen a different topic of conversation that September day, I would've met a different end—or at least a different middle. But I was beginning to learn that your life is a story told about you, not one that you tell.

Of course, you pretend to be the author. You have to. You

think, *I now choose to go to lunch*, when that monotone beep rings from on high at 12:37. But really, the bell decides. You think you're the painter, but you're the canvas.

Hundreds of voices were shouting over one another in the cafeteria, so that the conversation became mere sound, the rushing of a river over rocks. And as I sat beneath fluorescent cylinders spewing aggressively artificial light, I thought about how we all believed ourselves to be the hero of some personal epic, when in fact we were basically identical organisms colonizing a vast and windowless room that smelled of Lysol and lard.

I was eating a peanut butter and honey sandwich and drinking a Dr Pepper. To be honest, I find the whole process of masticating plants and animals and then shoving them down my esophagus kind of disgusting, so I was trying not to think about the fact that I was eating, which is a form of thinking about it.

Across the table from me, Mychal Turner was scribbling in a yellow-paper notebook. Our lunch table was like a long-running play on Broadway: The cast changed over the years, but the roles never did. Mychal was The Artsy One. He was talking with Daisy Ramirez, who'd played the role of my Best and Most Fearless Friend since elementary school, but I couldn't follow their conversation over the noise of all the others.

What was my part in this play? The Sidekick. I was

Daisy's Friend, or Ms. Holmes's Daughter. I was somebody's something.

I felt my stomach begin to work on the sandwich, and even over everybody's talking, I could *hear* it digesting, all the bacteria chewing the slime of peanut butter—the students inside of me eating at my internal cafeteria. A shiver convulsed through me.

"Didn't you go to camp with him?" Daisy asked me.

"With who?"

"Davis Pickett," she said.

"Yeah," I said. "Why?"

"Aren't you listening?" Daisy asked. *I am listening*, I thought, *to the cacophony of my digestive tract*. Of course I'd long known that I was playing host to a massive collection of parasitic organisms, but I didn't much like being reminded of it. By cell count, humans are approximately 50 percent microbial, meaning that about half of the cells that make you up are not yours at all. There are something like a thousand times more microbes living in my particular biome than there are human beings on earth, and it often seems like I can *feel* them living and breeding and dying in and on me. I wiped my sweaty palms on my jeans and tried to control my breathing. Admittedly, I have some anxiety problems, but I would argue it isn't irrational to be concerned about the fact that you are a skin-encased bacterial colony.

Mychal said, "His dad was about to be arrested for bribery

or something, but the night before the raid he disappeared. There's a hundred-thousand-dollar reward out for him."

"And you know his kid," Daisy said.

"*Knew* him," I answered.

I watched Daisy attack her school-provided rectangular pizza and green beans with a fork. She kept glancing up at me, her eyes widening as if to say, *Well?* I could tell she wanted me to ask her about something, but I couldn't tell what, because my stomach wouldn't shut up, which was forcing me deep inside a worry that I'd somehow contracted a parasitic infection.

I could half hear Mychal telling Daisy about his new art project, in which he was using Photoshop to average the faces of a hundred people named Mychal, and the average of their faces would be this new, one-hundred-and-first Mychal, which was an interesting idea, and I wanted to listen, but the cafeteria was so loud, and I couldn't stop wondering whether there was something wrong with the microbial balance of power inside me.

Excessive abdominal noise is an uncommon, but not unprecedented, presenting symptom of infection with the bacteria *Clostridium difficile*, which can be fatal. I pulled out my phone and searched "human microbiome" to reread Wikipedia's introduction to the trillions of microorganisms currently inside me. I clicked over to the article about *C. diff*, scrolling to the part about how most *C. diff* infections occur in hospitals. I scrolled down farther to a list of symptoms, none of which I had, except for the excessive abdominal noises, although I knew from previous searches that the Cleveland Clinic had reported the case of one person who'd died of *C. diff* after presenting at the hospital with only abdominal pain and fever. I reminded myself that I didn't have a fever, and my self replied: *You don't have a fever YET.*

At the cafeteria, where a shrinking slice of my consciousness still resided, Daisy was telling Mychal that his averaging project shouldn't be about people named Mychal but about imprisoned men who'd later been exonerated. "It'll be easier, anyway," she said, "because they all have mug shots taken from the same angle, and then it's not just about names but about race and class and mass incarceration," and Mychal was like, "You're a genius, Daisy," and she said, "You sound surprised," and meanwhile I was thinking that if half the cells inside of you are not you, doesn't that challenge the whole notion of *me* as a singular pronoun, let alone as the author of my fate? And I fell pretty far down that recursive wormhole until it transported me completely out of the White River High School cafeteria into some non-sensorial place only properly crazy people get to visit.

Ever since I was little, I've pressed my right thumbnail into the finger pad of my middle finger, and so now there's this weird callus over my fingerprint. After so many years of doing this, I can open up a crack in the skin really easily, so I cover it up with a Band-Aid to try to prevent infection. But sometimes I get worried that there already is an infection, and so I need to drain it, and the only way to do that is to reopen the wound and press out any blood that will come. Once I start thinking about splitting the skin apart, I literally cannot not do it. I apologize for the double negative, but it's a real double negative of a situation, a bind from which negating the negation is truly the only escape. So anyway, I started to want to feel my thumbnail biting into the skin of my finger pad, and I knew that resistance was more or less futile, so beneath the cafeteria table, I slipped the Band-Aid off my finger and dug my thumbnail into the callused skin until I felt the crack open.

"Holmesy," Daisy said. I looked up at her. "We're almost through lunch and you haven't even mentioned my hair." She shook out her hair, with so-red-they-were-pink highlights. Right. She'd dyed her hair.

I swum up out of the depths and said, "It's bold."

"I know, right? It says, 'Ladies and gentlemen and also people who do not identify as ladies or gentlemen, Daisy Ramirez won't break her promises, but she will break your heart.'" Daisy's self-proclaimed life motto was "Break Hearts, Not Promises." She kept threatening to get it tattooed on her ankle when she turned eighteen. Daisy turned back to Mychal, and I to my thoughts. The stomach grumbling had grown, if anything, louder. I felt like I might vomit. For someone who actively dislikes bodily fluids, I throw up quite a lot.

"Holmesy, you okay?" Daisy asked. I nodded. Sometimes I wondered why she liked me, or at least tolerated me. Why any of them did. Even I found myself annoying.

I could feel sweat sprouting from my forehead, and once I begin to sweat, it's impossible to stop. I'll keep sweating for hours, and not just my face or my armpits. My neck sweats. My boobs sweat. My calves sweat. Maybe I did have a fever.

Beneath the table, I slid the old Band-Aid into my pocket and, without looking, pulled out a new one, unwrapped it, and then glanced down to apply it to my finger. All the while, I was breathing in through my nose and out through my mouth, in the manner advised by Dr. Karen Singh, exhaling at a pace "that would make a candle flicker but not go out. Imagine that candle, Aza, flickering from your breath but still there, always there." So I tried that, but the thought spiral kept tightening anyway. I could hear Dr. Singh saying I shouldn't get out my phone, that I mustn't look up the same questions over and over, but I got it out anyway, and reread the "Human Microbiota" Wikipedia article.

The thing about a spiral is, if you follow it inward, it never actually ends. It just keeps tightening, infinitely.

I sealed the Ziploc bag around the last quarter of my sandwich, got up, and tossed it into an overfilled trash can. I heard a voice from behind me. "How concerned should I be that you haven't said more than two words in a row all day?"

"Thought spiral," I mumbled in reply. Daisy had known me since we were six, long enough to get it.

"I figured. Sorry, man. Let's hang out today."

This girl Molly walked up to us, smiling, and said, "Uh, Daisy, just FYI, your Kool-Aid dye job is staining your shirt."

Daisy looked down at her shoulders, and indeed, her striped top had turned pink in spots. She flinched for a second, then straightened her spine. "Yeah, it's part of the look, Molly. Stained shirts are huge in Paris right now." She turned away from Molly and said, "Right, so we'll go to your house and watch *Star Wars: Rebels.*" Daisy was really into Star Wars—and not just the movies, but also the books and the animated shows and the kids' show where they're all made out of Lego. Like, she wrote fan fiction about Chewbacca's love life. "And we will improve your mood until you are able to say three or even four words in a row; sound good?"

"Sounds good."

"And then you can take me to work. Sorry, but I need a ride."

"Okay." I wanted to say more, but the thoughts kept coming, unbidden and unwanted. If I'd been the author, I would've stopped thinking about my microbiome. I would've told Daisy how much I liked her idea for Mychal's art project, and I would've told her that I did remember Davis Pickett, that I remembered being eleven and carrying a vague but constant fear. I would've told her that I remembered once at camp lying next to Davis on the edge of a dock, our legs dangling over, our backs against the rough-hewn planks of wood, staring together up at a cloudless summer sky. I would've told her that Davis and I never talked much, or even looked at each other, but it didn't matter, because we were looking at the same sky together, which is maybe more intimate than eye contact anyway. Anybody can look at you. It's quite rare to find someone who sees the same world you see.

MARINA WATERS

JOHN GREEN is the author of *Looking for Alaska*; *An Abundance of Katherines*; *Paper Towns*; *Will Grayson, Will Grayson* (with David Levithan); *The Fault in Our Stars*; and *Turtles All the Way Down*. His books have received many accolades, including a Printz Medal, a Printz Honor, and an Edgar Award. John has twice been a finalist for the LA Times Book Prize and was selected by *TIME* magazine as one of the 100 Most Influential People in the World. With his brother, Hank, John has co-created many online video projects, including Vlogbrothers and the educational channel Crash Course. He lives with his family in Indianapolis, Indiana.

You can visit John online at **johngreenbooks.com**

Looking for Alaska

WINNER OF THE MICHAEL L. PRINTZ AWARD
A LOS ANGELES TIMES BOOK PRIZE FINALIST • A *NEW YORK TIMES* BESTSELLER • A *USA TODAY* BESTSELLER • A PBS GREAT AMERICAN READ SELECTION OF AMERICA'S 100 MOST-LOVED NOVELS • NPR'S TOP TEN BEST-EVER TEEN NOVELS • *TIME* MAGAZINE'S 100 BEST YOUNG ADULT NOVELS OF ALL TIME

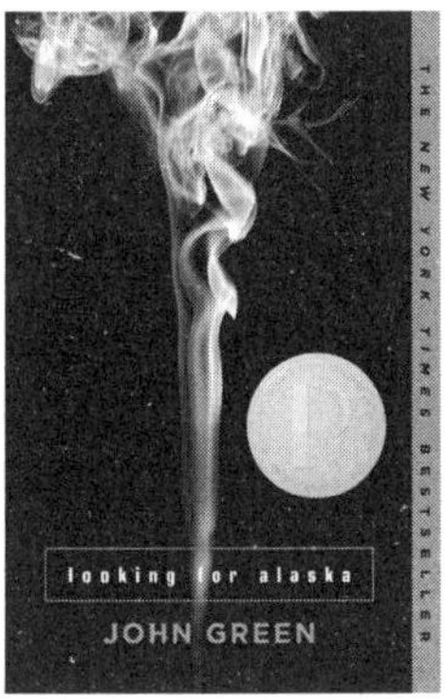

Miles Halter is fascinated by famous last words—and tired of his safe life at home. He leaves for boarding school to seek what the dying poet François Rabelais called the "Great Perhaps." Much awaits Miles at Culver Creek, including Alaska Young, who will pull Miles into her labyrinth and catapult him into the Great Perhaps.

Looking for Alaska brilliantly chronicles the indelible impact one life can have on another. A modern classic, this stunning debut marked #1 bestselling author John Green's arrival as a groundbreaking new voice in contemporary fiction.

"A gem of modern literature."
—GUARDIAN

★ "What sings and soars in this gorgeously told tale is Green's mastery of language and the sweet, rough edges of Pudge's voice."
—KIRKUS

PB: 978-0-14-240251-1 • HC: 978-0-525-47506-4

An Abundance of Katherines

A MICHAEL L. PRINTZ HONOR BOOK • A LOS ANGELES TIMES BOOK PRIZE FINALIST • A *NEW YORK TIMES* BESTSELLER

When it comes to relationships, Colin Singleton's type is girls named Katherine. And when it comes to girls named Katherine, Colin is always getting dumped. Nineteen times, to be exact. On a road trip miles from home, this anagram-happy, washed-up child prodigy has ten thousand dollars in his pocket, a bloodthirsty feral hog on his trail, and an overweight, Judge Judy–loving best friend riding shotgun—but no Katherines. Colin is on a mission to prove The Theorem of Underlying Katherine Predictability, which he hopes will predict the future of any relationship, avenge Dumpees everywhere, and finally win him the girl. Love, friendship, and a dead Austro-Hungarian archduke add up to surprising and heart-changing conclusions in this ingeniously layered comic novel about reinventing oneself.

★ "Fully fun, challengingly complex and entirely entertaining."
—*KIRKUS*

★ "Laugh-out-loud funny . . . a coming-of-age American road trip that is at once a satire of and tribute to its many celebrated predecessors."
—*HORN BOOK*

PB: 978-0-14-241070-7 • HC: 978-0-525-47688-7

The Fault in Our Stars

***TIME* MAGAZINE'S #1 FICTION BOOK OF THE YEAR**
A *TODAY SHOW* BOOK CLUB PICK • #1 *NEW YORK TIMES* BESTSELLER
#1 *WALL STREET JOURNAL* BESTSELLER • #1 *USA TODAY* BESTSELLER
#1 INTERNATIONAL BESTSELLER

Despite the tumor-shrinking medical miracle that has bought her a few years, Hazel has never been anything but terminal, her final chapter inscribed upon diagnosis. But when a gorgeous plot twist named Augustus Waters suddenly appears at Cancer Kid Support Group, Hazel's story is about to be completely rewritten.

Insightful, bold, irreverent, and raw, *The Fault in Our Stars* brilliantly explores the funny, thrilling, and tragic business of being alive and in love.

"Damn near genius . . . *The Fault in Our Stars* is a love story, one of the most genuine and moving ones in recent American fiction, but it's also an existential tragedy of tremendous intelligence and courage and sadness."
—LEV GROSSMAN, *TIME* MAGAZINE

"The greatest romance story of this decade."
—*ENTERTAINMENT WEEKLY*

"This is a book that breaks your heart—not by wearing it down, but by making it bigger until it bursts."
—*ATLANTIC*

★ "In its every aspect, this novel is a triumph."
—*BOOKLIST*

PB: 978-0-14-242417-9 • HC: 978-0-525-47881-2

MORE FAERIE NOVELS

MORE DARK FANTASY

BOB1152